MICHELLE ST. WOLF

The Accidental Bite

A Vampire Lesbian Romance

michellestwolf.com

First edition

Proofreading by Shane Tay
Cover art by Aries Nova Art

This book was professionally typeset on Reedsy.
Find out more at reedsy.com

Contents

Chapter 1

Taking one last sip of blood, Lillianna Markov threw the emptied blood bag in the trash and began to make her way back to her office. The lock of the executive break room clicked automatically behind her, ensuring no wayward or nosy employees would find their way in.

Her heels stabbed the plush carpet as she walked briskly back to her office. She needed to hurry if she was going to get everything done today, but she would. Settling down at her desk, she began to type furiously. She was nearly done with the report when an email from Eric popped into her notifications.

The subject line of the email mentioned the possibility of getting an assistant, and the preview of the body text caught her eye.

Hey Little Sis, this project has really been a big deal and you've looked terribly worn out lately. I've been thinking you should consider taking on an assistant...

She sighed in frustration as she switched applications and began to input numbers with increased force. "Little Sis" was hardly the way to address a work colleague, and yet, even though she had been working at Markov Incorporated for years, her brother still persisted in calling her by diminutive nicknames. If it was any normal family she would ask him to stop, but in the Markov Clan you had to earn your recognition over the years, not demand it. Throwing a fit and drawing attention to herself would not do her any favors in the long run, but she wished they would cut it out. She was an adult already, wasn't she? She wanted that respect *now*, not later.

Glancing out the window of her office, she could see all of her brother's and cousins' assistants at work in their cubicles on the center of the floor. Eric had at least a half-dozen, though most of the others were far less gluttonous. Most had at least three or four, but she had none. She didn't need them either; the assistants were hardly there to do real work, or work at all in some cases.

Speaking of which, she needed to get moving and get this report done quickly so that there would be time enough to go to the scheduled company blood testing later. Eric would rightfully chew her out if she missed it to work more, and she was loath to allow him any more reason to pester her about needing help in the office. Humans were a distraction; blood bags were more than good enough.

* * *

Dara West sighed as she punched in yet another figure into the computer. It was Monday, the office coffee was lukewarm, and, as if Mondays could get any worse, she had discovered mail this morning addressed to her ex in her mailbox. They had never even lived together! The day had been lacklusterly careening downhill ever since.

"Make sure you go after work to get your yearly physical done and stuff," her supervisor nagged as he moseyed past and she slapped the enter key again. "I want to check you off on it already."

"Yes, I will be sure to," Dara acknowledged monotonously while groaning inwardly. There went her evening. She was quite certain the company-wide memo had said that employees were free to take a break and go during work hours, but her supervisor would hear nothing of it interfering with his productivity ratings. Ratings which he did not deserve, by the way—Dara was the sole reason he ranked highly as a manager. But despite her skill, she was just another cog in the machine and interchangeable with the rest of the cubicle farm.

The good news was that Markov Incorporated paid a hefty sum more than her last job even though she did the exact same thing: creating financial models and compiling reports and figures into something more readable for her questionable bosses.

Dara adjusted her glasses and continued typing. After she finished this report, she would need to fix the errors that her supervisor had made when "correcting" her last report before he managed to give it to anyone. Then after that she should probably try to squeeze a snack in because of her missed lunch, and then there was the matter of the physical… Dara sighed again and leaned back in her chair for a brief moment. At least the financial outlook for the company was evergreen. Even if the future wasn't as rosy as it could be, there was little chance of anything unexpected happening to jeopardize her paycheck.

* * *

The windows of Markov Incorporated had gone dark before Dara even noticed. Even though it was late autumn and the days were growing ever shorter, she was still surprised when she looked up to see the inky black twilight. Though her boss was of little merit and the cubicles crowded, Dara actually did not mind the actual work. It was soothing in its own way to take a break from people and lose herself in data, and, best of all, her boss often dipped out early. Without him around, working conditions greatly improved.

She was just about to clock out for the night and go home when she remembered the company physical exam. She had better get that over with before tomorrow. Today had not started great with getting mail intended for her ex, but she had worked faster than usual so it was ending pretty good and tomorrow would be better.

Working at a company specializing in medical technology and pharmaceuticals came with certain perks—if mandatory blood draws could be considered a perk. She had been hired just a month after last year's physicals had been done, and still couldn't decide if that had been a good or a bad thing. Making her way across the cheap carpet of her floor to the elevator, she punched the button for the basement floor. The elevator dinged when it reached the floor and she found herself blinded by intense fluorescent lights.

Here below ground was where the bulk of the medical machinery and accompanying research was kept, as well as a modest company clinic. Behind the glass panes of the laboratories there were still researchers toiling away diligently, apparently just as unaware of the change in time as she had been, except unlike Dara they showed no sign of preparing to head home. Some fussed with vials of serum and tubes of brilliantly colored liquid, but the raw, impenetrable maroon of vials of drawn blood held Dara's gaze. She knew a lot of the research at Markov Incorporated concerned blood transfusions, but lingering on the thought made her stomach turn. At least her work upstairs was completely unrelated to all of that. Hurriedly, she walked to the end of the hall where the clinic was, signed her name on a clipboard at the front, and took a seat.

Several men with impeccable, expensive suits and dark hair loitered in the waiting room restlessly, working late as usual per their high status in the company. The higher level management and executives were easy to recognize: dark hair, pale skin, and an aura of aloofness when around the regular employees, as if they came from a different planet. The company's eponymous Markov family made up the entirety of the upper-level positions, and Dara was not even sure if one could be promoted without belonging to the family in some way. That suspicion was something her boss often lamented as stifling his own aspirations. However, business was thriving and did not appear to suffer despite what appeared to be an extreme case of nepotism.

While she waited for her own turn to have her blood drawn, a handsome, dark-haired man who looked to be one of the Markovs jauntily swung through the door medical bay and dropped off a fresh box of a dozen donuts. He looked around for a moment, giving a perplexed look after apparently realizing that whoever he was looking for wasn't there, and departed, leaving the box of donuts unguarded on the waiting room table. The still-warm scent of crispy glazed donut wafted through the room; Dara's mouth watered. Those were for her—*ahem*—everyone who got their blood drawn, weren't they? They wouldn't mind if she took her payment in advance, would they?

"Dara West?" A man's voice called, interrupting her steady inching toward the box. She stopped and looked back toward the clinic door, disappointed.

"Yes?"

"Come on in," the assistant beckoned.

Dara gave one last glance to the waiting donuts and reassured herself that they would still taste good even at room temperature. She followed the man into one of the rooms and sat down, eager to get this over with. The actual physical went splendidly—her blood pressure was excellent despite the recent stress at work, and the doctor assured her that her reflexes were quite good and her heart sounded strong. She wished it had ended there but, unfortunately, it did not. His assistant then returned to swab her skin with alcohol and pulled out a fresh needle to draw with. As he drew nearer, Dara looked away.

Donuts, she reminded herself. *Just a little longer and you get a donut.* A sting of pain—less than imagined, but certainly more than desired. Her grip tightened. Drawing blood took time, far too much time.

"All set," the doctor informed her as he slapped a bandage on her arm.

Oh god, it was over. Dara stood hastily, grateful that it was over. She wasn't even sure what the blood test was even for, but this donut was going to be the most delicious thing she had ever eaten. The medical assistant was informing her when she would know her results but she was more focused on making a beeline for the waiting room and the donut box. So intent was she on acquiring her sugary, crispy prize, she failed to register that there was a person beyond the clinic's entry door until it was too late.

Dara collided with her, the clipboard the woman was holding pushing back to smash into the vials in her other arm. Glass shattered and the clipboard clattered to the floor.

A mix of annoyance, frustration, and darkly rising anger were splashed across the woman's fine features. Dara had managed to avoid the spray of glass and blood, courtesy of the fallen clipboard, but the woman's crisp suit had taken the brunt of it. The once-white collar of her shirt was now coated thickly in dark red blood, and thoughts of sugar glaze fled Dara's mind in a rush with each congealing droplet that dripped, splattering, to the floor.

Dara cowered under the woman's vengeful glare as she towered over her. The medical assistant rushed out and immediately started calling for one of the lab techs to call for cleanup. Dara stammered an apology that would do nothing to aid in the serious dry cleaning the suit needed—and even then she doubted it would be able to save it—and was mercifully saved from the awkward purgatory by the doctor and his attendant ushering her along and out after they saw that she was unscathed. As she left, she cast a backward glance to the scene.

6

The doctor was murmuring an apology to the woman in hushed tones, but her eyebrows only creased further in a growing storm.

Dara walked down the hall past the other labs still in shock, got in the elevator once more, and as it dinged her arrival it hit her. She felt sick to her stomach, but not just because of the blood. *Dear god,* that must have been one of the Markovs. She had never screwed up something so badly in her life—not even with her ex-girlfriend.

* * *

A few days later, Dara dejectedly punched numbers into another report as her boss cleared his throat, looking over to her skittishly from the message on his screen.

"Upper management wants to see you," he said with a frown as he looked at the memo once more, as if it must be wrong.

"Is that so?" Dara replied as nonchalantly as she could as she looked up from the report she had been working to prepare.

"Strange, I thought that they would want to see me. It's about time for my promotion." He stopped, giving her a suspicious look as he closed the message. She could tell what he was thinking as he spoke again, the fake camaraderie in his voice replaced by rivalry. "Well, come back soon. We want to get a head start on the next project."

Dara could not say she was entirely caught unaware by upper management's request—the only surprise was really that it had taken so long. She had not heard anything in the last few days, but that merely meant that management was biding their time, building a case against her, and waiting to pounce. When glass got involved there was a good chance that someone was injured, and she doubted that other woman's clothing had protected her fully. Dara had hoped the woman had been unharmed, for both their sakes, but she was in for it now.

Her boss clearly thought that somehow she was jumping above him in the chain of promotion, and if she had the stomach to laugh right now she would have. Seriously, a promotion? More like Dara was on the verge of being fired. Even being good at her job, there were plenty more people in the company that could replace her *and* had not dunked someone in blood.

She lingered nervously at her computer, not really able to work when her nerves were jittery and also not wanting to face judgment just yet. Her boss coughed, cleared his throat, and gave her a look. He would not allow her to dawdle when the message had been given to him personally, as much as it was clear that he was still extremely jealous at the notion of her non-existent promotion.

Resigning to the inevitable, she trudged to the elevator. An upward bound carriage appeared soon, and few people returning from a late lunch waited inside as she joined them. *Office 6C, right?* Dara pressed the button for the sixth floor and the transparent plastic began to glow. A few of her fellow passengers' eyes widened and they shuffled away, making Dara more uncomfortable than she already was. Had rumors spread already? No, that didn't make sense. No one had cared about her presence until she had pressed the button for the sixth floor. What was it there, all iron maidens and thumbscrews? Or more likely: filled with pink slips.

When the door opened and dinged to announce her arrival to the sixth floor, she was all too eager to get off and away from the people staring at her. However when she took a good look around, Dara felt that she had been transported to a completely different company, but that couldn't be right—Markov Incorporated took up the entire building. But unlike the cheap carpet of her own floor, the carpet here felt thick and luxurious even through the soles of her shoes. Through the glass of the offices she could see real wood desks and furniture instead of chipboard, and even the modest amount of cubicles in the center of the floor looked a step up from the ordinary fare that she occupied normally. If her floor had been a factory farm for employees, then this was the grass-fed grazing pasture.

Office 6C was home to one *Eric Markov* according to the placard on the door. Dara knocked, and a cheerful voice welcomed her in to sit down in a comfortable leather chair. Eric had sleek dark hair combed back, well-defined cheekbones, and a boyish smile. Dara recognized him immediately. He was the man who had brought the donuts.

"Hello, Dara West, right?" he asked, taking her hand and shaking it firmly. "I've been getting the paperwork together for you and everything to make this go as smoothly as possible."

"The workplace injury slip?" Dara asked, looking confused. "I'll need to fill it out personally, won't I?"

Eric looked at her quizzically, a note of concern entering his voice. "Injury? You were injured?"

"No, I just thought…" Dara trailed off, realizing that she had no idea why she was actually here if it was not about the incident in the clinic. "What were you saying before?"

"Your relocation papers. Didn't your supervisor tell you that your position here was being—" he gestured his hands for a moment as he struggled for the right word. "—adjusted?"

Adjusted? While she could see how her boss had gotten the wrong idea, to Dara's ears that did not sound like a promotion at all, and, in light of the circumstances, was probably a punishment.

"But I like where I'm at," Dara lied. She still had a bad feeling in her gut about this. Even if Eric seemed friendly enough, the office horror stories always started with human resources being friendly before they dumped you into hot water. "Won't it be hard to replace me?" She knew for sure that without her, her boss's productivity would plummet, and although that in itself would be nice to see there was something that told her she should just stay put. This situation made no sense. Earlier this week she had had the biggest screw-up of her life and now she was getting sort-of-promoted, sort-of-not? Her refusal clearly dismayed him.

"I would that I could leave you be, but there's a grave need for a personal assistant for—"

"I'm not a personal assistant," Dara blurted out instinctively to correct him. "I work in finance."

"No?" Eric asked, frowning before he looked back to the screen and murmured to himself. *"AB negative, finance...went to university in...*But you make reports, right?" He asked, scanning through the information on his screen to find what he had missed. "Financial stuff?"

"Yes."

"Good! You would be just an assistant then. A sort of reports helper. I know this is a bit sudden, but management really would like to relocate you."

"Just like that?" Dara asked, confused. Why had it not mattered what job role she was fulfilling? Eric must have noticed the change in her tone and demeanor, because he immediately attempted to reassure her.

"In a good way, I mean. Think of it as a minor promotion, although your job won't be changing much. There are perks here! We have gourmet coffee in the lounge, there's reserved parking, and several times a week lunch is provided."

"Here?" Dara asked, trying to make sense of it all. This place was so nice. Too nice. "I'll be working here? As your assistant?"

"Oh no, not me, I have plenty," Eric said, gesturing through his office glass with a wave at several of the women working in the cubicles there. Dara had to hold herself back from frowning. *Plenty?* Dara wrinkled her nose. That was far too many for just one person to be employing. "You'll be with my sister, Lilly. She's nice. You'll like her.

Oh, and here, don't forget these," he said, foisting several pieces of plastic at her. After a moment, Dara realized they were gift cards, and, if her glasses weren't failing her now, that was quite a lot of cash on each card. It had to be a bribe.

"Oh, um, thank you." Dara felt awfully committed now, but she figured that was all part of Eric's plan.

"I'll go ahead and file the paperwork later today then. Thanks a bunch," he said, his smile wide as if a great burden had been lifted from him. "Let's go meet Lilly then." He stood, dusting himself off as if he was about to attempt a monumental task—or had just done so—and led Dara from the room down the hall to 6F.

Dara heard the furious clicking of computer keys before she saw the source of it. The typing sounded like two hundred words a minute at breakneck pace. Behind the desk was a woman with sleek, ebon hair, pale porcelain skin, and fine features that showed a strong resemblance to Eric's own except far more beautiful—at least what Dara could see of her from beyond the computer monitor.

"Hey, Lilly," Eric called, belatedly tapping on the office door in a perfunctory motion. "This is your new assistant, Dara West. Dara, this is my sister Lilly—"

"*Lillianna*," the woman preempted harshly as she looked up from the monitor. Irritation immediately took hold of her features, and with the familiar expression recognition kicked in. Dara's stomach sank as she realized they had met before. It was the woman from the clinic—the one she had dumped glass and blood all over. Dear god, this was *worse* than getting fired.

Her razor sharp gaze turned on Dara who was now trying her best to look as small as possible. "An assistant? I'm not like Frederick or the others. I don't need someone to fetch coffee for me. I can do it myself."

"Well yes, but you can't complete all those reports alone. You're wearing yourself out," Eric insisted. It was as if Dara had ceased to exist for the time being as they bickered.

Lillianna looked as though she would like to say more—a *lot* more—but she held her tongue as she looked Dara over with ice blue eyes that could have frozen her solid. The woman stood, and Dara found herself looking up. Dara had always considered her own height rather average, but good god, the woman felt a foot taller with those heels on.

"She looks familiar," Lillianna mused with narrowing eyes as she looked down at her.

"Well if she isn't, she will be soon. You'll be seeing a lot of her," Eric announced, settling a hand on Dara's back to urge her forward into the room. She resisted the survival instinct to grab onto the edge of the doorframe in a futile attempt to prevent her inevitable doom.

"I, uh—" Dara swallowed hard and stuck out her hand mechanically and the words followed. "—I'm Dara West. It's a pleasure to meet you."

Lillianna looked at her hand for a moment, and then held out her own in a superficial gesture. For a moment those ice blue eyes held a world of fatigue in them. Beneath the bristling, dark beauty, Lillianna Markov looked tired, stressed, more than a little ticked off, and exactly like the kind of boss that Dara wanted nothing to do with.

"Yes," Lillianna said, taking her hand as recognition at last gleamed in her eyes. Her lips twitched downward in a deepening scowl. "Nice to meet you."

Chapter 2

"Eric, what the hell? I told you ages ago that I don't need an assistant."

Lillianna stood rigid and displeased in his doorway, glowering. She had (mostly) kept it together in front of the newbie, but now that it was just the two of them it was time to let her brother know how she *really* felt.

"And I told you that you did, and I was right," Eric defended as he turned away from his computer to glare back at her. "After all, you matched her blood, and that hardly ever happens."

"And if it was common, you wouldn't have done this?" Lillianna asked skeptically.

"Well, no, I still would," Eric snapped, annoyed. "You need an assistant. You've been stressed, Lilly." She bristled at the nickname as he continued. "More than you've ever been since starting here. It makes me wish that you had stayed at the atelier—"

"I'll leave if I want to, Eric. You don't need to make my decisions for me," Lillianna interjected testily.

"Anyway, please take her as your assistant," he finished exasperatedly. "She worked in the general finance department. It'll help your reports."

"Because you don't think mine are any good?"

"Because your job is more than enough for three people right now."

"No it's not."

"Okay then, for two," he settled. "So it will be done by two. She's

13

going to be your assistant. I already filed the paperwork and marked her as your blood match."

"Shouldn't you have waited until you spoke to me?" Lillianna continued to bristle at being treated as the younger sister that needed help. The other vampires of Clan Markov might have quite a few decades, even centuries on her, but she had reached the age of human adulthood decades ago. Not all of that time had been spent at the company, but neither had any of it been spent slacking off.

"We have spoken," he pointed out. "Several times. Eventually I had to make an executive decision to take care of the situation."

Had he really sent that many emails in the past? Lillianna tried to remember. They all started to look the same after a while: useless and pestering. Perhaps he had mistaken her independence for stubbornness, or maybe she was just stubborn after all, though whether her family thought so or it actually was so it all ended in the same place—looking childish.

"Hey, don't look so down," her brother said when he noticed her pause and downcast look. "Her blood matched you with incredible consistency numbers—the highest the boys downstairs have ever seen. It's perfect, really. She's going to be good for you in more ways than one."

"It is unnecessary," Lillianna rebuffed, but she knew it was useless to resist any longer. It would look worse to refuse at this point; a highly rated blood match, or even a blood match at all, was what all vampires hoped for. "I am just fine with the generic bags."

"These things?" He pulled a blood bag from his lunch container and tossed it between his hands to warm it. "Suit yourself if you want to keep drinking cold blood, but we *all* need a little help sometimes. Just get used to it."

It was hard to argue against something that should be fine in theory. Her brothers and cousins had assistants, but they were older and no one treated them like a youngling with blunt teeth.

"We will see how she does with reports then," Lillianna relented finally, her glare still fixed. "If she's incompetent I'll be sure to let you know."

Eric gave her a shrug as she stalked out of his office back to her own to lick her wounds. A little help was fine, but when her family was involved it felt as though they saw her as needing a lot of help, and especially advice, all the time. This new assistant was just a reminder of the latest black mark against her—and one that had not even been her fault. There had been an issue when an incompetent oaf had mixed up several of the testing vials with blood bags and they were delivered to the break room instead of the lab. Eric had then asked her to ferry them down with her when she went to take her own blood test. She was just a few mere minutes later than she would have been had he not, and then she had arrived just in time to get roughly slammed into and every vial shattered. A huge pain not because her suit was destroyed in the process, but now she looked utterly incompetent as well as the reason as to why several employees had to be recalled to take another costly blood test.

And now the very reason for it all—the very same clumsy employee— was back and making things worse by getting in her way. Lillianna settled behind her desk once more to work, but it was difficult to concentrate on the spreadsheet when she could see Dara West's cubicle from here.

She had given her new assistant some material to work on and shooed her away as soon as possible, but the enticing scent of her lingered. When her assistant had been near, Lillianna had felt the pulse of blood within her, a scent sweeter than any blood before. It was the power of a blood match; a temptation that Lillianna had heretofore never experienced. The other night it had been covered by anger and the pungent blood spattered across her jacket, but now the tempting scent blotted out all competitors with its coppery warmth. She had firmly shut her door and hoped the air conditioning would clear it soon, but in the meantime it was impossible not to be distracted. Eric would have laughed if she had said that her new assistant was hurting her productivity instead of helping it, not to mention it would have been a surefire way to have her credibility ruined if rumors spread within the family.

Lillianna did not want or need a personal juice box, and it had not been a bluff to tell her brother that the blood bags were more than good enough to satiate her needs. Eric's harem of assistants were not only there to do his work for him, she knew, but to also satisfy his fickle taste in blood. At first the need for blood had been a fact of life, as it was for all vampires, but over the years she had grown to resent being so beholden to others for her continued health. By comparison, the blood bags were soothingly anonymous and there was no particular person to thank for them.

Looking through the windows of her office, she could see the woman in question diligently typing away at her computer, popping a piece of candy from its wrapper and into her mouth. The woman was young for a human, late twenties at most, and wore glasses. Her chestnut brown hair was cut in a simple style to her shoulder, just above her blazer. She had paired the jacket with slacks rather than a skirt, but she pulled off the understated style quite well and Lillianna would even say she was quite pleasant to look at. *Wait.* She noticed the woman's shoes—not heels, not even regular flats. She was wearing very ordinary and plain loafers. Perhaps Miss Dara West needed a primer on the dress code for the sixth floor.

No, Lillianna chided herself. *You're being as shallow as your cousins are. That dress code is only there to make sure they have eye candy. You wouldn't want a garish looking assistant anyway, and that's what they end up looking like when they try too hard. I'm sure those shoes are comfortable.* She took another look at the overly casual footwear and cringed; Markov Incorporated didn't even have a casual Friday. Those stupid loafers had better not reflect on her own professionalism.

Suddenly, her assistant looked up from her candies and toward her office. Their eyes met, and Lillianna felt caught. She looked away, pretending she had not really been looking at all. The air conditioning had cleared the air, and it was time to get back to work.

* * *

Dara sucked on the piece of mint candy, but it did little to ease the foreboding sense of doom that lingered like a dark cloud over her cubicle. She had found a lot of little snacks like that in the break room, and also the gourmet coffee that Eric had mentioned, but getting more jitters from extra caffeine was the last thing she needed.

As much as she had opined inwardly that being fired was better than facing the woman she had utterly embarrassed herself in front of, she wanted to crawl back to the job market even less. She had been carelessly tossed aside at the last place she worked despite her excellent numbers because the department had downsized and her boss had opted to keep his friends that did next to nothing rather than her. *Better off without them,* she had told herself, and she was: Markov Incorporated was a much better company and had weathered the poor economy easily, and now Dara absolutely did not want to lose her position here.

Unfortunately, it did not appear that Lillianna Markov was the forgiving type. The women she was working next to at her cubicle had been quick to fill her in on gossip and commiserate, though mostly they were feeling sorry *for* her, not feeling sorry *with* her. Eric was apparently night and day when it came to bosses, and the women next to her were all his assistants. They had let her know that even if she had not had the misfortune to collide with her in the clinic, Lillianna Markov's reputation was already rather questionable.

"Eric's a great boss," Katie, who worked to her left, explained. "But his sister, oh god. A workaholic if I've ever seen one. Feels like she *never* goes home."

"But you said all the Markovs work late?" Dara pointed out. "How do you know if you're not here to see it?"

"Well, yeah, we work late too," Katie said with a shrug. "Not that much though. We usually rotate." She gestured to her fellow assistants. "Rachel's on duty tonight." The woman who must be Rachel waved.

For reasons unknown, Eric Markov had six assistants, and none of them could quite explain it either. They were all gorgeous young things with tailored blouses and styled hair. Everything was higher quality on the sixth floor it seemed, including the employee wardrobes. Dara was beginning to feel out of place next to the sleek new computers in the cubicles and full grain leather couches in the break room. Even the bathrooms were pristinely clean. A niggling in the back of her mind was stuck on Eric's odd behavior and unexpected bribe of gift cards. Dara was almost certainly the latest in line of a revolving door of haplessly transferred helpers.

"What happened to her last assistant?" Dara asked hesitantly when there was a pause in the office chatter.

"Last assistant?" Katie frowned as she combed over her memories. Finding nothing, she turned to one of her fellows. "Candy, you've been here the longest. When was the last time Lilly—*ahem*—Eric's sister had an assistant?"

Candy thought for a moment, and then another moment, and then looked like she was having trouble retrieving this information like an especially slow computer whose disk space was all used up. "I can't recall her ever having one, actually."

Though Dara had been prepared for a horrifying tale of how the last unfortunate soul had been chewed up and spit out, there being no survivors left to tell the tale felt surprisingly worse. Nervously, she unwrapped another piece of mint candy and popped it in her mouth. Peppermint was supposed to help with stress and anxiety, but she was still waiting for those particular effects to kick in. She gave a worried look toward the office of her new boss, but nearly flinched when she found Lillianna Markov staring right back at her intensely, almost...*hungrily.* She looked away immediately.

Lillianna knew it had been her in the clinic, didn't she? Dara had better just rip the bandage off and get this over with. She needed this job, and metaphorically prostrating herself before her boss now could save her a world of trouble later. After taking a moment to psyche herself up, Dara rose from her cubicle and approached Lillianna's office.

At the first knock on the glass door, Lillianna's lips twitched downward immediately.

"Did you need something?" she asked when Dara entered. Her tone was cool but not as icy as before, but the intensity of her gaze was doing things to Dara's stomach again. "Yes?" Lillianna prompted again.

Dara opened her mouth to speak, but in that moment Lillianna rose from her desk and stood to her full height and it struck her just how intimidating Lillianna really was. It was not even just her height, but also the sharp contrast between her red lips, dark hair, and porcelain skin made for an ethereal and breathtaking beauty. Eric and the other Markovs may look similar, but somehow everything just looked better on Lillianna. The intended words caught in her throat, and then entirely forgotten as hesitation transformed into an impasse of indecision.

Maybe Lillianna did not remember who had crashed into her in the clinic after all—it had been a few days. Even if she *had* recognized her, bringing it up again might be in poor taste and make the situation worse when there was no need. And if she didn't recognize her, well, no need to kick the hornet's nest, right? Anyway, Dara had completely changed her mind about bringing it up, no matter what had happened.

"Did you want some candy?" Dara asked lamely, floundering as whatever plan she had to apologize crumbled. An unwanted heat crossed her cheeks. What an absolutely stupid thing to ask.

Lillianna blinked at her, that unnaturally intense hungry look in her eyes once more. The question registered painfully slow in the silence between them, until at long last there was another blink and Lillianna answered.

"I don't like sugary things," she stated simply.

"Oh." Dara's panicked gaze landed on a small yet exquisite lion statue on the side of Lillianna's polished mahogany desk. "That's a nice little lion." Dara cringed inwardly even as she spoke the words. What the hell was coming out of her mouth? These were social death throes.

"It's a miniature replica of a Barye bronze."

Dara did not really understand, but nodded anyway. "That's really cool." Unfortunately, Lillianna saw right through her ignorance. Oh great, her new boss was an art snob too.

"Is your report ready?" she clipped, changing the subject back to something pertinent.

"No." Dara squirmed.

Lillianna's expression began to sour as she raised a brow at her in open inquisition. "Then?"

"Just…uh…team building?" Lamer words had not ever left Dara's mouth. The slightly bluish, tired skin beneath Lillianna's eye twitched. "I'll be going now then," she added hastily. Dara beat a quick retreat back to the relative safety of her cubicle and sighed as she sat down at her desk once more. Good god, she hadn't been able to say anything coherent. She could probably do without speaking to her new boss for a bit. Quickly committing, she decided that for the rest of the day she was only interacting with spreadsheets, and then leaving as quickly as she could.

* * *

Lillianna took note that Dara West left exactly at five o'clock and not a minute later, but her departure was both a relief and an annoyance. While it was nice to have an alleviation of sanguine temptation, it was also clear that no one had taken the time to inform her new assistant that everyone on the sixth floor customarily worked later hours to accommodate the Markovs' unique sleep schedule. But of course Eric would neglect to mention that—this assistant was more of a white elephant than anything else. Humans needed more rest than vampires and could not stay up as late without their focus flagging. Prone to error and fallibility, these were a few of the many reasons that Lillianna had resisted accepting an assistant for so long; that, and simply being unnecessary.

The Markov clan of vampires stressed that a strong work ethic was the key to a long and fulfilling life and had subsequently shunned the excessive decadence that had overtaken many of the clans that had remained in Europe. One should not stagnate, but instead always be moving forward. However, with this new assistant, Lillianna felt that she had somehow become stuck in the mud.

Chapter 3

The next day when nine o'clock rolled around, Dara discovered when she walked in that Lillianna was not there yet; in fact, no one was. Dara wondered if she had shown up to work on a company holiday by accident, but the rest of the elevator had been packed with employees that gave her odd looks when she stopped off at the sixth floor.

Katie, Candy, and Rachel rolled in around half past ten along with several other assistants, saying their hellos and booting up computers and the coffee machine. From then on a steady stream of people began to arrive until at last Lillianna appeared at eleven o'clock sharp. She walked straight to her office with a sense of purpose, not even stopping to give Dara even a cursory glance.

Lillianna's blazer and skirt were pressed and crisp, and she wore heels so sharp they could have doubled as daggers. Her gait was strong and catlike in its grace, and Dara could not help but cast an appreciative glance at her calves before she caught herself and looked back at her screen.

"Why so late?" Dara asked when everyone had settled. "Company holiday? Half day?"

"Oh, I wish," Katie, who sat closest to her, laughed and gave a casual shrug. "But I suppose it's a nice perk that the sixth floor starts late. If you're not a morning person, at least."

Dara frowned. Eric Markov she could understand—the man seemed far too young looking for his position. Well, every Markov here looked too young to be promoted this high, likely the result of some degree of nepotism, but it was nearly time for lunch when Lillianna had strolled into the office! Dara had already pegged her as a cut and dry workaholic, but the sixth floor of Markov Incorporated was becoming stranger and stranger. It just did not add up.

Dara did not have long to dwell on it however, because shortly after her arrival, Lillianna began to send her a series of curt emails concerning a report she needed to have processed quickly. Not wanting to bug her again after yesterday's social fiasco, Dara sent her questions back by the same method, which seemed to work fine. She could do this job. She could handle her new boss and get through it. Dara glanced toward Lillianna's office, where the woman was furiously typing away. Well, probably. Maybe? She hoped so.

When the time came, she took a late lunch alongside Eric's assistants, and though they were a bit vapid they were also quite friendly and welcoming, which was more than she could say for her own boss.

"I still can't believe how nice the snack bar is here," Dara remarked as she opened a cupboard looking for tea sachets and instead found a wide variety of energy bars and trail mix.

"Well, apparently the executive lounge is even better," Katie replied before biting into her sandwich. The staff here were awfully generous, and more and more Dara could see that the assistants here were oddly pampered. With how much nepotism it seemed Markov Incorporated had, it didn't seem like much of a stretch that all of these attractive women might be here for reasons other than work, though the implications of such did not sit well with her.

No, Dara reminded herself, *you are definitely here for work and are not for office candy.* The same should be true for them... Plus, all six of them? Wouldn't that cause some major jealousy? Eric Markov was just promoted too far with all that nepotism and now needed several secretaries to hold his hand and do his work for him; that had to be it.

"Dara?" Katie asked in a concerned voice when she noticed that Dara was still staring at the bags of trail mix. "You okay?"

"Huh? Oh, I'm fine," Dara said, giving up on the tea and snatching an energy bar instead. "What were you saying? The executive lounge? Why did they make a separate one? They could have just added a couple locked cabinets and another fridge to save money instead of building two on one floor."

"Right?!" Rachel exclaimed. "What do they think we're going to do? Raid their private fridge?"

"Hey now, a lot of workplaces have issues with people stealing lunches even if ours doesn't," Candy pointed out.

"They provide so much of the food in the first place. You can't steal what's free," Rachel huffed, and Candy chuckled in response.

From there chatter devolved into the mundane as Dara ate her own lunch quietly. Her thoughts drifted away from shallow office gossip back to her work. She was going to need to get more information from Lillianna to complete the work she had been given yesterday, and then once she turned it in maybe Lillianna would feel differently about her. If she could appreciate how thorough Dara was with the work then maybe this could work out. If not...well, maybe Dara could suffer through it until her job could be "adjusted" again. She resisted wincing at the thought and instead concentrated on possible positive outcomes. Maybe she could just be Eric's seventh assistant. He was the one who got her into this mess anyway, wasn't he? Sort of. He had brought those incredible donuts, and then she had been so shocked after stumbling into his sister that she had never even gotten to try one!

Lunch came to an end far too soon, and soon Dara was shooting off an email about the required info. Only this time, no curt email was returned. Dara waited a bit. A bit turned to a half hour, and then an hour, and then who knows how long before Dara realized she was all out of things to do. She needed that new info. If she sent another email, she would be pestering her, but if she waited any longer, she might be faulted for being slow to complete the task. Glancing toward Lillianna's office, she saw her glaring at her computer and typing away, as usual. Timidly, she got up from her computer and walked carefully toward the door, as if her path was lined with booby traps.

Lillianna looked up when she knocked, her expression mostly a professional neutral edging on disdain, but bid her come in anyway. Dara opened her mouth and was just about to ask for the additional info when something caught her eye. Something dark and rust colored was smudged at the edge of Lillianna's ruby lips, and Dara could not help but stare at it in mute alarm.

"What's the matter with you?" Lillianna asked, her gaze becoming testy with the awkward, gawking silence.

"There's blood—you're bleeding," Dara blurted out immediately, embarrassed to have so obviously been staring at her boss's face and needing to explain.

Lillianna's perfect eyebrows flew up in alarm before she quickly reached for a tissue.

"I must have bitten my lip at lunch," she explained hastily as she dabbed the mark away. There was an unmistakable nervousness in her voice. It must embarrass her greatly to look anything less than flawless, Dara realized. The added emotion was surprising, but also strangely comforting. It made Lillianna Markov seem so much more...human.

The moment did not last.

"What are you here for? Lunch is over and it's time to get back to work," Lillianna ordered, her composure regained and posture rigid. Just like that, the glimmer of humanity was gone.

* * *

When the first part of the report came in, Lillianna was pleasantly surprised that there were no errors. In fact, checking Dara's work took longer than it should have simply because Lillianna kept checking and rechecking the numbers in disbelief. This was…good. Her brother had accidentally chosen someone competent despite the fact that the only thing on his mind had been her blood test numbers. Quite impressive really, even for an accident. In fact, the only person that had an accident today was herself, something she was still angry at herself for.

Lillianna pulled out a small mirror from her desk to check her lips for any trace of blood again. It had been terribly sloppy of her to have grown so complacent. She had not interacted much with the ordinary, human employees at the company for most of her career here, and the moment she had realized what Dara was saying she had panicked. However, her excuse about biting her lip had seemed to take, and she reassured herself a mere smear of blood on her lip was hardly something to hypnotize a human over. That should be reserved for biting and drinking from a human instead. Biting and drinking from Dara… so delicious.

She stared at the facts and figures printed on her screen, determined to focus on her work again, but the thoughts were slow to clear. The scent of Dara's blood in her office earlier had made it hard to think. Crimson ambrosia was just beneath her skin, waiting for her, and all Lillianna had to do was look into her eyes, bind her in thrall, lean down, and bite. Disgusted at the vision, she shook her head at the thoughts to clear them from her mind. She had drunk blood directly before; it wasn't *that* good, and it certainly had not been worth the dependent feeling that came with it.

* * *

"Trying to leave early?" Lillianna chided as Dara shut off her computer for the day.

"Five o'clock isn't early," Dara stated innocently as she continued to pack up, but the simple confidence in her voice was belied by the quickening pace of her heart.

"You never sent me the finished report I asked for."

"It's almost done. I promise I'll finish it first thing tomorrow," Dara assured her, giving ground. Her dinner with friends was beginning to look endangered.

"I have a meeting tomorrow first thing. It needs to be done today so that I can look over it before then," Lillianna ordered, steely eyed.

You could wake up earlier, Dara thought bitterly, but what she actually said held none of that defiance. "I didn't know that," she replied, her nervousness clearly coming through in her voice now. "Uh, I suppose I could stay to finish it then."

Lillianna's eyes narrowed with satisfaction. "Good."

She had just turned to leave when Dara spoke again. "Do you think that—"

"What?" Lillianna snapped.

"—uh—" Dara hesitated, cowering at that. "—you could share your calendar with me? So I just know in the future."

"I don't think that's necessary," Lillianna replied with a tone that brooked no protest, but then her expression unexpectedly softened as she considered the words' merit. "But I suppose I could if it would help you work."

"Oh, okay, thanks. I'll go get to work on that report then," Dara replied, relieved, before fleeing back to her cubicle for safety.

Dara went back to her desk, booted up her computer once more, and quietly texted her friends that she would be late. Disappointing a few people she hardly spoke to since college seemed like the safer option compared to finding out how much harder her new boss could glare. Sighing as she punched in a new set of numbers along a spreadsheet row, she idly wished the economy could hurry up and get better so there would be more good jobs around. She was paid well at Markov Incorporated, but was it well enough to forgo all life outside of it? Probably not.

* * *

Lillianna was disinclined to manage her mandatorily imposed assistant, but sharing her calendar with her was probably the least she could do. Clicking through a few buttons, she finalized the procedure and clicked okay. Now she could get back to work on readying herself for the meeting tomorrow without Dara's distracting questions or scent on her mind. Unfortunately, a minute or so after she shared her calendar, a notification popped up in the corner of her screen, eliciting a sigh of frustration.

'What's this?' Dara had written on her calendar as a comment for the next Tuesday where her schedule indicated that she needed to 'take home extra blood bags.'

Lillianna smashed the delete button so fast it was a wonder that her keyboard did not break. Then she hastily composed a flimsy email to tell Dara that the erroneous calendar entry was merely an inside joke or something or other and not to worry about it.

Damn it all, twice in one day she had messed up in front of her new assistant. If word got back to Eric or anyone else about these slip-ups, Lillianna was going to look so stupidly foolish. At least for today there was the small silver lining in that Dara was staying later at work properly now, as an assistant should. If Lillianna was going to have an assistant, especially an assistant that did good work, she was going to make sure she used her to the fullest. Even if Eric claimed that the job was fit for two people, with two people she should be able to get even more done than before, and she wanted her accomplishments to show it.

And furthermore, with how the tempting scent of Dara's blood was setting her back whenever they came in close proximity, her assistant needed to do more work to make up for it until she became acclimated to it. That would hopefully be soon, because Lillianna currently found it maddening. *These things just take time,* she reassured herself, though she was not really sure about that. She had never had a blood match before, and this hunger was worse than when her fangs had first come in as a child.

* * *

After the one o'clock meeting ended the next day, Lillianna strode down the hall back to her office with radiating pride. She was absolutely chuffed. The meeting had gone excellently; her proposal for the coming Graves project had been chosen over her cousin Frederick's idea and the ugly, astonished look on his face when it had been decided had been just perfect.

However, deep in the back corners of her mind, there was a small, niggling feeling that she did not really deserve the praise that she had been given. Dara had been the one to make all the charts and graphs in her presentation materials and report, after all, and because she had used Dara's report and only spent time checking it instead of creating it, she had been able to use the extra time to further prepare for everything else about her presentation. And now with the new proposal accepted, she was going to have more work and less time than ever, which meant that her new assistant was going to be doing a lot of that work too.

She hadn't cheated; Eric had *made* her take an assistant. It was just too bad if no one else's assistant could do real work and hers could. With her newfound justification, Lillianna brushed off the new, unfamiliar feeling of being undeserving. She had always gotten by without Dara before, and she could do it again. Just maybe a little slower, less snazzy, less...okay, maybe she needed to brush up her software skills a bit, but there was nothing stopping her from getting up to speed. Feeling as though she had something she needed to prove, Lillianna glanced toward Dara's cubicle, her pride warring with her desire for efficiency on whether to ask Dara or the Internet the key to more masterful graph equations and spreadsheets.

In the end, efficiency won out. Dara was not a Markov, so no one would know about this. Her pride was safe as Lillianna strode over to her assistant's desk and tapped on the side of the cubicle to get Dara's attention. Dara appeared to have been deeply engrossed in whatever she was looking at and immediately pushed her chair back and spun around when she realized that Lillianna was there.

Curious—and more than a little suspicious—Lillianna took a glance at Dara's computer screen expecting to see her haphazardly swiping the mouse to minimize online shopping or clickbait news articles, but there was nothing more than the spreadsheet Dara had been assigned at eleven o'clock that morning after finishing the last one and there had been no time for her to hide anything either.

"Did you need me for something?" Dara asked cautiously, as if bartering with a wild animal.

"You used a formula sequence in the spreadsheet that I had not seen before. I would like you to show me how to set up the sheet that way," Lillianna requested before adding, with some difficulty, "Please."

Dara looked shocked by her request at first, but then her expression morphed into a timid yet courteous smile accompanied by a nod. "Oh, of course. Was there anything in particular that you were working on?"

"I have some figures that we could use to get started on."

"Sure. Let's take a look on your computer then."

Lillianna returned to her desk with Dara in tow and got to work opening the files. The figures for the next project were straightforward and seemed the perfect candidate for learning with, or at least she had thought they were.

Once they got started, Dara was clicking various buttons and pulling out different sidebars at a rapid, yes nonchalant pace. As Dara leaned over to input formulas Lillianna quickly realized that what she had assumed was a single formula was actually several in sequence. It was so complicated that it made her brain hurt and contemplate going back to the atelier for real like Eric had suggested, but she banished the thought from her mind. Her family had never taken that work seriously enough. Learning just took time, but it could be done as long as one digested the material at a reasonable pace and practiced.

"So it's written like this?" Lillianna asked as she input one of the simpler parts of the formula.

"Not quite," Dara said as she leaned over her to correct the input with a degree of closeness that Lillianna was wholly unprepared for.

Lillianna's gaze was pulled from her screen to Dara's so close neck, noting the way the soft, brown locks curled slightly against the flesh, and the blood that pulsed beneath. Warm, soft skin thin just enough that a single bite was all it took to break the barrier to rich, coppery blood. She could see the faint bluish vein ever so slightly under the skin, and the muscles in Dara's neck tensed as she spoke words that

31

Lillianna did not hear. Just a bit closer and—

"Did you get that?" Lillianna blinked as Dara's words brought her back to the present. *Get what?* Lillianna blinked again dumbly as Dara looked at her. Out of the corner of her eye she spotted the spreadsheet with its overly complicated formulas.

"Yes," Lillianna replied automatically as she remembered the task at hand, despite having missed all of it. "My apologies, but I just remembered, there's a meeting I need to get ready for."

"Oh? Uh, yeah, sure," Dara said as she stepped away, confused and somewhat hurt.

Hurt? Lillianna noticed, but she did not dwell long on that thought. Spreadsheet education session successfully aborted, she made a beeline for the executive lounge. There was no meeting to go to at all, but the excuse got her out of her office and away from Dara's delicious blood. When she got inside the lounge she immediately rifled through the fridge for a fresh blood bag, and unscrewed the cap.

Vampires were supposed to hypnotize humans, not the other way around. She had known that the blood match was something that her brothers and cousins had all wished for, but this was more than she had imagined it would be. This was dangerous. She had not even tasted it, and yet now the chilled blood that the clinic provided was bland and flavorless on her tongue. The thrum of Dara's blood had held such promise: ninety-eight degrees of blessed sanguine delight that begged for Lillianna to take it right then and there.

Eric had to make things so much more difficult than they had to be, Lillianna groused internally as she sipped on her meal. *He just had to go and give me an assistant.*

Dara was good—too good, even, maybe. With her plain clothes and loafers she didn't look it, but she was crazy skilled at these spreadsheets. Before meeting her, Lillianna had thought herself pretty good at processing financial data. She did not make errors when she worked through everything, but her new assistant was just so much faster. Vampires lived a long time, and there was more than enough time for her to gain that speed, but...maybe not right now. If she just took advantage of Dara's speed for now while she had her, she could devote her time to more thoroughly fulfilling her other duties and worry about becoming speedier with spreadsheets after the human had turned to dust. That was the proper and efficient thing to do, even if having to rely on her bruised the edges of Lillianna's pride. A frustrated sigh escaped her lips as she finished the blood bag, having drunk it in record time.

A while later—long enough to pretend she had indeed been at some sort of meeting—Lillianna slunk back to her office. Wrinkling her nose as she looked back to the spreadsheet-in-progress that was still up on her screen, she moved the cursor up to the top right and closed out of the program. Opening her email, she attached the relevant information for completing it and clicked "send." If this was the price she paid to get ahead, then so be it.

Chapter 4

In the week that followed, Lillianna discovered that she had somehow underestimated Dara's ability to get work done. Perhaps she had been working with Eric too long and now naturally expected others to flake at a crucial moment, or maybe it was because, when she had been at the atelier, others getting involved when she was trying to work had only slowed her down in the past, and thus she had never considered that the opposite might be true at the office—at least when Eric wasn't involved. With her new assistant she was easily on track for all of her goals, or rather, her *former* goals. Now she itched to reach even further; perhaps instead of aiming for a promotion in the next couple years, she could get it by the coming summer if this new project with the Graves Group went well enough. The only problem with this plan was that her new assistant kept trying to leave right at five o'clock, even after Lillianna had made it clear that it was not happening. And then even despite that, yesterday, when Lillianna had been distracted by a meeting, somehow her assistant had snuck away on the hour.

The evening hours were prime time for vampires and she wanted Dara to be present in order to make the most of them. Due to the necessity of sometimes interfacing with human clients, Lillianna and the other vampires had been forced to adjust their sleep schedule to accommodate them somewhat, but there was something about the setting sun that just felt *right.* And although at times it was nice to be able to leave an email for Dara and then come in the next day with the work complete and waiting for her, Lillianna knew that it would be more efficient for them to be in the office at the same time working together into the evening—albeit safely an office away where Dara's delicious blood could not bother her. She would put a stop to this today, and therefore ensure her path to promotion.

She looked up, giving a glance to Dara who was working away on the work Lillianna had assigned her this morning, and resolved to talk to her later, when she was not interrupting her work. Productivity was important, after all. Standing, Lillianna moved from her office and down the hall to the lounge to take an early lunch so that she would have her own block of uninterrupted time to work unbothered by growing hunger. When she arrived at the lounge, she looked through the catered lunches in the first fridge, selecting a sandwich with capicola, salami, and peppers just the way she liked it and a small container of soup for the microwave. However, food was not all she was hungry for, and she moved on to the second fridge, carefully punching in the combination to unlock and open it to reveal...nothing.

Oh no. Lillianna scanned the shelves, hoping beyond hope that there was one, small, leftover bag of blood in the fridge, but there was not. The blood delivery today must be late. Her stomach whined at the injustice of it all. More than being inefficient, she hated being hungry, because then she could not be efficient, but she especially hated being hungry due to wayward delivery people being inefficient. Placing a preemptive hand to her forehead, Lillianna rubbed her temple. She felt starving already.

* * *

35

Shuffling the warm, freshly printed papers of her latest report in her hands, Dara took a peek over at her boss's office to check for danger, but Lillianna's head was down as she worked intently. Dara had just sent off the digital copy in an email, but for this specific report Lillianna had requested an analog copy to go along with it. Now Dara just needed to ensure it was safe to deliver it.

From working with Lillianna a week, she had quickly discovered that her new boss's moods held more variation than initially assumed. There were subtle differences in each scowl and glare that differentiated them from one to determine if the cause was frustration, deep concentration, or an email from Eric. Intense brooding appeared to be the default at work, though Dara briefly wondered what faces she must make when she was not working. Surely she wouldn't be glaring when she was chatting with friends, right? Or off work relaxing, or enjoying good food, or, well, actually, she probably just kept thinking about work through all of it.

Lillianna Markov was extremely driven, though for what Dara could not really tell. Not for love of work, though maybe money? Taking another glance at her boss as if it would divine some answers, Dara found none except a scowl as Lillianna leaned back in her chair and rubbed the space between her eyes. Scored from one to ten, the glare rated as a four on the danger scale. Dara winced. It had been a six earlier when Dara had checked at lunch, and four was probably as good as it was going to get today.

Dara adjusted her glasses as she readied herself to enter the lion's den. Taking the papers, she trudged from her cubicle over to Lillianna's office. Knocking twice, Dara was bid to come inside, but what greeted her when she entered was Lillianna's mood rapidly shooting up to a seven. She was not merely irritable now; she was frustrated too as she looked up from her computer and furrowed her brow at Dara's appearance.

"Here are the papers," Dara explained unobtrusively as she set the paper-clipped stack down on the edge of the desk.

"Thank you," Lillianna replied in a perfunctory tone, taking the papers immediately to examine. Dara edged toward the door as Lillianna's expression temporarily morphed to one of deep thought as she flipped through them. This was her chance to make a clean escape.

"Well then, let me know if you need any edits,

"Wait," Lillianna ordered before she could cross the threshold.

"Something wrong?" Dara asked, steeling herself up for the possibility that she had messed up a section.

"I need you to stay later tonight," Lillianna explained as she looked up from the papers.

"Again?" Dara asked before she could stop herself. From the unamused look on Lillianna's face, she really should have. "I had something important planned for tonight," Dara amended quickly, but it did little good. Lillianna gave her a scathingly skeptical look, as if she had heard this before—probably from Eric—and Dara's heart sank. She had been hoping to start going home on time now that she was all adjusted to Lillianna's workflow, but clearly her boss had other plans. "Well, I suppose I can stay." Dara agreed, not wanting to protest further when it was not worth it.

"Good." Lillianna set aside the sheaf of papers, stowing them beside a notebook that looked out of place on the otherwise neatly arranged desk. "Is there anything else?"

"No, that's all," Dara replied, excusing herself and heading back to her cubicle before she could be wrangled into anything else. She had been so preoccupied with Lillianna's facial expressions that she had forgotten where the real danger lay. Even if she actually did have plans for tonight, she had no interest in finding out if there was a bite behind Lillianna's bark.

Her mother would be more stressed if Dara was unemployed in this economy, and Dara would hate for her to have to pull any money out of her savings for her. She pulled out her phone and texted her mother that she would be a bit late tonight before once more looking toward Lillianna's office where she saw her boss pinching her nose. Dara frowned in bewilderment. *Do I smell bad or something?*

* * *

The lack of blood was making her irritable, and as the day continued Lillianna tried desperately to focus on work. However, without blood she was forced to settle for devoting the day to checking off more mundane, clerical tasks from her to-do list. Every now and then, errant thoughts of hypnotizing Dara and leading her away to somewhere private to feed flitted through her mind, but she continued to push them away. She would be fine tomorrow after a blood bag or two, and there was no need to give in to a short term temptation. Dara would not remember if she chose to do so, but she would, and that was the problem.

Lillianna had tried drinking blood from humans numerous times when she was younger, hoping that the repulsive feeling of dependency would go away, but it never did. After drinking from their lifeblood and feeling the pulse of their heartbeat beneath her tongue, the sensation of weakness tickled at her conscience long after the satiety had passed. She was stronger than any human, more sturdy, and from a long line of hunters of the night. She should not need to feel like she owed anyone else anything.

And she knew that if she drank Dara's blood even once she was not going to stop there. It was already worrisome that in one week she had come to rely on having an assistant to stay comfortably on schedule, but being an assistant addict was only temporary. She needed Dara to thoroughly trounce Frederick and his stupid smug face, and at this point she would do just about anything to keep her winning streak continuing against him.

Speaking of which, Frederick was increasingly moody these days. In the week following his loss at the meeting, he had been coming out of his office more to loiter around the shared space and cubicles. He glared at her when their eyes met, and a few days ago she had possessed the great misfortune of walking in on him in the lounge late at night when he was drinking from one of his secretaries. He had turned to look her dead in the eye and laughed when she sputtered and backed away, closing the door as quickly as she could. The incident still made her blood boil just thinking about the taunt. Frederick was her least favorite by far among her cousins, and from here on out he was going to be thoroughly thrashed when it came to work matters. She had been gaining on him before even without Dara, but now with her victory was all but assured. The Graves project was too big to go unnoticed if she was successful, and she would finally prove herself. Speaking of which, it was time for the evening meeting.

Sighing and rubbing her head in a feeble attempt to suppress her blood hunger induced headache, Lillianna rose from her desk and walked out to check on the cubicles before heading over. Her command to stay had stuck, and Dara was still chugging away as she passed. At least she more than made up from Lillianna's own lackluster productivity today, the silver lining being that she was getting the meetings over with for now and had something to do without losing the whole day to hunger.

* * *

As soon as she turned a corner and was out of sight of the meeting room, Lillianna breathed a heavy sigh of relief. Somehow, she had held it together at the meeting without snapping at anyone, but only just barely. Word had been received that the blood bags had finally arrived, but were now being processed in the basement labs and would not be available for another couple hours. Aside from that, her input on the project had been received well, but now there would need to be a few edits before she sent it off. It would be roughly half an hour for her to do it, but it was something Dara could probably do in about ten minutes, so that would not be a problem.

Walking further down the hall and reentering the cubicle farm, she began to make her way over to Dara's space to let her know about the edits when she realized that she could not see any chestnut hair peeking from above the low walls of the cubicle. Alarmed, her pace quickened the closer and closer she got to the offending cubicle, but when she arrived there the computer was off and Dara was already gone.

Damn it. A quick glance to the clock on the wall told her that it was a quarter to seven now, and she had been intending for Dara to stay at least until the hour. Now she was going to have to make the edits herself when she could have gotten a head start on tomorrow's draft. Lillianna fumed as she stared at the darkened screen and vacant seat. The air around Dara's cubicle still faintly smelled of her scent. It tickled Lillianna's senses and caused her to salivate. Irritation bubbled to the surface, turning to aggravation when it hit the air. Clearly being somewhat subtle about expectations wasn't working. Not that it usually did—Eric was thick as a brick when it came to taking a hint too and it made sense that people he sent her may take after him. Turning to the cubicle next to Dara's, Lillianna's focus honed in on Eric's assistant that was seated there. What was her name? Kayla? Karla? Katie? It didn't matter.

"When did she leave?" Lillianna demanded, jabbing a finger at Dara's empty seat.

The woman paled, her expression blanching as she realized Lillianna was speaking to her. "Er, I don't know, I wasn't paying attention. She mentioned she had to be somewhere and was late."

"Where?" Lillianna demanded.

"Rose Hill Cemetery," the woman sputtered.

"The cemetery?" Lillianna asked, incredulous. That was a new one. Usually the excuses she heard from Eric consisted of having to meet her cousins for billiards or drinks, and sometimes the cousins themselves were bold enough to claim that they had a business dinner to go to—though they were actually still just going for billiards or drinks.

"I think someone close to her recently died. She said it was the first anniversary of his death," her brother's assistant babbled.

"Did she say anything more than that?"

"No, not really," the woman replied hurriedly, clearly eager for this conversation to be over as she put her head down and tried desperately to look like she was working.

Lillianna was perplexed. Dara had not been throwing out flimsy excuses left and right like Lillianna's cousins and brother did, but it still shocked her that she had been telling the truth about having something important to do. She had said "his"—a man had died, but who? Brother, friend, father, husband? A quiet melancholy burrowed its way into her chest where all the fire and determination had been, and she did not like it. She sighed, sitting down in Dara's empty chair, and breathing in the last vestiges of both the reinvigorating and infuriating scent. Emotional troubles meant that Dara's work performance may take a hit, but even thinking that made her feel guilty. Compared to vampires, humans did not live long, but in recent years since leaving the atelier everyone she spoke to was a fellow vampire and it had begun to slip her mind that human lives were quite transient.

In truth, Lillianna no longer had much of a life outside the company—there was plenty of time for that later anyway—but she supposed that was not the same for others, especially humans. In her head it had not seemed like such a big ask to request Dara to stay later—Lillianna herself had done it for years now. Plus Dara was paid for any overtime she did when she came in early, but maybe that was not what she wanted. Maybe time was worth more than money, and maybe she had asked for too much. It had only been one week, but the woman seemed trustworthy so far. Perhaps, at least sometimes, even most times, she should simply allow Dara to go home more often without staying later so long as she got her work done.

She did not really understand why she felt this way—she didn't even particularly care about her assistant outside of her magnificent ability to crunch numbers—but wrestling with the uncomfortable sensation of nascent guilt was a bigger waste of time, and Lillianna was all about efficiency.

* * *

A chill breeze blew through the cemetery, sweeping golden, crinkled leaves over the dry grass. The rumbling sound of her mother's car faded into the distance as the autumn night grew still and quiet. Her mother had been teary eyed as she spoke about her father in a cathartic manner, though Dara had been unable to say or do anything except tightly curl an arm around her mother's shoulders. If there was any closure to be found at all, she hoped her mother had found it before heading home. Perhaps, now that he had been dead for a year, her mother would finally let him go. After all, her father had already let go of both of them a long time ago.

Standing by his graveside was more time with him than he had spent with her in the decade before his death, and it left her feeling empty and hollow. A part of her did not quite understand why they were visiting her father's grave at all; she didn't really know the man, but maybe that was why it hurt.

Chapter 5

Dara adjusted her glasses and yawned sleepily as she punched in another row of numbers. She took a sip of her iced latte, but there was only so much caffeine could do when she hadn't gotten any sleep. The workday was barely halfway through but she already felt so sluggish.

The college get-together she had attended last night had gone poorly, and sleep had failed to do more than blur the memory of it—well, maybe it would have if she had been able to sleep. The awkward gathering still hung like a moist, humid blanket around her thoughts and irritated her enough that the sense of peace that working with numbers usually provided evaded her. Thirty minutes after Dara had arrived at the venue, her ex had walked in with a new woman on her arm despite all of her old friends having assured her that she would not be attending. It seemed that she too wished to dispel any hopes their mutual friends might have had of them getting back together, or maybe she had just wanted to twist the knife. After the other woman casually called Dara "The Dropout," the rest of the evening was tinged with the sour flavor of betrayal and embarrassment and it had ruined the last vestiges of Dara's weekend, and now it was ruining the beginning of her workweek too.

Yawning once more, she got up to ask a quick question. When she knocked on the office door, Lillianna looked up, her eyebrows tightly knit. Upon seeing her in the doorway, however, her brows quickly unfurled. Dara resisted the urge to give a sigh of relief. Thank goodness, the brooding glare had just been from concentration.

"The current analysis is ready for me to send off, but I wanted to ask if you wanted me to wait until Eric sent me the preliminary Graves numbers to add for cross analysis. I thought they would look good together for presentation purposes," Dara informed her.

"Yes, that would be perfect. If you could stay later to do that when he sends them over."

"Will do," Dara replied, stifling a yawn. She was going to need to get more caffeine if she was going to make it through the day and overtime.

* * *

Through the glass of her office, Lillianna eyed her assistant sluggishly typing away at her computer. When she had come in this morning and said hello to her, she had immediately noticed that something was not right. Her posture was shabby, there was a noticeable purplish tone beneath her eyes, and her skin, while not quite as pale as Lillianna's own, was definitely too pale for a regular human. Normally employees looked better after a weekend of rest, but whatever had happened in the last few days to Dara was not rest.

Well, as long as she got her work done without errors it was none of Lillianna's business what Dara did with her personal life, except, well, ever since last week's mystery visit to the cemetery she had to admit she *was* curious. It irked her because, on top of reining in her desire for Dara's tempting blood, she now had to resist this too. She told herself that it was just a concern for efficiency and that, though humans were fragile, they were not *that* fragile. She would monitor the situation from afar. Just as she settled the matter and was about to get back to work, Eric popped his head into her office, only then giving a small, pointless knock on her door.

"Hey there, Lilly!" He started, ignoring the glare he got for using the childish nickname again. "Did you get the data I sent you combined with the other sheets?"

"No." Lillianna replied curtly, turning back to focus on work.

"But you're working on it, right?" he prodded.

"Dara's working on it," she said, trying hard to ignore him. "I'm working on the Graves numbers."

"Oh, is she?" he asked nonchalantly, glancing over to her cubicle. "Say, you're not working her to death, are you?"

"*No.*" The righteous annoyance she felt surprised even her.

"You know, I heard from Candy about how Dara's a whiz with spreadsheets. Maybe I should have kept her for myself. She'd like being well taken care of, I bet."

"I take care of her just fine," Lillianna snapped, her eyes narrowing. Eric got the message and shrank away.

"Well, I'll be looking forward to your email then, uh, thanks!"

Lillianna glared daggers at his back as he departed. Dara was *her* assistant, and she would be damned before Eric made any move to take her away. Unfortunately, she realized that could even be today: what if he helped her and got all the points for it? This was an emergency. The person who needed to help Dara was Lillianna herself in order to engender good feeling and loyalty. Eric had enough assistants as is, and he was not allowed to get his grubby paws anywhere near hers, even jokingly. And other companies had better keep away from her too. Frowning, Lillianna realized that that was much harder to do when she simply could not glare at a corporation to ward it off. She would need to take a more suitable preventative measure. Which meant maybe talking to her about more than work. *Ugh.* Lillianna swallowed hard, trying to tamp down her pride. She had better get this over with. The only thing worse than killing the golden goose was having it stolen.

Exiting her office to enter the cubicle farm, she zeroed in on her assistant immediately. Dara was still there, sleepily working away the same as before, and the sight made Lillianna's heart twinge with guilt. Was she overworking her? Maybe? She approached quietly, noticing that today even Dara's blood did not smell quite as enticing as before.

"Hello," Dara greeted her when she noticed her approach, her eyes suddenly gaining a sharper focus when she turned to her. "I got the data you sent and it will be ready by lunch."

"Thank you, I—" Lillianna wanted to say something kind and caring, and promptly found she was at a loss for words. Everything felt so hollow when she did not know the first thing about her assistant except that someone she had known was dead. She winced internally at the bluntness of the thought. She was so rusty. She had been persuasive once, maybe two or three decades ago. She could do that again. It was all in the name of efficiency, and there was nothing wrong with that. She quickly sprung to an idea. Eric had organized catering lunches for the assistants to ensure that their blood quality was top notch, but there was nothing stopping Lillianna from purchasing Dara even better food. This would be easy. Humans loved food like vampires loved blood. "—I'd like you to come with me for lunch, actually." She had meant it as a question, but it came out as a command.

* * *

"Aren't the lunches already catered?" Dara pointed out, confused by the sudden request. "I mean, I'll still go. It's just—"

"I'm not very fond of tuna sandwiches," Lillianna explained, her tone immediately softening from before. "And besides, this is for...team building."

"Team building?" Dara repeated, confused, maybe even a little alarmed. "Just the two of us?"

"We're a team, aren't we?" Lillianna asked, looking offended.

"Well, yes, of course, I just thought usually the team included everyone we worked with like Eric and—"

"Not Eric," Lillianna interrupted, looking disgruntled at the mere mention of his name.

Dara had not really understood what brought the sudden request on, but she was in no position to refuse either. As soon as she had sent off the email containing the files she had promised, she had grabbed her bag and trotted over to wait at Lillianna's office.

Now they were standing in line in a small bakery cafe down the street from the office building, with Dara nervously adjusting her glasses for the hundredth time. The scent of roasting coffee filled the air along with the sound of chatting lunch goers, but the air between her and her boss was dead silent.

"This place is lovely," Dara attempted, making a sweeping motion of the quaint interior before turning to the display case filled with brownies, tarts, cakes, and cinnamon rolls. "And the desserts look lovely."

"They are aesthetically pleasing I suppose," Lillianna conceded politely, but with far less enthusiasm than Dara, and then she suddenly remembered what her boss had told her before.

Crap. Dara had forgotten that Lillianna didn't like sugary things. She floundered mentally for something to say, and settled on the first thing that came to mind.

"What's your favorite color?" *Dear god, this isn't grade school, Dara!* She wanted to slap herself, but the words were already out of her mouth.

Lillianna blinked at her in response before finally answering as she stepped ahead in line. "Perylene maroon."

"Huh?"

"It's a pigment, sort of an iron red or blood color."

"And you?" Lillianna asked, turning the question back on her.

"Me? Er, I like blue I guess," Dara answered, grateful that Lillianna was playing along with her juvenile question.

"Just blue?" Lillianna pressed, tilting her head to one side, disappointed by the plain answer. Her ice blue eyes were inquisitive and demanding; they were such a pretty color, even if Dara always felt nervous when focused by them.

"Ice blue is nice," she decided.

"Ah, like the winter sky," Lillianna replied thoughtfully, tapping her chin. "It's getting colder, but lately the sky has just been gray." She motioned toward the windows of the cafe, where outside the dreary sky threatened to rain any moment now.

"Cold and wet," Dara agreed regretfully. "I hope by December things clear up at least. I'd like some snow."

"It doesn't snow here much, but up by my parent's place it snows all the time," Lillianna commented.

"That sounds beautiful."

"It is."

Another silence fell over them as they shuffled up in line, and for the life of her Dara could not think of anything to say. Her attention fell once more to the baked goods in the display case and especially the slices of creamy cheesecake and the fruit tarts whose slices of kiwi and strawberry were glazed with a sugary syrup. It sort of reminded her of those glazed donuts that she had never gotten to try when she had rudely collided with her future boss.

"Do you want one of those?" Lillianna suddenly asked, and Dara looked up. She was pointing to the glazed fruit tarts and cinnamon rolls behind the glass.

"Oh no, I'd better not. I'll get a sugar crash before work is over," Dara explained as she shifted her attention to the lunch menu hung behind the counter instead. "I'll just get the chicken pesto."

"Are you sure?" Lillianna asked, pulling out the company card. "You can get anything you want."

"Oh." She had not been expecting that, but it made sense. How thoughtful. "Thank you, but it's okay. Maybe the soup?"

"Coffee?" Lillianna asked. Dara figured she must look like she needed it.

"A latte, thank you." Dara wasn't used to the generosity, but she did like the food. Maybe it was a bribe to keep her staying late.

"Of course," Lillianna replied before approaching the counter. "One chicken pesto sandwich, a turkey artichoke panini, two daily soup specials, a latte, and an espresso with cream."

"I appreciate it," Dara replied awkwardly as they went to sit down at a table.

"No problem."

Maybe her boss had gotten over the clinic incident after all. Dara started to relax, but she couldn't find anything to fill the growing silence as Lillianna tapped her fingers on the table impatiently, clearly eager to get her food already and get back to work.

"What do you like to do off work?" Lillianna asked abruptly as she sighed and turned back to her.

"Huh? Off work?" Dara asked, caught off guard. In the past she had watched movies with her now ex-girlfriend, but now, sick of dating apps and reminders, she just found solace in the tried and true. "Nothing very exciting. Relax, I guess? I like sudoku."

"Just sudoku?" Lillianna probed.

"Sometimes I play solitaire or do the daily crossword puzzle," Dara conceded.

"My grandfather plays solitaire," Lillianna commented.

"I told you I wasn't very exciting," Dara chuckled.

Lillianna frowned. "I didn't mean it like that. Just that we had something in common since my grandfather taught me how to play when I was younger."

"Oh." The response took Dara entirely by surprise. Her ex had said that her hobbies were boring, and therefore by extension Dara was also. Although, it wasn't like Lillianna went out often with how much she worked. She had heard from Katic that the woman logged hours on *Saturday!*

"I'm not boring," Lillianna insisted, cheeks flushing. "I've just been busy. Postponing excitement and not having any are different."

Now it was Dara's turn to flush when she realized what she had done. *Dear god how much of that had she just said out loud? Do something!* "Uh, I didn't mean it quite like that either—I just—er—well, what would you do if you took a day off work?"

Lillianna took a moment to think. "Go to the zoo I suppose."

"The zoo?" Dara asked, entirely surprised by the answer. Okay, so maybe her boss wasn't boring. That was actually pretty interesting.

"I like to see the big cats," Lillianna explained. "They have this dangerous beauty."

"Wait, let me guess, you like the lions?"

"Well, yes, naturally," Lillianna replied, a sparkle of keen interest in her eyes, and the enthusiasm in her voice slowly building. "Did you know they used to live in Europe? But the humans there hunted them just like they did to vamp—*ahem*—other species, and now cave lions are entirely extinct everywhere."

"Really? When was that?" Dara asked, propping herself up on the table.

"The last of them died out during the time of Ancient Greece unfortunately. Oh, but are you more of a tiger person?"

"More of a little house cat person myself, actually," Dara replied.

"Oh? Do you have one?" Lillianna smiled, the gesture revealing her dazzling white teeth and two peculiar, pointed canines that stood out against her red lipstick. It was surprising, and yet also beautiful.

Coming back to herself, Dara shook her head. "I did, sort of. He stayed with me a long time, but it was actually my ex's cat, and when that ended, well…"

The corner's of Lillianna's lips dipped downward in a consoling expression. "I'm sorry." Dara, who had been carried away in the moment, suddenly remembered that Lillianna was her boss, not a friend. That was probably too much. "Has that been stressing you out?"

"No, no, that was a while ago. I'm fine, really. I just saw my ex unexpectedly over the weekend and—uh—" Dara floundered. Now she really had said too much. In the course of their friendly conversation about cute animals, it had begun to slip her mind that Lillianna was very much her boss.

"Oh," Lillianna sighed, relieved. "I thought someone had died again."

"Again?" Dara asked, bewildered.

"I heard you went to the cemetery."

Oh. Lillianna had heard. "No, everything's fine, really. It won't get in the way of work." She really needed this job after all. It didn't really matter if she was having a tough time when there was nothing in the market even close, with worse pay and hours anyway. Lillianna looked skeptical at her answer, but at that moment their number for food was called and she instead rose to retrieve it. Setting down her pesto sandwich, tomato basil soup, and latte in front of her, Lillianna began to eat her own food quietly while Dara poked at hers.

She didn't really understand what was going on. Lillianna was her *boss.* Replacing an employee once they had moved past their usefulness was just part of the job description, and yet they were sitting at lunch talking about cats both big and small as if they were friends. She wasn't even glaring, and sometimes she was smiling! She was certainly more friendly than Dara's old college friends had been at least.

"Are you feeling okay?" Lillianna asked. Dara's merely nibbled sandwich was telling on her.

"I'll be okay. I can start on the follow up data right when we get back," Dara assured her again, and then took a large bite of the sandwich as if to prove it. The pesto was delicious and savory, but did little to banish her sudden case of nerves.

"About that, well—" Lillianna cleared her throat, looking uncomfortable. "—I don't expect there to be as much overtime going forward."

"Oh, really?" Dara asked, trying and failing to feign nonchalance at the sudden turn of conversation. Her interest was obvious. This was the best news she had heard all week. "Then just nine to five?"

"Well, about that, I would like it if you did eleven to seven to match my own schedule, but I understand if that isn't doable now or always."

"Oh, I can try to match it. If you don't mind me asking, why does the sixth floor start so late anyway?" Dara asked curious now that the topic was broached. "It was never like this at my previous position."

"We Markovs have a genetic sleep phase disorder," Lillianna explained matter-of-factly, as if she had been asked this several times before and it was a ready waiting canned answer. "Just a family thing."

"Oh. That makes sense I guess. Well, I'll do my best. I think I can come in at those times most days."

"You can? Great!" Lillianna smiled widely, and her pointy canines flashed once more. "Thank you." In an unexpectedly warm gesture, she reached out a hand to place it across Dara's. "And please, go home and sleep tonight. You look…well, usually much better." Lillianna's smile turned apologetic, and this time the color in Dara's cheeks was not entirely from embarrassment.

Chapter 6

Booting up her computer for the day, Dara hummed to herself as she typed in her password and looked over her to-do list. Checking her calendar first thing, she saw that she was having another lunch date—*ahem*—meeting with her boss, and she was looking forward to trying out a new restaurant. Most recently they had gone to a nice Thai place, and the curry had been great. Lillianna had beamed with pride when Dara had told her that it was her favorite so far.

Speaking of, Lillianna had made good on her word and now in the weeks that followed she had begun to comfortably settle into a rhythm at work with her. When they had first started working together it was as if they were a snow globe that someone had viciously shaken, but now all of the fluff had settled at the bottom and begun to coalesce. Admittedly, Dara had done a little more overtime than she had wanted, but Lillianna was far more likely to ask than to order it.

However, it was confusing with how it felt like Lillianna flipped a switch outside the office. There was a certain sparkle in her eyes when she spoke about animals and old Roman architecture that was so very different from the determined, grim glint that resided there when they spoke of projects and deadlines.

"Dara?"

Dara immediately perked up at the sound of her boss's voice beside her. The woman's footsteps were strangely stealthy at times, and she hadn't noticed her approach at all.

"Oh hey, what's up?" Dara spun around in her chair to face her.

Lillianna still towered over her but Dara no longer found her quite as intimidating. She was still stern, but mixed in with all the hard edges was an odd sort of softness that she showed at times.

"Could you go and find this file for me?" Lillianna asked, pointing at instructions written on a slip of paper. "It's pretty old, so it isn't in the computer data. I'm pretty sure it's in the cabinets on the third floor, but I need to head to a quick meeting right now."

"Of course," Dara nodded, grateful for the opportunity to get up and move about. "I'll get right to it."

"Great. It shouldn't be that hard to find, and thank you," Lillianna smiled, revealing her teeth. The way her oddly sharp canines cut into her lower lip was quite attractive—bright white against a striking crimson.

Dara ignored the soft flutter in her stomach and nodded. Without her being frightening and glaring so much anymore, it was much easier to notice how attractive she was. Well, all the Markovs were attractive actually, as evidenced by how she had caught Candy and Rachel each staring dreamily at Eric on separate occasions.

Looking down, Dara examined the slip she had received as she headed toward the elevator. Exquisite, refined handwriting penned across the slip detailed the section and cabinet number, the elegance of which surprised her. Though she had never considered it before, she had expected that Lillianna's handwriting would be utilitarian and hurried like her attitude had often been when they met. But there were lots of little things like that Dara had discovered since getting on friendlier terms with her boss. Once, she had caught a glimpse of Lillianna's computer screen just after lunch and saw that during the break she had been looking at the website for a local art museum and checking the current show dates. Even if she had denied it before, it was proof that she had a life outside the office—at least if she had actually made it to the museum eventually. It seemed that Lillianna did have a soft spot for the arts. Dara had seen the little lion sculpture on her first day here, but since then she had also noticed a beautifully bound book on ancient Greek and Roman sculpture laying out on her desk one morning before Lillianna had arrived to work later to put it away.

Interrupting her thoughts, the elevator doors opened and Dara stepped out onto the third floor. Golden, incandescent light lit the dim floor, and the sound of shuffling papers came from the offices that lined the edge of the main walkway. The filing cabinets were off to the side in their own area, and Dara passed through the dimly lit, empty halls to get there.

Further into the floor, the three sections of records held over two dozen cabinets each. Their metal exteriors were worn with age, and nicks and scratches lined their sides after decades of use and periodic relocation. Reaching the edge of the cabinets, she looked at the slip of paper again.

Section R, Cabinet 3B

The metal of cabinet 3B creaked from disuse as Dara slid open the first drawer and coughed as a cloud of dust emerged from within. As she thumbed through the folders, the scent of old paper reminded her of a library, as did the sheer amount of physical files that Markov Incorporated kept.

Dara quickly realized that this particular drawer held a record of personnel, not the old financial documents she had been sent to retrieve. Giving the rest of the drawer a brief scan just to be sure it wasn't what she was looking for, she was about to shut the dusty drawer and look in the next one when a familiar name at the top of one of the folders caught her eye—*Lillianna M. Markov.* Dara suddenly had an abrupt and very strong urge to look through it. She knew she shouldn't, but the curiosity continued to itch, and after a long, conflicted moment Dara gave in—just for a peek. She would take a glance at her birthday and get her boss a gift to encourage the cooperative feelings between them and perhaps jockey for a raise. Yeah, this wasn't like, *weird* or anything.

Slipping the folder out, she brushed off the dust while stealthily suppressing a cough. In her old black and white photo, Lillianna was as darkly attractive as ever, those piercing eyes coming through even in monochrome. Even though the file had clearly been placed here quite a number of years ago, the photo of Lillianna looked recent. In fact, it could have been taken yesterday and Dara would not have known any different. The woman was aging like fine wine, or, actually, just not aging at all. The only difference was that she looked a lot less tired. So then, how old was she... Wait, what?

Dara did a double take. The line where Lillianna's birthday should be was conspicuously blank. She scanned the page looking for a date of filing. That wasn't there either. In fact, there were no dates of any kind listed on the document at all. Just an old residential address with the words "DEFUNCT" stamped across it in faded red ink, and educational credentials for schools she did not recognize. Giving up and placing the barren file back alongside the others, she felt foolish but also quite disappointed for reasons she could not quite pinpoint. She did not dwell long on the thought nor shame long, and instead quickly rifled through the other drawers to find the file and hurry back to the sixth floor. However, when she made it back to Lillianna's office she found it still empty. The cubicles where Katie and the others usually were were also empty, having already run off to lunch. The quick meeting wasn't turning out to be so quick after all, which Dara found troubling. She hoped that didn't mean that lunch would be canceled in favor of Lillianna eating at her desk. That had already happened once, and suffice to say Dara had been bummed the whole day. Dara was just about to leave the file on her desk before heading back to her own when she heard someone call out to her.

"Hello there," a man called, his voice dark and warm. His skin was pale, contrasting sharply to dark hair that was artfully combed with a lock of hair that fell across his forehead roguishly. Deep blue eyes were accentuated by sharp cheekbones and powerful, slanting eyebrows. "Looking for Lilly?" he continued, motioning toward the empty office.

"I'm just leaving this here on her desk. I need to get back to work," Dara informed him as she edged away. Despite his obvious resemblance to Eric, there was something deeply uncomfortable about this man. His eyes were such a deep blue, and—bizarrely—they seemed to be getting bluer by the second.

"Oh no, stay a while," he coaxed as he took another step toward her. Her instincts told her that this man was a threat and that she needed to leave *now,* but at the same time she just couldn't. She felt sleepy... paralyzed, but not alarmed by that at all. The world seemed to slow, and the stress of the day, the week, even the year, melted away.

"Dara! *Dara!*" a woman's voice cut through the haze like a knife to flesh.

The cloudy, tranquil feeling was gone, Dara found herself standing, several paces away in the opposite direction from where she had been heading and unsure of how she had gotten there. In front of her was the man, his extended hand dropping to his side languidly. His slick smile had vanished and his forehead wrinkled in immense distaste. Still dazed, Dara looked around for the source of the new, yet familiar, voice and saw Lillianna just down the hall.

"What the hell are you doing here?" Lillianna snarled at the man. She was rapidly closing the distance between them in a furious stride.

"Just stopping by, *Lilly,*" the man growled roughly, all his charm from earlier down the drain as Dara glanced between the two of them in confusion. Lillianna quickly arrived beside her and gripped Dara's wrist to pull her to her side.

"Frederick," she spat, her hand moving to curl over Dara's shoulder protectively. The tension was palpable and so thick that Dara simply held still like a deer in headlights for preservation. "You know what they say about tourists. Now don't *touch* anything and get back to your own floor."

"I have business here, just so you know," Frederick sneered haughtily, unwilling to allow Lillianna the last word.

Lillianna's ice blue eyes deepened in intensity, her glare so sharp edged that it could have cut glass. The savage animosity between them made Dara feel uncomfortable at having even been a spectator of it. It came as a relief when Lillianna dragged her from the hall and into her office, leaving the man behind as she closed the door behind them. Lillianna's gaze was still focused on the man's departing figure as he knocked on another office down the hall, entered, and was gone.

"...*knuckle sandwich for his afternoon snack...*" Dara heard Lillianna mutter under her breath as she continued to glare out into the now empty hall. Dara wanted to ask what the hell that was all about, but not when her boss was like this.

"Are you alright?" Lillianna asked after a minute when she turned away from the window. She began to look Dara over as if had narrowly escaped an attack by a wild animal. "I am terribly sorry. My cousin is—" Lillianna looked at a loss for words, her anger mixing with a different and far more potent expression. "Anyway, are you alright?" she repeated, examining her intently.

"I'm fine. It's okay, really," Dara tried to assure her, still unsure of what had even happened. Lillianna must assume that Frederick had done something incredibly untoward, but, while he had alarmed her, Dara's heart was racing now for an entirely different reason. Her face felt warm, as did the spot on her shoulder where Lillianna's hand had gripped her. Suddenly remembering why she had been outside Lillianna's office in the first place, Dara thrust the manila folder in her hands forward. "I got the file for you."

"Oh, I...right. Thank you." Lillianna took the folder from her and took a cursory look through the contents before flipping it shut again. "It wasn't any trouble to get it? No one bothered you there? Not like my cousin did?"

"No, no problems," Dara replied, feeling her face growing even more uncomfortably warm at all the care and attention she was receiving.

"Are you sure? No one spoke to you at all?" Lillianna asked, the worry still evident in her tone.

"Yes, really, I'm sure," Dara assured her again, eager to change the subject before she got a fever. "Anyway, I got the file so about the new—"

"Hey Lilly, did you manage to find that file I told you about?" As if on cue, Eric poked his head into the office. He had a sandwich in one hand and a bag of something dark in the other. Dara squinted. It looked...red.

"Yes," Lillianna replied curtly, clearly doing her best to ignore her brother as she continued to face Dara.

"Oh, good. So then you two will be able to get the report on my desk by Monday?"

"We were just now about to begin discussing the timeline after lunch," Lillianna stated bluntly.

"Right, well I'll let you girls get back to it then," Eric replied. He flashed them both a cheerful smile.

"I'm a little bit too old to be called a 'girl' you know," Lillianna corrected moodily, but Eric was already gone and down the hall. She gave a frustrated sigh and ran a hand through her sleek, dark hair.

The vague hint about Lillianna's age tempted her to ask, but it was utterly inappropriate and she had already transgressed enough boundaries today with that stupid file. Besides, it did not matter how old Lillianna was, she looked great, and it was not as though an unexpected gap in age was a deal-breaker. *Wait, deal-breaker for what?*

"Well then, let's go to lunch," Lillianna said, turning to her with an apologetic smile. Dara had seen her sharp canines peek out from behind her lips many times now, but this time it hit differently.

"Where are we going today?" Dara asked. She felt something in her chest twinge with feeling as Lillianna visibly perked up.

"There's this French Bistro I haven't been back to in a while. It's a little far, but I can drive us."

"It won't cut into the workday too much, will it?" Dara asked. "I mean, don't get me wrong, I would love to try it. It's just I know we're a little behind what with that extra set of data that got dumped on us."

"Well…" Lillianna's eyes drifted back in the direction that her brazen cousin had departed in. Her expression hardened, but then relaxed again as she looked back at Dara. "It's fine."

Dara wondered what sort of beef she had with her cousin, but had to admit that while Lillianna had been terrifying, she had also been so sexy—*ahem*—cool when she had showed up to grab Dara and chase him off. Dara felt a quantity of concern at what she had just thought about her boss. Guiltily, she stole a glance at her as they entered the elevator. Certainly, Lillianna was an attractive woman, and ever since she had stopped glaring so much it was more noticeable, but in that moment Dara felt like she was *the* most attractive woman instead of one of many that existed. Her heart skipped a beat at the revelation. *Crap.* She was starting to *like* Lillianna, wasn't she?

"You just have to try the warm shrimp salad," Lillianna explained as they exited the elevator and went out into the underground parking. "It has this creamy, lemon sauce that is just fantastic…"

Dara nodded along as she followed after her, listening but also becoming increasingly aware of how bad this was. Sure, Lillianna felt like a friend when they went on lunches together and she talked about lions and paint pigments instead of financial outlooks and deadlines, but she wasn't! Dara needed to nip this in the bud and firmly remind herself that this was her boss, not her friend, and certainly not her girlfriend. She had a bad habit of becoming too close to people and thinking way more of them than they did for her. Just because her ex had rudely dropped into her life last month did not mean Dara needed to go and make *another* catastrophic mistake in her love life, and, to make matters worse, Lillianna was already married to her job, out of her league, and almost certainly straight.

Chapter 7

It was half past two when a tingle ran up Lillianna's spine. Immediately looking up from her preparations, she scanned the hallway and cubicle farm for intruders. Between the cubicle walls she counted each head in Dara's section—eight cubicles and seven heads with an extra for whenever Eric got another one. Relaxing, she released a soft sigh of relief. Never before had she been so grateful for Eric's lack of control when collecting assistants. No one was going to try to creep on her assistant with all six of them present. As she watched, Dara adjusted her glasses and ran a hand through her hair before resuming typing, and Lillianna could not help but smile. She had acclimated surprisingly well since beginning to work with her, and even those dorky looking loafers had begun to grow on her.

Lillianna had not realized how much she had wanted a friend until she had one. This may have started with an awkward attempt to ensure that Dara's skills remained both at Markov Incorporated and with her, but the way it had ended up was more important than increased progress on financial outlooks and spreadsheets. Dara was pleasant to talk to and their chats always remained friendly, and when discussing various topics and hobbies the conversation felt more like a soft invitation to try something rather than a challenge to compete as it had always been with her cousins. Thinking of which, there was a certain cousin whose desire to compete had been ramped up lately.

Lillianna's mood immediately darkened as the storm clouds rolled in alongside her recollection. Frederick was the whole reason she was warily watching over Dara so closely now. He actually had the nerve to actually try to hypnotize her assistant, and it left Lillianna fuming at all hours of the day. How dare he try to steal her assistant for his gluttony. *She* was the one who was taking care of Dara and making sure she was healthy, not him! Though, Dara's excellent health might be part of the problem—she smelled, well, great: mouthwateringly delicious. However, that was only because Lillianna had been restraining herself and making sure that Dara got plenty of time for sleep and rest each night. That meant doing more everything else herself, and she was not doing extra spreadsheet work just because Frederick wanted gourmet blood. The man was such a glutton that he had been warned more than once for giving his assistants anemia, and the unfortunates in question were not even his blood matches—it was just that nothing was ever enough. Lillianna's hands were tied as far as retribution for his attempt went, but she could prevent another. She *had* to prevent another. What if she had not gotten out of the meeting in time to catch him and put an end to that affront to her authority? And then... *Urgh.* Just thinking about her smarmy jackass of a cousin drinking from Dara's neck made her want to puke.

Altogether worrying about both Dara and work together was just too stressful, and Lillianna needed to work to prepare for the business meeting tomorrow night. The date had been moved up when her grandfather had unexpectedly come into town early, and despite that under no circumstances did she want to appear disadvantaged by it. She had already sent an email to Dara warning her that she might need her to stay tonight, but, though Dara had said it was fine, it was one thing to warn her and another to actually ask. That was stressful too, and, as much as she hated to say it, she needed a break.

Just a short break, she told herself as she pulled out a spare notebook and uncapped a pen. After this she would feel better and then get right back to work straight all the way into the evening.

* * *

Throughout the day, Dara had felt eyes on her. She had caught Lillianna looking her way several times now out of the corner of her eye, and her boss was not even subtle about it. If Dara went down the hall to the water cooler for a drink, Lillianna somehow managed to hover nearby too. Dara felt almost flattered by the attention, though she knew she shouldn't for more than one reason. The most logical explanation was that Lillianna was worried that Dara was slacking or something with their deadline for the materials having been moved up to tomorrow. The woman was just plain odd when stressed, and right now she was even more stressed than usual.

Thinking back to the old photo she had seen in the file cabinet folder, Dara recalled that Lillianna had not looked nearly so tired back then, whenever "then" was, and far less brooding too. Taking a surreptitious peek back to Lillianna's office, she saw that Lillianna was working. She let her gaze linger, watching the woman's perfect eyebrows scrunch together in deep, angry looking thought. A few moments later, Lillianna looked up as she had often done today, but this time their eyes met. It was a pleasant sensation, not paranoid or nagging. Lillianna smiled, and Dara found herself smiling back as Lillianna waved at her, beckoning her to come to her office, which she obliged.

"Dara, I want to apologize in advance, but could you stay later tonight to help finish this prep stuff up?" Lillianna asked. "You already know about how the dinner meeting with the chairman got moved up. I just couldn't do anything about it."

"Of course." She had more than expected this after the warning about the change of dates, but what was on her mind was not the disappearance of her evening. Up close Lillianna looked tired and worn out, and Dara wanted to tell her to just go home and sleep, but that was neither her place as an employee nor even feasible at the moment.

"We're waiting on the last few documents, but they should be along soon. For now, how about you take the current data and..." Lillianna's instructions were clear and concise, but as she spoke Dara could not help but notice how her lips curved artfully on each word. The ruby shade of her lipstick suited her so well, and altogether she was just so— "Did you get all that?"

Dara abruptly snapped out of it. "Yeah," she said immediately. "Uh, but could we go over that last part again?"

"Just make sure to print an analog copy. I'm sure you've noticed that the company still makes use of printed copies a lot, but the chairman dislikes digital the most out of everyone. He vastly prefers the old ways."

"The 'old ways?' Does Markov Incorporated moonlight as a historical society?" Dara's comment earned her a smile from Lillianna.

"Kind of. I think he would prefer the sixteenth century, but he's settled for the fifties out of necessity," Lillianna conceded with a soft chuckle. She smiled, and pointy, pearly white teeth peeked out from behind ruby lips. This side of her was adorable.

Dara felt her cheeks warm and immediately forced her eyes away. *No, she scolded herself. Don't think about her like that.* Her eyes wandered the room for a distraction, latching on to the first thing she saw: a notebook left on the far side of Lillianna's desk, haphazardly flung open with a ballpoint pen still resting on it.

A lion was sketched across the pages, which was not in itself surprising considering Lillianna's admitted tastes, but what surprised Dara was that this beast was no stick figure. Intense shading brought bulging muscles and razor sharp claws brought the lion to life. An imperious scowl looked out at the viewer with glittering eyes, and a flowing mane had just begun to come into focus as the detail trailed off to the simpler parts of the sketch that had yet to be finished.

"Wow!" Dara blurted out, breaking the silence thoughtlessly. She stared with open mouth wonder at the sketch. "That's incredible! Did you do that?"

"Huh?" Lillianna turned around to look at the misplaced drawing. She had apparently already forgotten about it. "I just do it for stress relief every now and then. It isn't that special."

"No, it's great," Dara insisted. "I would put it on my wall."

"You would?" Lillianna asked, surprised and her expression thoughtful as if probing for sincerity.

"Yes, really."

"Then you can have it." With that, Lillianna carefully ripped the sketch from her notebook.

"Thank you, I'll take good care of it," Dara said as she happily accepted the paper. Out of the corner of her eye a shadow flickered as someone passed by outside in the hall and she immediately felt Lillianna stiffen beside her. Before she could even process what was happening, Lillianna had swiftly stepped to her side between her and the door and reached an arm around her shoulder protectively. Now Dara was tensing, flustered, and her insides doing a quick, impromptu imitation of a pretzel. "Uh—?" Dara blinked up at her boss as her face rapidly turned a florid red.

"Hey, I got your email, Lilly," Eric called as he walked into the office to join them without knocking. When he saw them he stopped and quirked a brow. "Something wrong?" he asked quizzically as he looked between them with growing interest. "Did I interrupt something?"

"No, it's nothing," Lillianna nearly growled as she immediately dropped her hand back to her side. She quickly moved on past the incident. "Did you bring us the files?"

Right, it was nothing, Dara ordered her errant thoughts that were attempting to leap to other conclusions. Except staying on track was hard when Lillianna was still so close that she could feel her body heat.

"Yep." Eric pulled a flash drive from his suit pocket. "Got them right here. Too big to email." As Lillianna snatched it from his hand, he raised a questioning eyebrow at her, which she returned with an unconvincing shrug.

"You were faster than expected," Lillianna said, brushing off his unspoken inquiry.

"Hey, hey, I can be quick when I need to be. I know you're going to that fancy dinner with Gramps tomorrow night. Can't have Grandpa's favorite girl unprepared," Eric replied with a grin.

Lillianna was patently unamused. "Thank you again for the data, Eric, but we really need to get to working on this."

"Sure, sure." Eric said nonchalantly before leaving as quickly as he had come. Dara was about to awkwardly follow him when Lillianna stopped her.

"Wait, you need this," she said as she held out the flash drive and Dara took it. All the venom that had accumulated when speaking to Eric had drained from her face and left Lillianna looking apologetic. "Sorry about grabbing you like that. I've just been a bit jumpy ever since my cousin tried to bother you," she explained. "I won't do it again."

"It's okay, don't worry about it," Dara replied before heading back to her desk. Lillianna's cousin must have affected her something awful for that reaction. Maybe he was a womanizer, and considering how many suspiciously beautiful assistants Eric had, that didn't seem all that far-fetched that Lillianna's other relatives might be similar. As for herself, she felt more disappointed at the apology and promise of no repeats than she would like to admit. This was going to become a problem soon if she didn't manage to rein it in better, but she could not find it in herself to be that worried yet.

* * *

"Oh, joining me tonight?" Katie commented after the others had left for the evening. "It's real nice here after seven. Real peaceful, and it feels like the time goes by fast too."

"Sounds nice. What does Eric have you working on tonight that's so important?"

"Oh, this and that. Nothing too big, really, just a few things to keep everything on schedule. Personally, I don't think it's that necessary but I'll take the easy overtime. You?"

"Huh." Well, Dara could not say she had not expected Katie's job in general to be easier than hers, but overtime for nothing was new. In contrast, there were multiple data sets already pulled up on her screen waiting for her. "It's sort of too complicated, but Lillianna says she needs it in time for tomorrow night's meeting."

"Ouch, doesn't sound like a lot of leeway," Katie gave her a sympathetic smile. "Best of luck getting that done!"

It quickly became apparent that time was not flying by Dara like it did for Katie, but it was also not as though she would be busy on this fine Wednesday evening, or at least not anymore. She had previously reserved her Wednesdays to have dinner with her mother, but in the last few weeks that had changed: her mother had gotten a new boyfriend. And while it was good that her mother had a new man in her life and not just Dara, her only child, most of the weeknight dinners had turned into date nights with Jack. Even Thanksgiving had centered around him despite the newness of the relationship, and she wasn't quite sure how she felt about that.

Previously, Dara had been the last link to her father that her mother had fiercely held onto, but now that she was released from that obligation it left an empty spot in her life and calendar. However, people moved on to a different phase of their lives, and that was just the way things were. Now her mother was enjoying herself spending time with her boyfriend, and Dara was, well, spending her evening with her boss working.

She got to work pasting in numbers and placing formulas as she fell into a rhythm and soon her other thoughts and worries began to slip from her mind. In the background she could hear Katie and one of the other boss's assistants chatting about their weekend plans. One of them was going to go to a bonfire or something, but Dara was too in the zone to pay attention to who exactly, and the exact meaning of their words faded into the background as she worked.

At some point Katie flitted off to help Eric with something, and someone else across from her who worked for a different Markov went home. Then the assistant she had been speaking to got up and left in the direction of the bathroom, and by the time Dara looked up from her work again she was the only one left at the cubicles. Katie's bag was still there on her desk, but Katie herself had been gone for quite a while now. Dara was nearly done with her work so she decided to take a break and stretch her legs. The halls of the sixth floor were eerily empty as she strolled through them. The sparsely placed windows were black against the night, through the darkness she could make out the pinpricks of street lamps as shoppers and diners braved the chilly autumn to socialize and run errands.

She was just coming back from the bathroom and nearly to her cubicle when she heard a strange noise. Someone was moaning in pain. Alarmed, Dara cautiously followed the sound of the noise to the edge of the cubicle area. Maybe someone had slipped and fallen and that was why they had not been able to make it back to their desk. Heels were dangerous like that—what people really needed were a trusty pair of comfortable loafers like her own. Stopping at the corner and looking ahead, Dara abruptly realized she had heard wrong. There was no pain or injury. Instead, it was Katie leaned up against the wall, head thrown back and nails digging into the shoulders of Eric Markov's charcoal designer suit. His mouth was glued to her neck, sucking as she moaned in pleasure.

Dara backpedaled so hard that she slipped and fell on the carpet with a thud. She expected them to hear her and investigate, but they appeared too engrossed in their own activity to notice her—yet. The moans were now growing closer as activity escalated and Katie's back slid against the wall, the sound of her moans growing ever closer and in that moment Dara wanted to be anywhere but here.

"I'm not done yet..." Eric crooned.

Katie gave an intoxicated giggle in response, the edges of her voice fuzzy as she spoke incoherently. "My, what big teeth you have..."

No, no, please shut up, Dara thought as she scrambled frantically back to her desk to cower. It was not any of her business if Eric was having some sort of steamy office affair with Katie, and she did not want it to be. He could be making love with all six of them as long as she didn't have to see it. She had been idly curious about the whole situation before, but now Dara wanted none of it. More giggling and soft whispers that Dara did not want to hear followed, and then ever closer footfalls that beckoned her doom.

Oh no. Dara's eyes widened hard when she realized they were heading toward her still. They were going to enter the cubicle area soon, and dear god Dara did not want to be in here for it. She began a frantic search for a better hiding place. Under the cubicles? No, they might pass by hers and notice her in their peripheral vision. Not that the odds of that happening were high when they were so busy with each other, but it would be beyond awkward if they did. Dara started to make her way down the hall, but it was too late.

"Oh, *Eric*," Katie moaned, her voice unbearably close now.

Dara panicked, grabbing the first door she came to and squeezed herself inside. She tumbled into Lillianna, knocking the much taller woman off balance as they both slammed against the ground. Dara's forehead smacked into Lillianna's jaw and she yelped in pain.

"The hell—?" She heard Lillianna exclaim as she rubbed her jaw. The papers that had been in her hand scattered in the air and settled all around them. Dara's forehead throbbed angrily as she looked up and found that Lillianna really was well and truly glaring at her. "What the hell were you doing?"

Dara's heart was beating a rapid staccato pace against her ribcage. First the awkward thing with Katie, and now *this*. "I was—they were—" Dara sputtered, unable to form a coherent thought as her stomach twisted into a tight, fluttering knot. She could feel Lillianna's stomach muscles tense beneath her as she sat up. The warmth of her body permeated through the fabric of her blazer.

"Um, I was avoiding—avoiding—" Dara attempted, pointing toward the door.

Lillianna's expression darkened as she gripped Dara's forearm to lift her up and disentangle them both. "Frederick?"

"Sort of?"

"Sort of?" Lillianna quickly looked outside the office glass. "I don't see anyone."

Oh thank heavens. Dara inwardly breathed a sigh of relief.

"Are you hurt anywhere?" Lillianna asked, her face and voice full of concern as she looked her over.

"I'm okay," Dara said, rubbing her forehead a little as if to prove it. "It was my fault anyway. I'm sorry, I wasn't thinking."

At the mention of Frederick, Lillianna's glare had melted away entirely. "You have the right idea to stay away from him," she said, reaching out to give Dara's hand a tight squeeze. There was a pause as Lillianna's ice blue eyes looked deep into hers, and Dara lost track of anything she might have wanted to say. Sensing that things had turned awkward, she changed the subject. "I was just going to ask you about these," Lillianna said as she leaned down to collect the papers from the floor and hand them to Dara.

"Oh, what are they for?" Dara asked. It was hard to even see the numbers when all she could think about was how warm she felt. Lillianna was concerned, she cared about her, and they were all alone at night. *Stop, hold it right there,* her conscience abruptly butted in.

"You're holding them upside down," Lillianna said, laughing a little and moving to correct the papers. God, her smile was so pretty. "Perhaps you've stayed too late."

"No, no, we're almost done. I'm alright."

"Well, alright. You see, with this data I was thinking about taking this and…"

Dara listened quietly and as she followed along everything began to make sense. Not just for the figures printed on the paper, but also the soothing way Lillianna's voice enunciated each word of instruction everything began to slot into place. Almost subconsciously, Dara leaned in closer, and she realized she could smell the subtle, sweet scent of her perfume—a heady mix of vanilla and black plum that begged her to lean in ever closer, a siren's call coaxing her to lay her tired head across her Lillianna's shoulder and just stay there. Dara now had no doubt about it at all; she really had a problem. Her mother had a new boyfriend, and all Dara had was a pipe dream.

Chapter 8

"You really stayed late last night," Katie commented sympathetically as she settled into her desk for the day and noticed the stack of papers already sitting on Dara's desk. "Lillianna really works you hard."

"It's alright," Dara assured her as an aura of awkwardness settled over the cubicle farm. She had been hoping that Katie would not come in at all today, but alas, she had just been late. After last night, she could imagine why.

"Did you get enough done at least?" Katie asked casually as she booted up her computer. "Won't miss the deadline?"

"I did. You?" Dara returned politely, though she did not want to know.

"Oh, of course. Eric's request was pretty simple—they usually are. I don't know why he can never find the client meeting times though. He needs to have better notes or an address book or something so I don't have to help search his office for scraps of paper all the time."

Searching through notes—so that's what they were calling it now. Dara cringed inwardly at the thought. "That's too bad you had to stay late for that."

"They're paying me. It works out." Katie shrugged in an unruffled manner as if nothing out of the ordinary had happened last night at all. But Eric had been going at her so hard that even with makeup the hickeys on her neck would be unmistakable—*wait.*

Dara paused in disbelief as she saw smooth, unblemished skin all along Katie's neck. From this close she should easily be able to tell where Katie had tried to hide the evidence, but there simply was none. She stared with increased intensity at her, trying to find something—anything—but there was nothing out of the ordinary there at all. Well, nothing except the very fact that there was nothing when there absolutely should be. There was not a single discoloration or even the barest hint of a bruise or hickey on Katie's neck, but Dara was sure of what she had seen last night.

"Something wrong?" Katie asked, noticing Dara's prolonged attention. "Need another coffee after last night?"

"Maybe I do," Dara admitted, though not for the reasons Katie thought. This was beyond weird, but she couldn't have imagined the whole thing, could she? She certainly had not imagined colliding with Lillianna in her office. *Well,* Dara thought in an attempt to comfort herself despite the dissonance, *at least they're very discreet about it the rest of the time.*

"Dara?" Lillianna called from her office.

"Oh, gotta go. We're still working on it today, so I won't be able to talk much. Good luck!" Dara explained quickly before quickly scampering off and away from the case of the disappearing hickey. However, in the short amount of time that she had been extricating herself from the awkward conversation with Katie, Eric had appeared with a file in hand and occupied Lillianna's office. Dara waited patiently outside the office, not wanting to crowd them and potentially cause a tripping hazard like last night.

"Hey, sorry, it's a bit late but here's the file," Eric said. She could see him hand over a thin manila folder, which relieved her. She did not need any more massive sheets of analog data to wrestle with.

"A bit?" Dara heard Lillianna grumble. "You transferred her here over a month ago. The least you could do was bring me the file on time."

"I just misplaced it for a little bit. You know, if we could keep more digital copies..."

"You know we can't do that," Lillianna stated firmly.

"I know, I know. Anyway, I'll email you the project stuff. You'll see it soon."

With that, Eric left, unaffected whatsoever by the pointedly unamused look Lillianna was giving his back as he strolled easily back to his office.

"He's always late, isn't he?" Dara said as soon as Eric was out of earshot and she took his place within the office.

"Yes, he is," Lillianna agreed as she shook her head. "Something about taking it easy to provide stress relief."

"He's nicer than your cousin though, at least?" Dara attempted.

"That's not a very high bar to cross." Lillianna's expression went dark for a moment, but then quickly cleared. "Anyway, I wanted to talk to you about the ordering of the..." As she spoke, she slid the folder Eric had delivered into her desk, but not before Dara noticed that it had her name on it.

Dara followed along, grateful that today's work was relatively simple and easy. In fact, she might even finish early. Lillianna was halfway through the explanation of the topic when she suddenly stopped speaking. Her eyes were glassy as she looked forward, seeing but not really seeing Dara.

"You okay?" Dara asked.

Immediately, she snapped out of it and shook her head. "Just hungry." Lillianna was not the type to space out, but she seemed to be hungry a lot lately.

"Time for an early lunch, then?" Dara asked hopefully. Or rather, an on time lunch for the rest of the world.

"Not, today, no," Lillianna replied apologetically. "I'm going to be spending any extra time going over the presentation."

"Oh." Dara tried to quell her disappointment. Thursday had been a very consistent lunch day, and she had begun to take it for granted. "Well alright. The progress report is that tough?"

"Well, it's the company chairman, so of course."

"He doesn't cut you any slack for being your grandfather, huh?"

"Maybe a little, but a lot of others will be there too, and I don't want to mess up in front of anyone. It has to be perfect," Lillianna admitted.

"Perfect?" Dara asked.

"Well, as close to it as possible at least." Lillianna gave her a tired shrug.

"Huh." Glancing to the side of Lillianna's desk, Dara thought she saw a sketched lion paw among the filled wastebasket, almost certainly thrown away in a fit of stress, but didn't say anything more about taking a break. Even if she wanted to see her boss relax, it was not her place to advise her on that sort of thing. "Well, I believe in you," Dara attempted, but it just felt corny. She wanted to help, but all that she could manage further was a generic, "You're going to do great."

"Well, I—" Lillianna began, but then her eyes went glassy again for a brief moment, then quickly refocused once more. "—uh, thanks, I really appreciate it."

"Anytime," Dara said with as bright a smile as she could muster even though she wanted to frown inside at this predicament. Lillianna had to be stressed out of her mind with how often she was blanking on her today.

* * *

Lillianna gripped the lacquered wood of the bathroom countertop and glared at the droplets of blood that were rapidly darkening in the sink. She had been so furious with Frederick that she had clenched her fangs right into the inside of her lower lip. Breathing deeply, she steadied herself, but it was difficult. She had been so stressed as of late that even among the scent of wine and desserts she had just wanted more blood. It was a natural reaction, to be sure, but she had already drunk two bags earlier at the office.

Still, despite all her stress at the impending dinner meeting, everything had gone without a hitch thus far. Her grandfather was now looking through the materials she had given him after her small presentation, and she had not started something with her cousin no matter how much she wanted to. She just needed to head back and finish speaking with him about it while everyone else finished up their dinner. It would not be hard, and then a promotion within the next couple years was practically assured. At least, as long as she did not turn this into a boardroom brawl in the meantime. Lillianna narrowed her eyes at the mirror as she recalled Frederick's final words to her after already asking several subtly heckling questions in the Q&A.

"I see you've been making good use of your assistant," Frederick had commented, his tone dark, smug, and self-satisfied.

His comment was inane, and her grandfather had not even been listening—the man far preferred his puzzles and cards to anything social—but Lillianna had caught every undertone it held. He had made countless comments all through her tenure at Markov Incorporated thus far, but this time it was far more personal—because it included another person. Not only was it a dig that her current success was reliant on another, but it doubled as a threat. Dara was invaluable to be sure, but Lillianna was still ten times better than Frederick even without her assistant. And just because she could have made do without did not mean she was about to relinquish Dara to prove it. That feeling of dependency, of one's own worth, talent, or even life being contingent on another—she hated it. Teamwork came with the territory in the company, she knew that, but she preferred to keep as much of her own work separate as possible.

Her thoughts drifted further from the present, back to earlier that evening when she was still at the office where she had noticed every movement of the muscles in Dara's neck as she breathed, spoke, or turned her head to look up at her. With all the stress it had been so tempting to just take a bite. Just once—except that was going to lead to twice, and then thrice, and then she was going to hate herself if she felt like she owed Dara any more than she already did. She would not even want to see Dara at that point, and that...that made her upset, and perhaps that was what irritated her the most. It was not just her work, or blood, or anything that Lillianna had expected, but something else too—Dara's company. She just liked her being around. She did not really know what to make of that, but now was not the time. She had been hiding in here long enough.

Her pulse slowed as she took another calming breath and steeled herself up for any further taunts from her cousin. Rising from the sink with one last deep breath, Lillianna left the bathroom and made her way back to the private dining room where her grandfather and others were waiting. The space was dimly lit by candles, and soft lamps, with a crisp, white tablecloth and the scent of well-prepared food and wine. Along the table sat a number of relatives and loyal business associates, their faces lit by candlelight as they sipped wine and chatted about the various business topics and inter-clan gossip. The dinner had been delicious, but it had been hard to let her guard down long enough to enjoy any of it properly and her slice of cheesecake remained untouched. Upon spotting her Frederick, who was seated a few scant seats down, smirked once more, his fangs gleaming in the candlelight in a silent taunt. She refused to meet his eye, instead training her gaze back to her grandfather and waiting expectantly for his appraisal of her work as she did her damnedest to ignore Frederick's very existence.

"Excellent work," her grandfather said as he at last looked up from the papers. "The Graves will be very pleased with this, and I expect their alliance with us to continue many years into the future."

"Happy to hear it," Lillianna replied cordially as her ego inflated.

"I hear the woman that runs their branch on this side of the pond is quite the stickler," Frederick interjected.

"She is, indeed" her grandfather stated thoughtfully, thumbing his well trimmed black beard. There was not a bit of gray there despite his age. Distinguished cheekbones and an air of wisdom in his eyes set him apart, but no one human would ever guess that he was actually centuries old, except perhaps the certain distance he had with his descendants. "But I think this passes the test."

"Excellent," Lillianna replied, shooting a quick smirk of her own to Frederick as her grandfather was distracted with the papers again.

"Although—" he began, looking down at the papers again, a pensive yet troubled expression coming over his face. "—there is just one thing."

The smirk immediately vanished from Lillianna's face and, much to her dismay, returned to Frederick's. "What thing?"

"Frederick, those files you received from the client earlier today, did you bring them?"

"Of course," he said smoothly as he reached for his briefcase below the table. "I have them right here."

"Files?" Lillianna asked cautiously as she kept her eyes on her grandfather. Frederick was making a big show of going through his briefcase behind her and she did not care to see it.

"Well you see, the Graves main branch sent us over some new data earlier today that was mainly related to things Frederick is working on, but if we applied it here to your project as well it would be quite excellent in my opinion."

"And your opinion is excellent," Frederick added unhelpfully as he flipped through files.

"It would be quite the task, but with the two of you I think you could get it done tonight in time for my meeting tomorrow," her grandfather continued, entirely oblivious to his grandson's attempts to butter him up.

"I will be able to do it myself. Frederick's help won't be necessary," Lillianna spit out immediately at the first mention of working with her cousin. No way in hell was she working with him, not after all he'd done to rankle her in the office by attempting to pounce on her assistant. And no way was he getting any more credit for this than absolutely necessary either.

"Are you sure? Your work ethic is admirable, but I would need it ready first thing tomorrow," her grandfather asked, looking at her with concern. It was the same sort of concern he had shown when she had been a mere child and had hurt herself in the forest. She had been so small then, and the concern that had welled up in his eyes then had been just the same.

"I'm sure. It will be fine," Lillianna pressed, gentle despite inward defiance. He acted as if she had not changed, but she *had,* damn it! She was more than capable of doing this without Frederick's slimy help.

"I will be awaiting it then, thank you Lilly," he said, letting it drop. As he said so, she could hear Frederick's dark mirth as he chuckled behind her.

"Here it is," Frederick said, a barely suppressed grin on his face as she turned back to him. From his briefcase he produced a thick folder of papers bearing the cracked wax seal of the Graves crest. Lillianna nearly did a double take at the size of it, but tried to look unconcerned as she took the folder and casually examined it, but now she understood why Frederick had not fought her on it when she cut him out. This was a *lot* of data for one night, and he had absolutely known it.

"Is there a digital copy of this?" Lillianna asked hopefully.

"Nope, that's all that was faxed," he replied with nonchalant smugness, a forkful of pasta already halfway to his mouth as he gleefully delighted in the problem he had just dumped on her.

Lillianna narrowed her eyes at him. He was probably lying, but since it sounded almost feasible she could not call him out on it here in front of her grandfather. Vampires in general preferred to stay off the Internet when possible to avoid leaving permanent footprints. When sticking with paper and analogue records, files could simply be "misplaced" or covered up when necessary to hide their existence—like hiding the fact that her grandfather had been chairman of Markov Incorporated for longer than any mortal's lifespan.

As he ate another forkful of pasta, he continued to grin at her, delighted in what he knew was going to be a painful night. He hoped she would fail—thought she would, in fact, unless she backed down and begged for his help. As if she ever would. She suppressed the urge to snarl as she turned back to her grandfather and instead smiled graciously.

"It will be ready and waiting tomorrow when you wake up."

* * *

Frenziedly typing away on her laptop, Lillianna took a moment she did not have to check the clock in the bottom right corner of her screen and winced. Doubt and a growing sense of doom were becoming harder and harder to stave off as the hours grew later. The night was still young, but by her calculations she had not made enough progress to believe that the trajectory would allow her to finish before she grew tired enough that even a vampire would begin to make careless mistakes, and she could not make any mistakes if she was to pull ahead of the pack. Lillianna groaned and shut her laptop for a brief respite. As much as she hated it, she needed help.

Handily, she knew someone who did this sort of work flawlessly and in record time. What was not handy was that it was a damn Thursday night and she had already had Dara work overtime yesterday. And Dara surely had better things to do tonight, even if it was just playing sudoku or solitaire. She was human after all, and there were only fifty-two Thursday nights in a year, and only so many years in a life. It would be unreasonable to ask Dara to come in, and there was not even a veneer of fairness to even the thought of it.

But if she didn't ask then she was going to look unreliable in front of her grandfather and worse, a fool in front of Frederick—something that was looking more and more assured by the moment. Lillianna eyed her work phone left out on the coffee table, and warred with the outcomes. On one hand there was the possibility that Dara was not going to like her very much. She might even look for a new job, or it could be the start of their budding friendship unraveling when work came before proper consideration. That probably wouldn't happen *just* yet, or maybe Lillianna needed to be grateful that it hadn't happened already. In order to keep that from happening she needed to stop taking so much, or maybe...maybe she just needed to give back more. If their relationship was more symbiotic than parasitic then she need not feel so reliant either.

For now though, she needed to swallow her pride and evade the very real possibility that she would hear Frederick's hyena-like laughter in her dreams for months or years. She picked up her work phone, unlocking it and scrolling to Dara's contact information that she had saved there when she first was transferred in and never used. She did not want to think about what would happen if Dara said no, but it was a real possibility. If only there were digital copies and then this would somehow feel like a smaller request to send over, or if she had gone and used the scanner at the office, but no, that also took time she did not have.

Please say yes. With resignation and nervous hope, she tapped a finger to the glowing screen. Soon, Dara's voice came over the line, clearly surprised and confused at the sudden despite the lateness of the hour.

"Hey Dara…it's…" Lillianna fumbled at first, unsure of even what to say, but eventually launched into the crux of the problem as if she were a presentation at a board meeting and she needed to make her pitch. Dara was receptive at least when she offered a significant boost in pay for the time. "Yes, I know. It's an emergency. I really, *really* need you to help me with the project. It's due tomorrow morning. No, really, it has to be you." Dara's voice rattled off several questions and terms from the other side of the line. She still sounded very surprised yet almost—happy? No, Lillianna was just so grateful that she was receptive to unexpectedly working at unreasonable and awful hours that she was hallucinating. No one would be happy to be working at this hour. "No, you don't need to come in tomorrow, take the day off. Takeout? Yeah, whatever you want and then some. No, not the office. My place. Bring your work laptop. The address is…"

Finished and the matter settled, she hung up the phone as a deep wave of relief flooded through her. The work was not over yet, in fact it had hardly begun, but with Dara's help she felt assured that it would all turn out. It had been far easier to convince her than she had thought it would be. Too easy really, Dara must be a saint. Slumping down on the couch, she dropped her phone before immediately picking it up again and dialing the number of Dara's favorite Thai restaurant, which sounded like a great idea now that she thought of it. Despite already having had dinner tonight, she was still just so hungry.

Chapter 9

"And, done!" Dara declared triumphantly as she tapped the send button on the email. Project phase one was well and truly complete, addendum and all. Wincing as she looked at the time, she closed her laptop and set it aside next to the empty takeout boxes and scattered papers.

"Good," Lillianna groaned, leaning back into the sofa. "I don't want to see another spreadsheet ever again."

"Aren't you going in to work tomorrow?" Dara pointed out. Lillianna had promised the day off to her, but said nothing of herself.

"Yes." Lillianna groaned again, covering her eyes.

Lillianna's apartment was not what Dara had been expecting. She had imagined a place with an abundance of sleek, black furniture and sparse, utilitarian lodgings reminiscent of Lillianna's perfectly pressed blazers, but what had greeted her instead was an abode more suited for the interior of a cottage than city apartment. Rustic landscapes by a painter whose name escaped her now were hung along the wall, and a wealth of small, intricate sculptures of figures and animals alike dotted the oaken bookshelves. Warm lamplight cast a cozy glow over the room, and on top of the coffee table there was a book on the sculptures of Ancient Greece and Rome which had been pushed aside to make way for laptops.

"It wasn't so bad. I quite liked working from home. Well, your home anyway. You ever thought about doing that more often?"

"I have, but if anyone's not present in the office there's a general assumption that they're not working," Lillianna complained. "They think I'm sketching all day even if all the work comes in on time."

"But you get so much done? Much more than Eric, that's for sure."

"Well..." Lillianna gave her a soft, almost sheepish look. "Thanks," she murmured quietly. "It isn't all me though. I really appreciate everything you do, and thank you especially for coming tonight."

"Happy to help," Dara replied, beaming despite her tiredness. At first she had felt foolish showing up at this hour, dragged along by her wayward feelings and the promise of the day off and pay, but when she had seen how panicked Lillianna was upon her arrival it felt like she had made the right choice. She felt valuable and irreplaceable. Wanted. *Needed.* She had not felt enough of that in her life, but she liked the change, even if it was just for work. As long as she didn't do anything for free, it was probably fine to bask in the glow of praise. Probably, anyway.

"If it wasn't so late I would say we should celebrate," Dara said as she began to pack up her things and stow her laptop in its case. She wanted to stay and bask in it longer, but with work over there was no longer any real reason she was here sitting on Lillianna's couch—just that she really wished she could stay.

Lillianna perked up at that suggestion. "We should. Wait here," she said as she got up from the couch. "I have just the thing."

Before Dara could even ask what that thing was, Lillianna had disappeared down the hall. The sound of footsteps migrated to the apartment kitchen, soon followed by the opening and closing of cupboards and pantry before Lillianna returned holding a fancy looking bottle of wine and two glasses. Setting it down on the coffee table, she went about uncorking it as Dara's eyes drifted to the label. She did a double take after she read the vintage.

"Wait—" Dara began.

"Don't like wine?" Lillianna asked, stopping mid-cork.

"No, I love wine, but isn't this a bit too nice for the occasion?" she asked hesitantly. This was starting to actually feel like she really *was* special, not just an especially useful cog in the machine.

"I'm never going to drink it otherwise. My brother gave it to me years ago, but I never have anyone over to drink it," Lillianna explained. "We should just have it."

"Well it looks lovely." Dara watched as she finished popping the cork and began to pour a glass. She bet it tasted lovely too.

"I'm glad you reminded me. I almost forgot I had it," Lillianna said with a small laugh, her pointy canines showing as she did so. She finished pouring the glass and handed it to Dara. "So what are you going to do on your three day weekend?"

Dara sipped her glass and considered it. "I think I'll get myself a nice meal, a warm bath, and a movie."

"No sudoku?"

"Well, yes, that too, but I wouldn't call it an event. It's just sort of there."

"I was going to try it myself, but I haven't had the time. I did a little research and read that it could help with stress reduction."

"You need that?" Dara asked, feigning shock.

"I'm too tired to tell if you're joking," Lillianna laughed and took another sip of wine. "But of course I do."

"Good to see that even the best of us are still just human," Dara said with a small chuckle.

"Human?" Lillianna asked, her expression confused until she shook herself awake. "Uh, yeah."

Dara snorted. "Good one. You almost had me there like you were a robot or something. And you? What are you doing on your three day weekend?"

"I'm not taking the tomorrow off," Lillianna reminded her.

"Well, your two day weekend then."

"Probably call my mother," Lillianna said after a moment's thought.

"You talk often?"

"Yeah, my mother is always worried about me."

"Mine too."

There was a pause as they both sat on the couch, drinking wine as the conversation faded out. There were so many things Dara wanted to ask her, and yet knew she really should not. Instead she enjoyed the wine and Lillianna's quiet company. A few minutes passed by peacefully like this, but then Lillianna turned to her and spoke.

"Why didn't you finish college?" Lillianna asked, breaking the silence. The question took Dara by surprise. They had never spoken of it, and, now that she thought about it, she had not even known Lillianna knew about it. As if reading her mind, or more likely her expression, Lillianna added, "Eric finally got your file over to me, and I saw in your resume that you got a lot of credits but never quite made it through."

"I wanted to finish," Dara began, trying to explain, but the words came out in a rush. Not having the opportunity to finish was a sore spot for her, and one that made every hunt for a new job more arduous than it should be. It just felt shameful. It hadn't at first, back when she had every intention of going back to finish up, but now, several years after the fact and hurtful doubt from others, she knew that wasn't happening. "I just couldn't afford it."

"Scholarship ran out?" Lillianna asked, tilting her head to the side sympathetically. "That happened to a lot of my classmates."

"No," Dara said with a soft sigh as the recollection flooded back. She had still had her scholarship, but it wasn't enough to cover things. Transferring to a state school was tricky with trying to get financial aid and she had been in the process of figuring that out when she got her big break. "My dad decided to do something else with his money, and so when one of my part-time job offers turned into full-time I went with it."

"...Huh?" Lillianna's head tilted further. "What did he do with the money instead?"

"One of my dad's other kids started at a private high school and he decided to pay for them instead."

"Other kid?" Lillianna appeared perplexed and extremely curious at this development. "Your brother? Sister?"

"Half-brother. We've never really spoken though, so I'm not sure I would really call him a brother at all," Dara admitted. "But he was my dad's favorite. I mean, it was never my money to begin with. I suppose I should be grateful he even paid for part of it at all." Dara knew she should not share all this, but with the wine and lateness of the hour, the words kept spilling out.

"Oh." Lillianna leaned back on the couch, seemingly having a hard time taking it all in whether from the wine or the sudden solemnness it was hard to say. A wave of embarrassment crashed over Dara, and her collar felt hot. She looked at her nearly gone wine glass, and then back to her laptop bag. She should probably go now. She was just about to get up when she was stopped by a hand being placed across the hand that rested in her lap. The sudden touch surprised her, so much so that she flinched in surprise.

"Oh, sorry," Lillianna said, pulling her hand away as Dara reddened further. "I just—well, have you thought about going back to finish it?"

"I don't think I can," Dara said quietly, looking at her wine. She felt far too embarrassed to look at Lillianna now. It was not that the touch bothered her at all, just that she had really, *really* not expected it. Lillianna did not want her like that; she was just being friendly. And why would she? Her own father had not even wanted her. He'd found a new wife, had new kids, and only begrudgingly paid for a couple years of college before finding an excuse not to that was softer than a

89

simple "no."

"The company has a fund for things like this. I can get them to approve you," Lillianna told her with a flash of that beautiful, pointy smile.

"You—what?" Dara asked in disbelief. "But won't that get in the way of work? I won't have time."

"The approval won't be ready until next fall. I could ensure things are light enough that you won't get caught up in crunch times while working on your schoolwork. Of course, this is only if you want to work on it after hours. It's not that the degree would change the fact that you're already talented, but if you want it you can have it."

"I—um—wow, thank you. I don't know what to say. That's wonderful. Thank you," Dara replied, nearly speechless as her earlier resolve began to melt away.

"Let's drink to that then," Lillianna replied, pouring more wine into her glass.

"I can agree with that." Dara returned the gesture with a smile of her own. "This stuff is really good."

"Have as much as you want."

It felt like Lillianna really did want her. *As an assistant,* she reminded herself. *Just an assistant.* But inside she could tell that what she was feeling was rapidly progressing beyond crush to something much more difficult to staunch. Lillianna Markov was just her boss, even if sitting here on her couch drinking her wine sure did not make it feel like it.

* * *

"—and that's why the lions on the coat of arms look so strange. The closest thing to it is the artwork of tigers on the Japanese mainland when they only had the skinned pelt to reference and not the living, breathing thing," Lillianna finished. Dara looked dazed at the sudden influx of information.

"Wow, you really know a lot."

"Just art history courses and museum visits," Lillianna explained. "Though I think it would have been so much more fascinating to live through those time periods."

"But then you wouldn't be here?" Dara pointed out, cocking her head to the side, clearly fuzzy with wine but making a good point—at least from a human perspective. What Dara didn't know was that Lillianna actually would still be here—as long as the vampire hunters hadn't caught her in the centuries between anyway.

"Do you want more wine?" Lillianna asked, changing the subject away from anything vampire related.

"Oh, I'd better not. I've had plenty," Dara replied, swaying as she tried to get up. Lillianna immediately reached out a hand to steady her. She felt delicate, but that was no surprise because all humans were. Even so, there was something that felt more fragile about Dara. Something that needed protecting.

"Don't stand up so fast. Here, sit down. I'll get you something."

As she left, Lillianna tried to recall how many glasses she had poured for Dara, and, more importantly, how many humans were normally supposed to stop at. The answers to both questions remained elusive at the edge of her fuzzy thoughts, dulled by wine and the late hour. She was no longer in sync with the normal rhythm of vampire sleep and it felt difficult for her to be so tired and yet revitalized by the night all the same. For humans, the night was for rest, but for vampires the night was for hunting, prowling the forest in search of travelers and drinking their blood. *Blood.* She could smell it, the sweet scent wafting from Dara as the woman sighed and laid her head against the soft leather of the couch and closed her eyes. Her glasses smushed up against her face and her chestnut hair fell across her eyes. She looked adorable, like a lost little lamb in the woods. Lillianna breathed deep, tasting the air on her tongue, floral and fruity fragrance of the alcohol overlaying the sweet scent of blood beneath skin, then she forced her gaze away.

Getting up off the couch, she went to her small kitchen to get Dara a glass of water to help sober up. She filled it from the tap before setting it on the counter and opening her second, smaller fridge. Looking inside at the chilled blood bags, she took one out and removed the cap. Just as she took her first sip, she heard Dara call out sleepily from the other room.

"Lillianna?"

Dara needed her. "I'll be right there," she replied automatically, recapping and setting the blood bag back down. She picked up the glass again and headed back to the couch to find Dara right where she left her, the only difference being that she had found the energy to set her glasses down on the coffee table.

"Thanks," Dara murmured drowsily when she caught sight of the glass of water in Lillianna's hand.

As she drank, Lillianna watched the muscles in her throat contract and relax in rhythmic timing, forcing her to remember that it was not just Dara who was thirsty. No longer did wine coat Lillianna's tongue, but blood. A single taste from the blood bag and her senses had rapidly heightened. Instinct demanded that she finish the hunt. Saliva flooded her mouth. The world felt blurry, as if she were underwater and struggling to reach the surface. She needed blood like it was air, but not the cold bag left on the kitchen counter. It was as tasteless as water compared to the precious pulse within Dara's neck.

"Here," Dara said, her words sleepy as she held back out the empty glass.

Lillianna leaned forward, her hand brushing the warm skin of Dara's fingers as she took the glass in her hands, deftly placing it onto the coffee table. She placed her other hand on Dara's cheek to steady her, and she leaned into the touch, closing her eyes as Lillianna drew ever closer. The expression looked familiar, but there was no thought to spare for why that was as she changed trajectory at the last moment to dip below Dara's lips to her neck and bite. Her sudden movement jostled the coffee table and the empty glass rolled and fell with a soft thud to the carpeted floor as rich, warm blood flowed into her mouth from lips locked to warm, soft skin. The salt of sweat and coppery metallic tang blended together to augment the sweetness beautifully, and Lillianna was enthralled. Nothing in the world nor even the blood of others compared to the sweet ambrosia on her tongue. She was a predator that roamed the night, the top of the food chain. Nothing and no one could stand in her way.

Dara tensed at first, but then her muscles grew slack as the relaxing qualities of vampiric saliva took hold. Her breathing slowed, then rose to a breathy cadence as the euphoric properties of the saliva hit her. She moaned, twitching at the otherworldly sensation as it entered her bloodstream. Then the sound of her breath faded into the background more and more and there was nothing in the world but Lillianna and sweet, sumptuous blood.

You're going to hurt her! A part of her came back from her blood high to reality and screeched loudly in unwelcome protest.

Lillianna's eyes snapped open and she pulled away as if burnt. Dara's eyes were dilated as she blinked at her and shivered slightly at the after effects of the saliva. Lillianna's tongue snaked out and licked a stray droplet of blood from her lower lip, tasting it still even as she looked on in shocked disbelief at what had just happened. The bloody pinpricks on Dara's neck were rapidly coagulating in the air with the help of her saliva. Her eyes closed lethargically, her mouth slightly as she let out a soft, contented sigh.

Fear shot through Lillianna's stomach like daggers of ice. She had hurt Dara—*no, she'll heal. The saliva will take care of that.* But that thought did little to comfort her. Physical pain was not the only thing she was worried about. There was an unbearable feeling of intimacy and dependency just as she had remembered from drinking blood decades ago while she was still at the atelier, except this was ten times worse, and yet also ten times better. It was impossible to push away something that just felt so *right.*

Oblivious both to Lillianna's warring thoughts and the world entirely, Dara continued to breathe in and out, her breath steadying and her lips and cheeks a rosy pink from exertion. The pinpricks on her neck were already healing and would be gone before the sun rose to burn away the night. Minutes passed, and then many more as Lillianna stayed there, unable to leave but equally unwanting to remain with the evidence of her bloody mistake. Finally, she retrieved a warm, wet cloth from the kitchen and wiped away the evidence. As she looked back at the burgundy stains upon the cloth, a sick feeling curled in her stomach and overrode the satiated glow of fresh blood. Revulsion rolled over her drowning her as she sat in silence beside Dara's sleeping form, but nothing changed. Time passed, still unchanging, and eventually Lillianna rose from the couch and returned to her own bed. She laid her head down on the pillow and hoped that tomorrow when she woke up this would all be a distant dream.

Chapter 10

When Dara awoke the next morning she blinked in the dimly lit room for a minute, confused at whose couch, pillow, and blanket this was before abruptly recalling the events of the prior night. A note was on the coffee table apologizing profusely for the previous night along with a few bills to buy breakfast to "help with her blood sugar" and wishing her a good day off. The spare key was placed a short distance away for locking the door behind her when she left.

Dara sighed wistfully, looking around the empty living room. Lillianna had already left for work, and now Dara could not help but have her heartstrings twinge: somehow the scene felt almost domestic. Her ex had never wanted to live with her, and although at this point Dara was grateful she hadn't, it was something she had yearned for to have someone in her life besides questionable college friends and her mother. Well, it was at least a nice little bit of make believe.

Sleeping on the couch had been more comfortable than she would have thought, with only a slight ache in the side of her neck from the experience and a budding hangover from the excess of wine. It couldn't be helped though, as there was no way she was going to have been driving herself home after all that wine and at that hour of the night. Yawning, she collected up her laptop bag and purse to head down to the covered parking. She drove home, poured herself a bowl of cereal, and was just considering if she should go back to sleep or hop in the shower when a bizarre recollection of last night hit her like a freight train going two hundred miles per hour.

Images of being roughly pushed against the wall flooded her mind, but there was no Eric or Katie in this dream as it had been in real life. Instead, Lillianna's piercing, ice blue eyes demanded something far more enticing than overtime, and Dara had been more than happy to give her whatever she wanted. Dara shivered as she realized just how true that was even when she was awake. Especially if it felt anywhere near as good as it had in her dream.

Dara pushed her bowl of cereal away and groaned as she hid her face in shame from no one in particular. This was her boss! Forget domestic, this was absolutely lurid! The freight train had left the station a long time ago. She didn't even know if Lillianna was like that in bed, or what she—*no! Stop thinking about it!* She bit her lip guiltily. Maybe she shouldn't have given in to her desire to be helpful to Lillianna last night. Maybe she should have kept her distance. But Lillianna's voice had been tinged with pleading desperation, and Dara had so very badly wanted to help, or perhaps to prove that she was useful, or both. When all was said and done she had felt unique and irreplaceable, just like she wanted to be, and yet now when she stepped back to really look at it she felt so cringey. She had just done overtime for her out-of-control crush, well, for that and extra pay. There was the Thai food and three day weekend too. Maybe this wasn't so embarrassing, except she was pretty sure it still was. Her Freudian dreams needed to cut it out or this freight train was going to veer off a cliff into a river. Though at this point maybe that would not be a bad thing—at least the train would stop then.

Dara's phone pinged with a notification, and she nearly shrank away when she saw that it was from Lillianna, but she was going to face her again on Monday anyway. It was not like Lillianna could see her humiliation from over a text at least.

I wanted to apologize again for last night.

Aw, that's so sweet, she feels guilty about the overtime. Ahem. *That was very nice of her to say that,* Dara corrected her thoughts mentally. She hit a few buttons on her phone to reply in a proper and professional manner.

No problem. I was happy to help. See you on Monday.

There was a long wait for a reply as Dara became increasingly nervous until she remembered that Lillianna was in the office today, and probably busy too. It wouldn't do to distract her or worry away her three day weekend. As long as she had not suddenly started talking in her sleep, then everything would be fine. Giving up on her cereal, she tossed her phone onto the couch and headed for the shower. Cold water was sure to banish these heated thoughts.

* * *

Unable to focus, Lillianna looked away from her computer screen and back at her phone again. She double checked the text for any sign or hint that Dara might remember last night in any way, but there was none. Dara was just being cheerful, professional, and polite. She relaxed somewhat at this realization, but it was still damn near impossible to focus on her prep for upcoming meetings today. Fool that she was, she had not even hypnotized Dara before she drank from her the prior night. It was pretty much the first rule of vampiric feeding and she had blown it. Her only saving grace was that she was pretty sure Dara had been tired enough and imbibed enough wine that the euphoric effect of vampire saliva had mixed with it to create a sort of confusing stupor, and humans generally believed vampires were a myth so anything she could remember would be reasoned away as false.

Vampire saliva acted both as a natural painkiller and potent drug. The effects were extremely pleasurable for humans and Dara was no exception. Her racing pulse as Lillianna drank from her neck was not caused by fear, but by pleasure. She remembered even now how Dara had moaned and panted as she lay beneath her. At the time, all Lillianna had focused on was her blood, but now there was a distinct aftertaste of how soft and delicate her body had felt against her too. Her face felt hot just thinking about it. Drinking blood from another had always been awkward, but this was different. Dara was cute with her dorky loafers and unusually chipper mood when completing reports. She was not supposed to be sensual or erotic, and the images that flashed through Lillianna's mind were incredibly incongruous to the rest of Dara's image. She probably should not have seen that side of her assistant, and yet a part of her wanted to see it again while another told her that what she had done was wrong. Lillianna tried to push the feeling away, but it held fast. Before, it had been an inconvenience to feel reliant on humans, but the sticky, residual feelings of guilt were new. Drinking blood was what vampires *did*. Always and forever and, even if she had never liked it very much, she should not feel so terrible about it.

As it was, Lillianna felt a growing sense of shame and discomfort in the pit of her stomach. A blood match's blood was supposed to make you feel great—a lighter body, stronger limbs, and a sharper mind, but Lillianna just felt awful inside. The world felt simultaneously brighter and darker than it ever had before, a sharp contrast between intelligence and instinct, the fool she was and the sage she wished to be. She was weak, and her sight was now merely sharp enough to see it.

The sudden swell of desire had been unlike any prior temptation she had experienced before. There had always been a choice before and the ability to resist, to hold out just one more moment until she could make space between her and the seductive call of lifeblood upon her tongue. But somehow last night's siren call had slipped past her in an instant. Even in the kitchen she had not been herself. She should have run away, not walked right back to Dara with the glass of water. It should have been obvious what would soon follow from returning, but the gears of her mind had snagged and whirred uselessly in place when it came to foresight and reason and she had no longer been thinking straight. To deny herself in that moment had been as unthinkable as attempting to perish of thirst and dehydration while floating in a pool of pure water. Instinct had taken over, and that was the end of it—powerless. She hated it, and hated herself for it.

Lillianna rose from her desk, resolving to simply take an early lunch. She should have been able to relax today with Dara safely out of the office for her three day weekend and Frederick having nothing to taunt her with, but that just wasn't happening. Walking out past the cubicle farm, she passed by the empty spot at Dara's desk and a pang of sadness struck her. Despite her being intertwined in the cause of Lillianna's additional stress, she still wanted to feel close to Dara and yet also safely a million miles away.

On the side of the cubicle was pinned the sketch of a lion she had given her, still only half-finished and imperfect, but it warmed her heart to remember that Dara liked it. Beside it was a photo of Dara with an older woman there that bore a strong resemblance to her. Her mother, Lillianna decided. She should probably call her own mother soon, except she did not even know what she would say. She had thought that Dara needed protecting from her cousin, but in the end the one she had needed protection from most was herself. Looking back at the lion sketch of it standing regally as it overlooked a cliff, she sighed wearily, feeling it all the way to her bones. Being a big, tough hunter of the night was a romantic notion until she actually felt like one.

* * *

Lillianna's eyes roved over glazed fruit tarts with kiwi and strawberry, dark chocolate brownies, and creamy slices of cheesecake among other sinful delights in the glass bakery case. She didn't usually eat these things as they were too sweet, but come Monday morning her impending dread had spilled over and the meager apology she had given over text did not seem like enough at all, even if Dara may not remember anything at all. A sense of unease clung to her like a tailored suit adjusted one size too small, and she would do just about anything to soothe it. She was now at the small bakery cafe down the street from the office, and she needed to hurry up and pick something or she would be late, except she could not decide what Dara would like best.

"Going to order?" the clerk asked, when the last customer ahead of her in line filtered out. She was holding things up now.

"Yeah, uh, how about—" Lillianna glanced back at the case. Most of the things inside were too sugary for her to like much, but they were all so pretty. "—one of each?"

"Sure thing," the clerk nodded, ringing her up and handing her a heavy box of baked goods when she was through. Surely Dara would enjoy something among all of this.

When she walked through the elevator and onto the sixth floor, she felt a wave of relief wash over her when she spotted Dara at her cubicle as usual. Somehow, that simple fact made everything feel normal and like every other day, which, after this weekend, was a very good thing. She walked slowly at first, as if Dara might bolt if she approached too quickly, but then assumed a more assured stride as she fell into her usual rhythm. Dara was typing away at something, probably one of the less significant reports that wasn't due for weeks, but after getting more feedback on Friday it was time to get her on board with the new phase of their project for the Graves Clan.

"Good morning," Lillianna greeted her as she reached the cubicle.

"Oh, hey there," Dara replied, looking up at her only to have her eyes quickly dart away again and her cheeks flush.

The latent dread in Lillianna's stomach sent a lone tendril up to her heart. Did she remember? No, that couldn't be it. Even if the behavior was odd, a blush was not the proper reaction to discovering that vampires were real and your boss was one of them. If Dara remembered being fed from she would not even have shown up to work today. Instead, the flushing in her cheeks was likely due to a hopefully mild case of fever caused by anemia, which in turn had been caused by her reckless blood drinking. Guilt plucked at Lillianna's heartstrings as she hoisted the heavy box of baked goods onto an empty spot on Dara's desk.

"I got these for you. As an apology—I mean a thank you."

"They can be both. Oh these all look great!" Dara exclaimed as she peeked under the lid. "Thank you!"

Seeing Dara delighted heartened her, and Lillianna found herself smiling as she cleared her throat and continued.

"We're starting up project phase two today, so could you meet me in my office in about fifteen minutes?"

"Alright," Dara nodded, before her eyes bashfully darted away once more and then back again. "Thank you again." Her cheeks were still rosy, and the potential anemia worried Lillianna.

"Are you feeling alright?" she asked, concerned. "You didn't catch a cold over the weekend, did you?"

"Oh no, I'm fine. Never been better, really," Dara assured her.

"If you need to go home early, you can," Lillianna said, though she decided not to push the matter. She would just keep a good eye on Dara. For all her worry, things had turned out fine and it seemed the wine had covered for her foolish mistake of not covering her tracks like a proper vampire. Now that she could see that all her worrying was for nothing, she wished she had done more over the weekend rather than just fretting. She could have gotten more headway on the Graves project, but alas, her mind had been preoccupied. She was just finishing up organizing last phase's reports and adding the final touches to the timeline for phase two when Dara arrived at her office.

"Hey," Dara called as she entered and closed the door behind her.

It was then that it occurred to Lillianna that there was something different about her today. Something she had not noticed in her rush to speak and deliver the apology box to her at the cubicle. Then it hit her. Dara was not wearing her glasses.

"Did you get contacts?" Lillianna asked. She felt a strange sort of inner conflict at the loss of such a distinctive accessory.

"Oh that, well, I just didn't need them today I guess?" Dara replied with a note of confusion in her voice and shrugged. "I've heard of eyesight degrading with age, but never getting better. Maybe I'm just lucky?"

"Must be," Lillianna agreed, but she found it difficult to share in the gratitude for the auspicious luck. The glasses had suited Dara particularly well and now Lillianna...missed them? An odd feeling, but they had indeed looked adorable when she found Dara so sleepy that last night that she hadn't taken her glasses off. Well, it had looked cute, but glasses in general were inconvenient and that had probably hurt, just like it had hurt at first when she had bitten Dara's neck. The image of Dara panting and laying back across her couch flashed through her mind, the two pinpricks along her neck just beginning to rapidly congeal as Lillianna issued a primal command that she lean back down for more. Lillianna harshly pushed the sudden desire away, willing to lock it deep below the surface once more where it belonged.

"Did you have a nice weekend?" Dara asked as she fished something out of her pocket. "Oh, and here's your spare keys, sorry about falling asleep on your couch."

"Oh, that," Lillianna paused again, unsure of how much to share. "Thank you. My weekend was as good as it could be, given the circumstances."

"And what circumstances were those?"

"That my weekend was only two days long," Lillianna quipped. The comment earned a chuckle from Dara. "And how was yours?"

"Quite good considering that I didn't struggle with that at all," Dara smiled at her widely, revealing her teeth, dazzling, genuine, and *sharp*.

Lillianna's grip on the papers she was shuffling went slack, causing them to fall to her desk. Her gaze fixated on Dara's smile. It was not just the lack of glasses that was different today. Sometime between last Thursday night and now Dara had grown fangs.

"Is something wrong?" Dara asked as she cocked her head to the side. A sudden silence had fallen between them and the timing—immediately after a joke—was undeniably odd.

"No, nothing," Lillianna said with a polite, and very forced, smile. The world had turned itself upside down in a mere moment and now her head felt like it was spinning. "I just—just need to go find another file I forgot. Give me a bit."

"Alright. I'll go grab a drink of water then. Be right back."

Dara trotted off down the hall to the water cooler, and Lillianna stared blankly at her back in muted panic. Like hell nothing was wrong. She needed to get Dara out of this building—out of the country even—before anyone saw her teeth!

But what to say to her to get her to leave? What sort of excuse would make sense when they were clearly about to start an important phase of the project that she absolutely needed Dara for? A sudden work-from-home assignment? Employees loved that nowadays, didn't they? Maybe she could spin it as a reward for all her hard work. Except she did not really want to be separated from Dara, even if it was a necessity. *No, don't be ridiculous. This is an emergency! Get her out!* Quickly, Lillianna rose from her desk to halt the disaster unraveling before her. She was hot on the heels of Dara's trail to the water cooler and was nearly there when suddenly she nearly collided with Eric.

"Congratulations, Lilly!" he exclaimed excitedly as he clapped her on the shoulder, effectively waylaying her. "I didn't think you had it in you!"

"Huh? Thanks?" Lillianna replied, feeling slighted at his admitted lack of confidence in her. She already knew he didn't think that highly of her as the kid sister, but he didn't have to say it out loud. "I put in a lot of work you know, so it makes sense that Grandfather liked it." She glanced down to the water cooler again where Dara was alone. Thankfully, no one seemed to be heading in that direction to join her.

"No, not that, although I heard you did a great job on that too. I mean great job with your new assistant!" He clapped her on the shoulder again. "Or should I say girlfriend? Maybe fiancée?"

"Huh?" Lillianna stopped looking at the water cooler and turned to face him fully. Eric had her full attention now as he waggled his eyebrows impishly at her. "What do you—?"

"No need to be so modest. You staked a claim!" he grinned and gave her a cheesy thumbs up. "I'm bummed that you put me to shame by finding someone first, but at least I get some credit for setting you two up. Well, sort of."

That was—this was— "What?" Lillianna could not believe the words she was hearing. This had to be wrong. He couldn't really be saying—

"Your blood bond! I'm not blind, Lilly," Eric chuckled. "I'm happy for you. She's cute."

Lillianna blinked at him dumbly, the gears inside her head whirring uselessly until finally they clicked into place. Eric had already seen Dara's teeth, and he knew that Lillianna had envenomed Dara, but he also thought that they had done a lot more than that together too. Of course it was only natural that he thought that they were together when a blood bond was such a big step, but something inside her twisted at the notion that she and Dara had not done all of what he assumed.

"Um, thanks," Lillianna managed as Eric continued to look at her expectantly, her throat unbearably tight and head still spinning.

"Hey Eric," Dara greeted as she returned from the water cooler. Eric's grin grew even wider, and Lillianna's stomach sunk even further. Any moment now he would make a sophomoric comment to Dara about her bedding her boss. Vampires she could explain away with disbelief and jokes, but innuendo would be near impossible.

"Well, I'll leave you two to it then," Eric said as he headed back to his own office to work. "Great job again!" he called over his shoulder with a small wave. Lillianna could not help but release a sigh of relief as he left. She could hardly believe it. Eric was being mature for once. It was...uncharacteristic.

"Thanks!" Dara called, waving as he left. "So, the Graves project?" she asked, the two little teeth clearly visible when she spoke.

"Yeah," Lillianna answered, deflated. She just wanted to curl up somewhere and wait until this century had passed. She was never going to recover from this humiliation, and she hadn't the foggiest idea of how to back out of this without ruining her reputation with her family, her relationship with her assistant, or both.

* * *

As soon as she got back to her apartment that night, Lillianna rushed to her bedroom and began pulling boxes of stored summer clothing out from under her bed until she at last found what she was looking for: an ancient, dusty tome bound in leather with the Markov crest engraved in gold across the cover. Flipping through the pages of the codex, Lillianna scanned until she found what she was looking for: the finer details of a vampiric blood bond.

The bond is created when a vampire injects their venom into a chosen human after careful consideration and the approval of both the human and one's clan.

Lillianna winced. She had really botched this badly. This was not just a mistake like drinking blood without hypnosis, instead it was practically a violation of her. Even Lillianna's family would be furious if they found out she did this by accident. Hers would be the story they told for centuries about "that time Lilly was an idiot." The blood bond relationship was supposed to be symbiotic, not parasitic like the relationship between vampires and humans normally was, except right now Lillianna felt like the biggest, sloppiest parasite that had ever walked the night, and she probably was.

The blood bond is of mutual benefit to both vampire and human, which becomes a dhampir after the bond is complete. As the venom takes hold, the human gains a lengthened lifespan to match the vampire's own, and stronger senses, endurance, and resistance to illness, albeit not as strong as a true vampire's. To make the bonded lifespan permanent and gain greater resistance, the dhampir must then ingest their bonded vampire's blood. After the change, the dhampir will require regular injections of venom to continue to reap the benefits beyond lengthened lifespan. However, if the dhampir never partakes of the bonded vampire's own blood, then all changes will begin to fully revert once injections cease and they will eventually resume mortality.

Lillianna breathed a sigh of relief at those final words. Dara was not stuck like this. Dara did not have to pay a price for Lillianna's own incompetence. Dara's teeth may be sharp now, but it was not as though she was going to suddenly use her newfound canines to make the bond permanent by accident. She could still be human and live a normal life, and she would not need to be grilled on vampire secrecy and to avoid vampire hunters and accidentally appearing on late night news.

Her grandfather had oft drilled her when she was younger that while many humans imagined they wanted immortality, the actual results frequently turned out to be something less than they imagined. Living forever when your friends and family didn't was really not so fun. After realizing how short lived humans would be in comparison, Lillianna had kept to socializing mostly with other vampires. Dara was an exception to that rule, but just the same she felt sad when she thought about her growing old and passing on. It had only been just over a month since she met Dara, and yet she felt so attached. But that was selfish and ridiculous. Blood bonds were for lovers, not office assistants. Unless...

The memory of Dara's panting, parted lips and dilated eyes surfaced to the top of Lillianna's mind with sizzling intensity. She could recall being faintly aware that Dara's breasts were crushed against her own as she had pressed her down against the couch and felt her heart thudding in her chest. The carnal memory was deeply entangled with the taste of iron-rich blood, but under that craving was something instinctively dark and possessive. A new, smoldering hunger curled beside the guilt in the pit of her stomach.

She had drunk blood from humans before, but it had never played out like that. She pressed a hand to her forehead and breathed evenly until her heady thoughts became placid once more. The intermingling bloodlust had fried her brain, she decided. A blood bond was a weighty decision that she would make when she was older, wiser, and far less foolish, not something that she simply bumbled into.

However, even if the veneer of professionalism between them was stretching thin, what she did know was that she needed to protect Dara. If her grandfather found out what she had done there was a good chance that she and Dara would be separated "for their own good." Dara might be fired, or worse, relocated somewhere within the company—perhaps with Frederick. Lillianna felt herself tense at the mere possibility. The very thought of Dara with that slimeball of a cousin made her want to vomit and rage in equal measures. This was *her* mistake, and she could not allow Dara to pay for it. Even if Lillianna was deemed the least qualified person to have her as her assistant, it did not matter when one of the possible alternatives was Frederick. His appetites went far deeper than just blood, even if— Lillianna looked down at her hands, clenching them—maybe hers did too.

Shutting the codex on that thought, she roughly shoved it back beneath her bed to collect dust for another several years. Whatever her feelings for Dara she had were beneath the surface of sanguine hunger, she was *not* like Frederick in any way that mattered. Closing her eyes, she leaned back on the bed and rubbed her temples, but thoughts of Dara continued to confusingly intermingle with her appetite for blood.

Chapter 11

Turning her head to the side, Dara angled her mouth to get a better look at her teeth in the bathroom mirror. Sharp canines glinted under the overhead lighting. The teeth had served as extra precaution lately to avoid biting her lip or tongue by accident and aside from that they did not bother her physically, but the sudden change was still just so odd. She had to remember to ask about this at her next dental checkup. Perhaps pointy canines could come in late just like wisdom teeth. At first it was hard not to do a double take when she saw them in the mirror, and she had wondered if she looked strange to others until she remembered that Lillianna also possessed similarly pointy teeth and was quite attractive.

She sighed wistfully at that last thought. The last few weeks had been filled with many lingering looks on her end, but those brooding, ice blue eyes remained distant and deeply troubled. She had hoped that Lillianna's stress levels would go down or at least stabilize after the big meeting with the chairman, but if anything they had only increased. Dara's crush continued to impel her to help, but Lillianna had not given the opportunity to do so, instead always herding her home at the earliest she could.

Leaving the sixth floor bathroom and heading back to her desk, she passed by several windows. Chilly winds nipped at the world outside, but inside the building was cozy and warm. December was flying by, but she was not really sure how she felt about that. It had not been a bad year, but at the same time she would have liked something a little...*more*. More than the little gifts of glazed fruit tarts and chocolate brownies from the bakery, or Thai lunches every now and then, or just saying hello at the office. As much as she enjoyed her little books of sudoku puzzles and the occasional television show at home, it would be been nice to have someone there on the couch watching with her.

However, even spending the holidays alone was beginning to sound more appetizing that spending them with her mother and Jack. He was nice and all, but spending Thanksgiving with him and her mother had been awkward, and then afterward the two of them had run off to his parent's place to celebrate it "for real" anyway. Last time her mother had called her it had only been to ask for advice on what to buy Jack's young nieces and nephews for Christmas, and Dara had a feeling that she was going to be an afterthought again. Perhaps she could just feign illness and save herself the hassle.

As she neared her desk, she peeked inside Lillianna's office to find her boss was thoroughly engrossed in the screen and whatever documents lay there. Dara sighed. Perhaps romance could have been on the forecast for this holiday season if she had picked her women better. Even if Lillianna Markov looked nice, she was surely trouble underneath. Either that or Dara was having a bad case of sour grapes. Sensing something, Lillianna looked up, but Dara looked away just before she could catch her staring.

* * *

The brisk weather had grown ever frostier in the week that had passed, but Dara's fangs showed no signs of returning to normal and Lillianna was growing more nervous by the day. To make matters worse, that wasn't the only thing lingering: her wayward feelings concerning her unnaturally strong attachment to Dara were only growing stronger, which was both worrisome and oddly elating. The latter sensation was rather alarming. Where had her sense of reason gone? This was not the time to blow up her life any more than it already was. The explanation that most readily came to mind was that the venom injection had caused her to develop these feelings more strongly as a reflex, to "take responsibility" so to speak for the ancient ancestral rite of the blood bond, but that was ridiculous. It was becoming clear that she liked Dara and thought about her often, but an *eternity?* It didn't sound bad per se, but Lillianna was very young by vampire standards, and she could not even fathom making such a decision at the present. Furthermore, Dara had never consented to such a thing, and it needed to be undone as quickly and quietly as possible. Lillianna just wanted things to go back to the way they were, right down to Dara's glasses.

At least she's still wearing her loafers, Lillianna comforted herself. Some things never changed, though she hated to think of what *would* change if Dara were to find out just what had transpired that fateful night. The possibility that Dara would hate her left an acidic taste in the back of her mouth that rivaled the sense of inevitable doom she felt about her family finding out about the mishap.

Restlessly, Lillianna looked up from her computer to check Dara's location and found her safely stationed at her cubicle still clicking away at the keyboard. As the single benefit of Lillianna's big mistake, Frederick would not be going anywhere near Dara's neck now. Courtesy of Dara's new status as a newly minted dhampir, hypnotism would no longer work on her, not to mention that everyone assumed they were together and drinking from someone else's fiancée was about as off limits as you could get. But even though she was no longer in danger from Frederick, there was the chance that Eric or someone else might make an offhand comment about their supposed trysts, and Lillianna could not have that either. No one could be allowed to get anywhere near Dara. That feat had actually not been difficult at all to accomplish. All of her relatives on the sixth floor had gotten used to her prickly reputation long before this and had quickly given "them" space, or at least everyone but Eric anyway. He kept showing up time and again to ask meaningless questions and just smile warmly between them as if they were part of some zoo exhibit. "Exhibit B— The youngest Markov and the biggest mistake a vampire ever made." Even caged lions had more dignity.

When the time came and Dara's fangs subsided, Lillianna would quietly pretend to her brother and cousins that she had called it off, ask for space yet again and for no one to bother Dara about it, and then that would be that. Claiming that things "just hadn't worked out" would be far less a smear on her reputation than to admit to it being an accident, and also not unprecedented. Cold feet was always a risk when revealing the truth of vampires to a potential mate, and everyone knew that.

Potential mate... Lillianna's eyes were drawn back to the scene of Dara chugging away at the financial data at her desk. She shook the thought from her head. She had a promotion to collect, and it was not the time to be sidetracked by drunken instincts.

"Hey Lilly," Eric called as he popped into her office unannounced yet again—it was starting to happen so regularly that perhaps she should set a timer to predict it. "Do you have a moment? I wanted to talk about your plans for the solstice."

"What do you need?" Lillianna replied, her voice steeled to be cool and professional despite her troubles and stress.

The winter solstice, the longest night of the year, was very important to vampires and quickly approaching. The Markov's pagan traditions stretched back to before the advent of Christianity in Europe, though many of her ancestors from that period had perished during the vicious crusades against vampires that had followed the continent's conversion. The modern festivities were greatly toned down compared to what she had been told was a veritable bacchanalia in the past, but it was still relaxing compared to work which was something she could have a bit more of considering how stressed she had been lately.

"Well, I saw that Dara hadn't marked her vacation days yet for next week except on the twenty-fifth," Eric commented as he glanced toward the cubicles at the woman in question. "She *is* coming, right? I've been looking forward to having her over and so is Mother."

Lillianna froze, completely blindsided by this retrospectively obvious snag in her holiday plans. Even if Dara was not actually her blood bonded partner, everyone's assumption that she was meant she would be expected to attend the solstice gathering too. But she wasn't. She couldn't. Except her mother expected her to be there. The image of her sweet mother's disappointed, teary face flashed through her mind. Her father had always been the stern parent, the future head of the clan, and her mother so loving. She could not bear to disappoint her, and not allowing her mother to meet her supposed fiancée was a snub she was not likely to soon forget.

"About that—" Lillianna began to say, but the words she had intended to say caught in her throat. Something else came out instead. "—I was just about to tell her myself, actually."

"Oh, great!" Eric exclaimed cheerfully. "I'll let you get back to work so we can all finish up in time then. Thanks!" He shut her office door jovially, strolling down the hall humming without a care in the world despite having just blasted her plans to smithereens yet again.

"No...problem," Lillianna replied to her empty office, still dazed by the sudden strike of inopportune social lightning. Her grandfather's disappointment was something she avoided because it hurt to feel less than or unworthy, but her mother was different. It wasn't intended to punish, it never had, and yet Lillianna could not bear to shatter the heartfelt hopes her mother had for her. She was delaying the inevitable, she knew, but at least months from now she would not have to see her mother's disappointment when she told her quietly over text that they had "broken up," or, better yet, Eric just told her for her.

But how the hell was she going to pull this off now? This was too much. She should just come clean, except that would not help either. Admitting she had messed up was going to affect Dara, herself, and everything in between from the Graves project to her entire career. She just couldn't. She stared at the facts and figures strewn across her screen, seeing without seeing, and began scrambling furiously as a thought occurred to her. It sounded stupid, bizarre, and ridiculous, but so was the fact that she had accidentally envenomed Dara.

She had already committed to playing this part and pretending later that they had broken up. What would it hurt to let Dara in on part of the secret? That would make it easier, in fact. She would no longer need to guard her from half the secret, and instead only from one part. It was not like her family walked around loudly proclaiming their inherited vampirism every few seconds; it was a rather mundane secret when everyone had it.

The next several minutes were spent pulling up everything from her bank account and current cash on hand to searching up documents concerning the legality of what she was about to do. From what she could gather it probably wasn't quite right, but neither was concealing the true ages and identities of your employees and Markov Incorporated did that all the time. For hours she went over the details, what she would say, and the contingency plan for if this all went wrong—which wasn't much, because there was not much worse this situation could get. However, when the time for Dara to go home drew near, Lillianna knew she had better make her move before Eric got impatient and mentioned it again himself.

As she rose and glanced toward Dara's desk, she gathered her nerve and reminded herself that Dara was an excellent assistant. She had helped her with many things before, and this was just the latest in a long list of assignments, even if it wasn't official business. This new plan sounded stupid, oh so very, *very* stupid, but was also the only thing that could possibly work to take back control of the ever worsening situation. All she needed was to just get Dara into her parent's place and be visible for a day or two until the solstice, and then they could even leave early if it proved too much.

"Yes?" Dara looked up at her expectantly as she arrived at her desk.

"We need to talk about next week," Lillianna informed her before glancing around the area and catching Eric's eye as he peered out from his office. He smiled at her enthusiastically and gave her a hearty thumbs up. "Could you come to my office to discuss this further?"

* * *

Dara could tell that Lillianna was very tense as they entered the office together, and she gave her space as the other woman settled into her chair. Lillianna laid one hand on her desk, her fingers rubbing the smooth grain of the wood as she fidgeted restlessly.

"You said there was something you wanted to talk about?" Dara asked unobtrusively as she shut the door, leaving them alone.

"Well, it's just that—" Lillianna began, but the words trailed off, leaving only silence in their wake. Her brows furrowed in mute frustration, clearly having difficulty with the words she wanted to say. There was something else there too, something Dara could not quite place. Dara tilted her head to the side questioningly, waiting as her nerves tensed in anticipation. Had their deadline been moved up?

The project canceled? Was she being relocated to another department? She did not like that last idea at all, but it was hard not to catastrophize as Lillianna searched for the words for what appeared to be a weighty topic. "It's about next week," she said finally, repeating her earlier statement.

"Yes?" Late next week was Christmas. Perhaps she wanted Dara to work over the holiday, which wouldn't be the worst excuse to skip being the third wheel with Jack and her mom.

Lillianna looked visibly pained, like the words had caught in her throat and were beginning to choke her. This was beginning to worry Dara. The silence drew on, becoming awkward until finally Lillianna broke it once more.

"Dara, we're...friends, right?"

"Yes?" Dara tried and failed to hide the surprise in her voice, but, as much as she wanted that to be true, she was reminded that this line often came before an outrageous favor. *Don't allow her to take advantage of you just because she's gorgeous,* a little voice in the back of her head reminded her.

"What I want to ask isn't as your boss, but as your friend. Would you be free next week to take a trip?"

"A business trip? Well, I was going to take Christmas off."

"We can be back for that," Lillianna assured her. "And I'll pay you well." Her eyes glanced nervously toward the door, as if paranoid someone might hear the exchange. "Is ten thousand alright? It's going to be roughly three to six days."

"Ten thousand?" Dara blurted out, her brain snagging as she stared blankly at her in shock. This had to be shady. No one could be throwing that sort of money around in this kind of economy. That sort of nest egg could be the start of a down payment for someplace more permanent than her current lodgings.

"Shh!" Lillianna hissed, her eyes darting toward the door again. "You can't tell anyone about this, alright?"

"I understand," Dara said blankly, her brain still trying to wrap itself around the offered sum. "What do you need me to do? Spreadsheets?"

"Goodness no. It's...I'm going to visit my family, and I want you to come with," Lillianna explained. It sounded almost too mundane until she added with solemnity, "I need you to pose as my fiancée."

Dara stared, bewildered. Somehow if Lillianna had told her she needed to remove a kidney for the black market it would have sounded more plausible. Nothing made sense about this. Not when her boss was not even gay. "But I'm a woman?"

"You have to be. My family knows that I'm a lesbian, and—oh." Lillianna's brows furrowed in consternation as she seemed to realize she had overlooked something very important about this whole plan. "I apologize. It did not occur to me that the arrangement would make you uncomfortable." She frowned and it appeared that she was trying to conjure up a backup plan, but Dara's brain sprang into action and jolted her into action before things could get any more offtrack.

"No, no!" Dara held up her hands. "I'm perfectly comfortable with that, really, I mean I'm also into women—er, I thought—I didn't realize that you, uh, that *you* wouldn't be uncomfortable." *Dear god, please stop rambling before you put your foot in your mouth.* Dara nearly cringed at herself. At least she had only said she was "into women" and not "into *you.*"

"My family will expect us to be affectionate with one another," Lillianna informed her, looking at her seriously. "It needs to be convincing."

"I understand," Dara replied quickly, her brain still unable to quite comprehend the magnitude of the office. Being cuddly with her boss? Her gorgeous boss? She couldn't believe this was happening. It felt like she had fallen asleep at her desk and was dreaming. "But why me? Why—I mean, why anyone at all?" It felt too good to be true. This had to be some bizarre scam.

"It's important to my family," Lillianna replied, her expression quickly becoming guarded. "I can't say anything more than that. The real reasons won't affect you in the slightest, I promise. Your part simply is what it is. I will deposit half before the trip, and the other half after. Ten thousand should be enough for the secrecy too, I trust?"

"Of course, I understand," Dara nodded, unwilling to jeopardize the potential nest egg even if something about this deal still felt off. People did not just hire fake fiancées, and especially not people like Lillianna who could easily get a real one if she wanted.

"We'll go over the details later in a place more private," Lillianna said, her stress noticeably lessening at Dara's agreement. "Do you have any questions now?"

"Do I need to bring any presents for Christmas?" Dara inquired, suddenly remembering what was next week.

"It's fine. We don't celebrate Christmas actually," Lillianna replied.

"Oh, I'm sorry," Dara apologized. "I just assumed. Hanukkah?"

"No, not that either," Lillianna said, shaking her head. "Anyway, don't worry about that. There's some traditions and stuff, but I will go over anything you actually need beforehand."

There was a pause in their conversation, and though Dara did not like the silence, she could think of nothing to fill it. The situation was novel, and nothing in her life had prepared her for it.

"I guess that's that, then?" Dara said finally.

"Yes, thank you. I suppose we should get back to work then. I'll be in contact soon," Lillianna said, her manner returning back to what she usually was like here at the office. "But on your private number, not the office."

"Right, okay," Dara nodded. "Talk soon." She walked out of Lillianna's office and closed the door solidly behind her.

She looked around at the cubicles, offices, anything, trying to make sense of her surroundings, the world, and what the hell had just happened.

Chapter 12

Lillianna waited restlessly on her apartment couch, checking the time once and then again. Dara would be here soon. She had not been sure about inviting Dara over again after what had happened last time, but as the planned trip crept up on the calendar she had been forced to relent as there was nowhere else to prepare for the impending trip. Between the Graves project and everything else in the whirlwind of a week, they had scarcely had time or privacy to even finalize the details of their agreement over clandestine lunches. However, nothing unintended should happen during this visit; she had prepared well in consuming an excess of blood—so much so that the thought of drinking more almost made her sick. Despite that, she was wrestling with the idea of drinking yet another *just to be safe* when the doorbell finally rang.

"Hey," Dara said, nervously tugging the strap of her bag on the doorstep of the apartment. Chilly, December air blustered in through the open door.

"Come in, come in," Lillianna greeted, ushering her inside so that they could get to work. "Have a seat. Do you want anything to drink?"

"I'm good," Dara answered as she settled onto the sofa and laid down her bag. "I wouldn't want a repeat of last time. Sorry about that."

"You were no trouble," Lillianna assured her. Though Dara had a point about "last time," it was not her who was the cause of it. "But if you're all set then let's get to what I told you about." Lillianna sat down beside her on the couch closer than she would if they were truly just boss and employee. Dara began to fidget at the closeness, as was expected, but was not so bothered that she pulled away. So far so good. "So the main part of this is you need to stay close to me and act affectionately. Hugs, hand holding, that sort of thing," Lillianna explained, reciting the parts of the plan she had gone over before. "But I also thought we should know a bit more about one another than we normally would for a work colleague, don't you agree?"

"Right," Dara nodded before her tone turned joking as a reaction to stress. "What were you thinking we should start with? Favorite colors, childhood memories?"

"I already know that. You like blue. Ice blue," Lillianna reminded her. "Or did it change?"

"Oh." Dara blinked at her, surprised that she had remembered. "We did talk about that a while ago, didn't we?"

"Yes. Now then, my father's name is Octavian and my mother's name is Natalia," Lillianna began, jumping right into it. "He works as a doctor, though mostly in research now and does a lot with the company. My mother is an archivist."

"Archivist? Like a librarian?"

"Yes, sort of." Lillianna wasn't sure how to further explain that her mother spent much of her time combing through centuries of vampire records in order to organize and catalog them. Thankfully, Dara did not ask.

"How did they meet?" she inquired instead.

Lillianna opened her mouth to speak, having heard the story so many times that she knew it by heart, before she remembered that it was not exactly appropriate for the uninitiated. Her mother, being terminally ill, had been saved by her father and turned into a dhampir to heal her, but she could not say that to a human. "She was his patient," she finally decided. "And he fell in love."

"That sounds very romantic," Dara said, smiling at the touching story. "Do they get along well?"

"It is, and they do," Lillianna answered. Her mother was the one person her father was not overly serious with—at least when he thought no one else was around. "What about your parents? I've seen the photo of your mother in your cubicle. Are you two close?"

"Yeah, we are," Dara said before considering it for a moment. "She has a new boyfriend though so we haven't been in touch quite as much lately. Her name's Shannon and she's an elementary school teacher."

"I see. And your father?"

"His name is—was David. He passed away last year," Dara said, her voice growing quiet by the last word.

"Oh. I'm sorry," Lillianna replied automatically, but from the wry smile Dara gave her it was not the right thing to say.

"Don't be. I lost him a long time before he died. I told you about the situation with my half-brother. It's probably not the greatest thing to mention to your family though. If it comes up I should probably have a different cover story ready."

Lillianna shook her head. "You don't need to do that."

"But this is all pretend anyway?" Dara pointed out. "And this feels just so...heavy. Won't your parents think you can do better than someone like that?"

"Someone like that?" Lillianna asked, perplexed. "Like what?"

"Someone whose father abandoned her. You know." Dara shrugged awkwardly, and Lillianna realized what she was saying. She bristled at that notion that Dara was not good enough to be her fiancée, her lips pressing together in irritation as she considered the unseen people that would condescend the both of them. Her sudden aggravation abated when she saw how uncomfortable Dara had become as she fidgeted more thoroughly under her gaze—as if she wished she had never brought up the point at all.

"That's—well, it's better to pretend as little as possible, isn't it? It helps keep the story straight," Lillianna insisted, deciding to deal with the tangled feelings of defensiveness irritation another time.

"That's true," Dara conceded.

Except it wasn't true, at least not in the sense that it was the real reason that Lillianna did not want to lie about it. Secretly, perhaps embarrassingly, she wanted her parents to meet Dara—the real Dara, not a pretend version of her. Their engagement was pretend, yes, but that did not mean that anything else had to be. In fact, the realer the better. After all, she was proud of her assistant.

"Anyway, we shouldn't have to recite our entire life's story anyway, but I just didn't want us to look surprised if something came up in conversation," Lillianna continued, moving on smoothly. Though Dara's admission about her parents reawakened Lillianna's curiosity about the topic of her father and his death, she did not want to forcefully dredge up unpleasant memories. She would wait until Dara herself wanted to tell her more on the topic. "Don't worry about it. Let's just move on to the next part of practice for now." In her determination to move on from the sensitive subject, Lillianna went ahead and moved her hand to Dara's waist before she realized she should have waited for an answer.

"What practice is that—" Dara began to ask, before her face immediately flushed pink. "Oh. Right."

"Sorry," Lillianna said, pulling her hand away again. Dara looked horribly conflicted at the tepid touch. That wasn't a good sign. "But we need to, you know, test this out before the big day."

"No, no, it's fine. I just wasn't ready. That's why we're practicing, right?" Dara explained hurriedly, her pink cheeks flushing even further. "It's fine, really."

Are you sure? Lillianna wanted to ask, but at the same time the question was impossible. Dara *had* to be fine, or this plan was never going to work, and she could *not* allow things to spiral out of control again. "Okay," she said instead, and reached her hand back out to clasp Dara's waist. She could feel Dara quiver when she first made contact, her ribcage expanded and contracted as her breath rose and fell, and the warmth of her body through her sweater. Emboldened when she did not pull away a second time, she pulled Dara closer, pressing her against the side of her body, and curled her hand around her. At the same time felt something else curl below her stomach, though she did not dwell on it because Dara's hammering heart was growing more alarming by the second.

Sometimes when Lillianna had been a child, the delivery of blood had been late. When that happened she would go into the forest to hunt. The deer then had been so panicked when she caught them, their eyes wild with fear before they were lulled into a hypnotic calm. Their wild heartbeats had made their blood flow freely as she fed, and she had thought nothing further of it. Now however, Dara's reaction caused her immense concern.

Could some deep part of her instinctively recognize that Lillianna was a hunter of the night? Did she remember something about that night before, even a sliver? Though not on the level of life-or-death, the physical reaction was already absurd. Unless, instead of fear, it was...*attraction?* Lillianna pulled back to examine Dara, attempting to appraise the situation, but between ruddy awkwardness, timorous apprehension, and sprinting heartbeat mixed together it was difficult to tell what was going on, except, maybe, that would be nice if it was attraction. The thought had never occurred to Lillianna before, but now it drifted like a buoyant cloud through her mind. Wait, why did she even care? She shouldn't. Besides, why would Dara like *her?* She was the boss who had only gotten to know her in the first place to make sure they stayed on good working terms and kept her loyal. It was only after she had gotten to know her better that she had realized Dara was sweet, unassuming, and deserved someone far better. The once buoyant cloud of thought scattered in the winds of pessimism.

No, this extreme physical reaction must be caused by a primal, instinctive fear of vampires that Dara's senses were alerting her to. Vampires were predators after all, even if Dara did not consciously realize that Lillianna was one. She had always prided herself on being intimidating before, but for situations like these it would have been better to be small and adorable like Dara. She needed to calm her down and get the adrenaline to subside for this to work. She may be a vampire, but she was not a threat. The questionable truthfulness of that last thought made her squirm. *At least not a threat tonight.*

"Not so bad?" Lillianna asked hopefully despite knowing full well it was not. She took Dara's hand, and thumbed across the pulse of her wrist. Dara's pulse was not calming down at all.

"Um, yeah," Dara mumbled, sounding dazed. "Sorry, my hand is sweaty."

"Your hand is fine," Lillianna assured her, but it was very clear that Dara was not fine. Something was greatly agitating her, and it was only going to get worse from here when she dragged Dara into a lair of vampires come Saturday. However, it was not as though Lillianna's entire family was like Frederick. For the most part he was an unfortunate stain on the Markov name, and Dara was going to be fine in the end even if she felt uneasy about it.

"Do you need a break?" she asked. "We can go ahead and go over the packing list."

"No! I mean—ah, no, I'm fine, really," Dara exclaimed hastily at Lillianna's suggestion. "Let's keep going."

Lillianna eyed her questioningly, trying to determine the extent of the adrenaline in Dara's veins. Her heart rate had actually increased more when she had suggested that they stop, which was...odd. *Maybe she really does like...no, quit thinking about that.* It just must be that the bribe of money she had offered was more tempting than she had realized—not just an offer Dara wanted to take, but could not refuse.

"Let's hug then," she decided, and Dara gave a quick nod. This should not be asking too much.

Dara was soft, warm and rather timid at first, but that quickly began to dissolve as Lillianna embraced her. She snuggled into Lillianna's side in an unexpected display of bravery. *There, not so bad.* Lillianna held her tentatively, then more assuredly as they settled together, but as she pulled her closer she discovered once again that her heart was beating like a thousand scared rabbits running from an entire congress of owls.

"Are you sure you're okay?" Lillianna asked, instinctively holding her tighter despite that obviously not helping at all when she was the cause of the distress. Maybe this *was* asking too much.

"I'm sorry," Dara whispered quietly, but the sentiment made no sense to Lillianna's ears.

"What for?" she asked, pulling away to get a good look at her. Dara was red as a tomato, her eyes darting away instead of lifting to meet her gaze.

"I just feel...guilty," Dara admitted, edging away on the couch while looking like a wounded animal.

"Guilty?" Lillianna asked, her heart sinking. This couldn't be good.

"I mean, if we're going to do this, I thought I should tell you that—" Dara's throat bobbed as she swallowed thickly. Her words didn't come, and if her heart was hammering before it was now positively about to burst.

"Relax. Just relax," Lillianna said, trying her best to calm her down. "You don't need to worry about any of that." Dara's eyes looked down and away from her, but Lillianna could hear her heartbeat slow somewhat so she continued. "You can keep your secrets, like I keep

126

mine."

"But I—I really—" Dara tried again, her heart rate ticking up once more.

"You don't need to tell me," Lillianna repeated firmly.

She was curious, just as she had been about Dara's dead relative in the past, but now that she had accidentally gotten the truth about Dara's dead father her curiosity fell flat. It truly did not matter what it was that was bothering Dara, or what other sordid family history she had that she felt compelled to confess, but it could definitely wait until Dara was actually ready to tell her—if she even deserved to hear it. And if liked her then—well no, Dara couldn't like her like *that*, because if Dara liked her then—then—*then what?* Lillianna did not know what happened next, because it had not been part of the plan.

"Okay," Dara said finally, still looking nervous. "Let's try again then," she decided after fidgeting a bit more. "If it's okay?"

"As long as you're alright." Lillianna offered her a calming smile.

She held out her arms, allowing Dara to acquiesce and lean into her before wrapping her arms around her and pulling her close. Dara nestled her head between the crook of her shoulder and her neck in a way that felt all too natural. It was easy—*too* easy. Her body fit against her like it had been made for this, and slowly her pulse calmed to a gentle thudding melody against her chest. Lillianna could smell the sweet, strawberry scent of her shampoo. Blood scent still tingled at her nose, but it was not all consuming. Instead, a different feeling rushed up to the surface—hungry yet gentle, possessive yet protective. It itched at Lillianna's mind, to pull Dara closer, to keep her with her, safe. To revel in more than just her blood, but the simple feel of her skin.

But just like the temptation of Dara's blood, this was going to get Lillianna in hot water again. She had not turned out to be all that great of a boss after all, doing this to her assistant and then asking her to help make it up, even with pay. The mess of feelings should have stopped at respect and appreciation for Dara's competency, not the tangled morass it was now. But none of that mattered; she was sticking to the plan now. Pretend, persevere, and part company to settle things with minimal fanfare at a later date. Her vampiric instincts for finding a blood bonded mate were fried, and that was not reason enough to jeopardize the promotion that she had worked decades for in favor of an assistant she had barely known for a couple months. It did not help that Dara very well could reject her offer outright if she knew the truth, and damn quickly too. Lillianna needed her to play this part a little longer. She would keep Dara safe from Frederick, from termination, and from herself.

They stayed there for a moment, just taking in the peacefulness of it. Dara's heart remained calm, and Lillianna grew more confident in her plan. This was going to work, and she had made the right decision in asking Dara for help with this. She was loyal and trustworthy, which was a surprise to Lillianna to realize she felt that way. Even if they had not known one another that long, she knew that Dara would not let her down. Things were under control.

"Oh. I almost forgot," Lillianna remembered suddenly, breaking away from the hug and reaching into her pocket for the item she had picked up earlier. "You should check the sizing."

Without further elaboration, she dropped the ring into Dara's hand. It felt strange, just handing it to her. Rings weren't meant to be parceled out; they were supposed to be lovingly gifted from down on one knee. However, the disquiet in her heart was swept aside as Dara reacted with just as much astonishment as if she had been down on one knee. She stared at the small piece of metal in disbelief, clearly having not quite thought through the plan this far herself. Lamplight reflected brightly off the ring, glinting as she turned it over reverently in her palm.

"How much did this cost you?" Dara asked, the shock in her voice tangible as she examined the gemstone set in the ring. It was not a diamond, but instead a ruby so deep and rich that it resembled blood set in gold. It was a Markov tradition from more recent centuries, but still something that Lillianna's family would expect to see.

"Don't worry about that." Lillianna shook her head as she could tell Dara's heart rate was picking up again. A frivolous hope began to grow again in her chest, despite her best efforts to squash it. "You can keep it after this is over, just consider it part of the payment. And you need to wear it at the office even after we get back, so don't forget." Lillianna looked at her again expectantly, but still Dara hesitated.

"I mean, it just feels a little strange," Dara explained as she continued to turn it over in her hand and admire the craftsmanship.

"You have to wear it," Lillianna sighed. Clearly she was not the only one feeling awkward about just handing over engagement rings. "Here, just put it on." She took the ring back before Dara could protest and reached for her left hand. She slipped the ring on—a perfect fit, which was good because getting a rush adjustment done tomorrow would have been a pain. There was something else too that felt perfect; it just felt *right* to put the ring on. She was asserting a claim, to show Frederick and everyone else that they couldn't have Dara. And Dara looked happy about it, which made her happy too. Well, mostly happy except for the fact that it was becoming increasingly impossible to ignore the obvious.

* * *

The ring felt unusually heavy on her hand as Dara gripped the steering wheel. She was at the last stoplight before home, and still in disbelief at what had just transpired. When she arrived at the empty house she made a beeline for the sink, splashing her face with cold water several times before glancing down at her left hand again. The ring was still there with the ensconced ruby gleaming brightly, more luscious and deep than a pomegranate seed. It was the same shade as Lillianna's lipstick.

Dara's thoughts began to drift at that notion, back toward meandering dreams and unspoken fantasies, but she reined them back in. What a disaster. Tonight she had nearly confessed that she was practically in love with Lillianna straight to her face.

So, so guilty, she chided herself. She had thought that her heart was going to burst. For the first dozen mild touches she had been absolutely paranoid that Lillianna was going to realize that she had the biggest crush on the planet. Her skin felt like it was made of rice paper and entirely transparent. She wanted to cuddle with her boss, yes, but it did not feel as good as it should when Lillianna didn't know she liked her. Though maybe this was for the best that she had said nothing in the end. It had shocked her to find out that her boss was a lesbian, but perhaps that was worse. After all, now instead of an unattainable straight woman Lillianna was simply just not interested. If she had actually been into her she would not have needed to pay her to pretend: she could have just asked her out for free. Whatever it was that her boss felt compelled to throw money around to prove, Dara was not special beyond being readily available. Which left her wondering: why was Lillianna really doing this?

Pretending to be engaged potentially toed the line on legality, and whether or not it crossed the line into fraud depended entirely on *why* Lillianna wanted her to pretend, which Dara still had no clue about. It was a bit late to worry about that though, as the first half of the money had already been deposited in her account, and now she even had a ring on her hand. She was at least one step ahead of being scammed herself, so it wasn't like she was being duped unless she was about to get kidnapped and have a kidney removed for sale on the black market. Dara winced at the thought, looking sadly at her abdomen in the bathroom mirror after wiping water off her face with a towel. Goodbye, kidney, sacrificed thoughtlessly on the altar of yet another, hopeless love. She needed to quit doing this; she only had two kidneys after all, or perhaps only one after all was through with this trip.

But that was silly. This was her boss, and even if Markov Incorporated was a medical technology company that Dara still wasn't sure what exactly they did, she was pretty sure they did not engage in black market organ sales. Besides, more than doing this because Lillianna was gorgeous and her brain short-circuited whenever she looked at her with those sharp, ice blue eyes, or because she really could use the money to pad her savings, she could tell that Lillianna really did need her for this. Dara knew it was just because she was available, and that she was in no way really her fiancée, but it was just so nice to feel necessary for once. Lillianna could have had just about any woman be her assistant to ask this favor of, but in this moment that assistant was her, not Katie, not Candy, not Rachel, or anyone else, and that meant she was essential.

Chapter 13

Seven in the morning sharp, Dara's phone alarm began to buzz, tearing her from fitful sleep into the world of the waking. She blinked at her phone, nearly turning it to snooze when she saw it was Saturday, before jolting awake when she remembered that today was the day of her big trip.

She hopped out of bed and headed to the bathroom to get ready and brush her teeth. She had already packed last night, and although Lillianna had assured her that the trip was not going to be long or anything, Dara had slipped into spending a little bit more time than necessary picking out the most attractive clothing to wear. The Markovs, judging by the crispness of Eric's suits, were not ugly sweater sorts of people. It's just, Dara would feel a bit better if she knew what sorts of people they really were. Lillianna had been somewhat vague about them at the "practice," but she really hoped they were the sorts of people that would like her.

Dara spat out her toothpaste in the sink and sighed as she leaned against the countertop. Her roommate was still out on night shift and the house was empty as she went about collecting her things and getting dressed in the quiet stillness of the morning. She had just finished getting ready when her phone vibrated again, this time with a text from Lillianna, and Dara hefted her bag out the door of her little duplex. She spotted a familiar black sedan waiting by the curb and headed over. Lillianna got out of the car to help her load her bag into the trunk, and as she did so her gaze drifted back to the little duplex Dara had emerged from.

"Do you live here alone?" Lillianna asked after she finished and settled back into the driver's seat.

"I have a roommate, but she works as a nurse," Dara explained as she buckled her seat belt. "So I almost never see her. Sometimes I forget she's even there."

"Huh." Lillianna squinted out at her home again, her expression unreadable. "Not your girlfriend then?"

"Of course not," Dara sputtered, taken by surprise. "I wouldn't do that! I mean, if I was dating someone I couldn't be your fiancée!"

"Good point," Lillianna's eyes broke away from the house to look back at Dara. "Sorry. I didn't mean to say you would do that. I guess I just assumed you'd had someone with you when I saw the place. It's cute, sort of cozy. Built for two."

"Oh. Yeah, it does sort of look like that, doesn't it?" Dara answered, deflating.

Lillianna's guess was closer than she could know. When Dara had first moved into the duplex her then-girlfriend had very nearly moved in with her.

"Yeah, but I'm glad you're not. If you weren't single right now I'd be in trouble." Lillianna flashed her a smile that was both apologetic and grateful. "Again, thank you for doing this for me."

"No problem." Warmth bloomed in Dara's chest at those words, tight and snug. She had been right after all, she *was* necessary.

The engine started with a low rumble as Lillianna turned the key in the ignition, and the car steered away from the little duplex and toward the highway. The familiar sights of the city soon disappeared behind them and were replaced by empty fields and desolate, old farming shacks. Icicles clung to the edges of the corroded tin roofs, and in the frosty fields there was no longer even a solitary cow to poke at the dead grass. They did not speak much as they drove on, and though Dara could tell that Lillianna was feeling as apprehensive as she was about putting this illusion to the test there was something very comforting about the hum of the engine and Lillianna's quiet company. Before Dara knew it, she had leaned back, closed her eyes, and fallen asleep.

Around lunchtime, Lillianna gently shook her awake. They ate at a small roadside diner and filled up at a gas station before continuing on their way past yet more fields and fallow farmland, plus the occasional cow. Splotches of raindrops began to hit the windshield intermittently and gray storm clouds formed on the horizon. They had been driving for hours and although Dara knew that Lillianna had said her parents' place was quite the drive, they did not feel any closer than when they began.

"How long do we have left to go?" she asked eventually, casting a glance to the heavy sky. The clouds' purplish glow cast a heavy shadow across the horizon.

"Have you ever heard of Red Moon Campground?" Lillianna asked, keeping her eyes on the road.

"No, is that close?"

"Practically next door to the place. We're not far now, maybe an hour left at most," Lillianna informed her.

Lillianna's estimation was indeed correct. Not long after their conversation, the cows and fields were left behind as the road turned and tucked into a dense forest. The tangled branches of the barren trees overhead clawed and crowded out the already meager winter sunlight. The winter days were short already, but the area's gloom was more a product of the thick, interlocking trees than a shortage of daylight. Off the side of the road, camper vans were tucked into dark edges of the forest with their inhabitants already hiding away for the stormy evening.

A sign at the side of the road indicated that they would soon enter "Red Moon Campground," but Lillianna paid it no heed and instead went down an unmarked path so well hidden that at first Dara thought they were driving into the forest itself. Branches parted and soon posted signs now informed them that they were on private property accompanied by warnings of trespassing. Soon after, they came to a wrought iron gate that had been unlocked and thrown open for the day. They drove on past before coming to a bend in the road and a copse of trees that narrowly hid the barely visible structure beyond it. Curiosity itched at Dara as she leaned forward to try to get a better look, but Lillianna slowed the car to a temporary halt.

"We're here," Lillianna stated quietly, her voice calm, determined. "You remember, right? When we go in there, we aren't talking about this anymore. We have to stay in character. We're engaged."

Dara nodded. The first five thousand dollars had been well enough a reminder that she needed to not mess this up. Lillianna was counting on her, and so was her future down payment. Satisfied, Lillianna revved up the engine once more, and they passed through the bend into an open meadow where Dara nearly had a double take.

Lillianna had continually referred to the residence as "my parents' place," which was more than a little misleading to say the least. To say more, the Markovs lived in a straight up mansion complete with colonial facade and ornate columns that lined the porch and framed the door. The ancient red brick had long since faded to rust, and much of it was hidden by large swaths of ivy that snaked up the walls and grasped at windows. Yellow lights flickered from within, peeking out from behind thick curtains to reveal silhouettes of the already arrived guests.

Dara did not have long to dwell on the building's ancient beauty, as no sooner had she opened the car door to grab her bag from the trunk than a drop of rain fell from the sky and slapped her shoulder. A flurry of even larger raindrops quickly followed as the coming downpour picked up pace. Before Dara knew it, Lillianna had already grabbed both their bags and was hurriedly hefting them both to the front porch. She knocked heavily with the solid brass knocker attached to the front door, and, just under the rumble of distant thunder, Dara could hear voices within growing closer. Suddenly, the door swung open and revealed a young woman in the doorway.

"Lilly!" she exclaimed upon seeing Lillianna.

"I've missed you," Lillianna greeted as she pulled the young woman into a tight embrace before standing back and gesturing to Dara. "Mother, this is Dara. I'm glad you could finally meet one another."

Dara's brain short-circuited at that. *Mother?* As in, Lillianna's *mom?* Not like, an honorific title for the leader of a convent of nuns? By looks alone, the woman could hardly be any older than Dara, so how could she have given birth to her thirty-something boss?

"Dara, it's lovely to finally meet you," her mother gushed, turning to Dara with a wide smile that flashed her teeth. Behind her lips poked two sharp canines, just like her daughter's. She pulled Dara into a hug, squeezing tightly.

"It's great to meet you too," Dara replied, relaxing. She realized now that she had been very nervous about Lillianna's parents liking her, and much of her stress had dissipated as she was welcomed so warmly.

"Come in, come in," Lillianna's mother said, ushering them inside before hugging them each again in turn. She was around Dara's height, and although she could see the family resemblance to her daughter, her features were far softer. They shared the same ebon hair, but her eyes were a honey brown rather than ice blue, and her voice held the faintest hints of a faded accent that Dara could not quite place.

"Is everyone else already here?" Lillianna asked, glancing around the house as they migrated to the den. It was warmly decorated with furniture whose styles ranged from baroque to Victorian with even a little art nouveau thrown in. On the wood paneled walls hung numerous paintings depicting everything from serene Arcadian landscapes to mythological scenes of Greek gods warring over mortals in classical style. In some ways it felt more like she had entered a museum than a home with how the paintings crowded even the hearth, and yet somehow the curated collection fit together better than it had any right to. As she observed the decorations, the warm, wafting scent of cooking meat and hearty mashed potatoes made its way to Dara's nose, and her stomach rumbled happily at the expectation of dinner.

"Very nearly," her mother answered before turning back to Dara. "Oh, you're adorable! It's a shame that Lilly kept you such a secret."

"She's my assistant," Lillianna countered defensively, as if that explained everything, laying a protective, practiced hand on Dara's waist.

"Oh, I know. Eric can't stop talking about how he set you two up," her mother laughed. "He's so proud."

He what? Dara thought, blinking in silent confusion. Eric had set them up? Since when?! She smiled as blithely as she could as the two of them went on about something she clearly had no clue had even been happening behind the scenes.

"He exaggerates," Lillianna said, shaking her head and allowing her hands to drop to her side. "He told me I needed an assistant to help with work, not my dating life."

"I do not!" Eric piped up as he came down the stairs. "She was your perfect match, but I had to rig the test's final selection so that none of the other matches got seniority. You really needed her in more ways than one, you see, so I had to."

"You did *what?* Eric, that's not what the test is for, it's—" Lillianna caught herself, as if she was about to say something she suddenly remembered she shouldn't. "—anyway, where is everyone else? I thought that Uncle Titus was going to be over."

"They're at Leon's place with father," Eric supplied. "They'll be over for dinner soon enough."

"I see."

"These are beautiful paintings," Dara commented, eager to change the subject to something she could contribute more on. She was pretty sure she was supposed to be ingratiating herself.

"Aren't they?" Lillianna's mother perked up at the mention. "Tav's grandfather—Lilly and Eric's great-grandfather—made most of them, but some of the great-aunts and uncles have some up here too."

"Oh wow, that's really cool," Dara exclaimed, walking over to get a better look at them. "So you have a whole family of artists?"

"I'll go put our things away," Lillianna offered suddenly, going to pick up their bags again.

Lillianna's mother nodded, but quickly returned her attention to Dara and the paintings. "Yes, they were actually quite famous, too. It's under a pseudonym, but one of their great-grandfather's paintings actually hangs in the Louvre and..."

* * *

No sooner than she had tossed the bags onto the floor of her room than Lillianna flopped down onto the mattress with a heavy sigh. Books detailing muscle groups and anatomy lined the shelves beside miniature replicas of Barye lion statues just like the ones in her office. It was the same house, the same family, the same dead ancestors she had never even met requiring the highest of respect and reverence, and the same feeling of inadequacy when compared against their achievements. Perhaps in a thousand years she would have been able to make it to the Vatican too, if she were even allowed to exhibit by then. But she wasn't, and that was that.

The door creaked open behind her and interrupted her dreary thoughts, and Lillianna instantly recognized who was there. The way she stepped, hesitated, and the cadence of her breath.

"There you are," Dara said as she entered the room. "You had the right idea with retreating up here. As soon as your mother left to check on the food, Eric wanted to know who made the first move and which one of us cried during sappy movies. Said he bet money on it."

Lillianna could feel the bed shift as she sat down on top of it. She groaned, sitting up on the bed and turning to Dara. "I wish that he'd stop doing that. Our grandfather hates gambling, but all of my cousins love it. He keeps going on about how if his father or aunt were still alive they'd be ashamed of their vices."

"Would they? Your relatives are very impressive. Your mother was showing me all of their paintings. I see where you get your artistic talent from," Dara commented.

"I don't think I could be compared to them. She told you the story about the charcoal sketch in the Louvre, didn't she? And probably about how one of his oils is in the Vatican."

"Now you've got to be pulling my leg," Dara said, smiling and shaking her head. "Is he *really* in the Louvre, or is your mother just overly enthusiastic about the family history?"

Lillianna was quiet. She did not know how to explain to Dara that all of it was true, made believable only because the vampires who had made those paintings had been born hundreds of years ago—only a few generations for vampires at most, but dozens upon dozens for humans. They were history itself.

"Let me show you something."

She stood, beckoning Dara to follow, and walked out into the hall, past a half-dozen other beautifully illustrated paintings crammed onto the wall, to stand at the entrance to the bathroom and point inside. Dara hesitated for a moment, unsure of what she was up to, but eventually came to stand beside her and saw what she was pointing at. It was a painting positioned opposite the mirror, just above the towels. It was alone in the bathroom, and rather different in style—more modern compared to the ones downstairs, with brighter colors and an emphasis on the movement of the muscles as the singular lion draped itself gracefully across a sunlit rock.

"You did this," Dara stated finally, recognition dawning on her. "It's a lion too, your favorite."

"I did," Lillianna agreed. "And they are my favorite."

"It's the best painting I've ever seen."

"You're sweet," Lillianna said, shaking her head ruefully.

"No, really!" Dara insisted.

"They certainly wouldn't put me in the Louvre."

"Then maybe the stuff at the Louvre isn't as good as we all think it is," Dara asserted resolutely, and for a brief moment Lillianna was bolstered by that resolve—but only for a moment. Then she sighed and gave the painting a stern appraisal.

"It can't even be hung downstairs. Did you see where my family put it? In the bathroom. Near the toilet for goodness' sake. I know there was hardly any space left in the house, but still."

"Why didn't she just move one of the paintings downstairs?" Dara asked, clearly confused.

"Because those paintings have always hung there, even before I was born," Lillianna said with a shake of her head. "My father would see it as disrespect to their memory to move them now, and it's hard to compete with anyone who's already dead."

"That does sound like a problem," Dara said before adding thoughtfully, "Artists do tend to become more valuable after they pass on."

"Maybe if I died they would put me downstairs, but maybe not," Lillianna stated dismally, shutting the door to the bathroom to banish the painting once more. She did not want to think about how long she had spent simply detailing the fur on that thing only to have it be hung in the bathroom.

"You can't do that!" Dara insisted. "The bathroom is still a step up from being pinned to the fridge. If the space is already taken then you just have to find a new space."

"You mean build my own house?" Lillianna asked dubiously. She did not even display her own artwork at her apartment. It felt counterfeit to nominate herself for display when what she really wanted was to be recognized by others for merit alone.

"Something like that, I mean, I don't know." Dara flailed her hands futilely in front of her. "We go to museums to look at dinosaur bones but don't even notice when things go extinct all around us. People in general just have an obsession with things we've already lost so much that we forget about the things we have right now."

"Huh." Lillianna had not expected something so sagelike.

"Even I like dinosaur bones," Dara admitted guiltily. "But it's just a bit silly at the end of the day to like them more than other things simply because they're gone."

"It doesn't rule out the possibility that the things already lost were simply better than what is left, but I like that thought. It's sweet of you to say that."

"Dinner's ready! Everyone's here, come on down!" Lillianna's mother hollered up the stairs, cutting the moment short.

"Coming!" Lillianna called back before turning again to Dara. "You're going to meet my uncle, and—" Lillianna frowned when she remembered who his children were. "—his family."

Chapter 14

Reaching the bottom of the stairs, Lillianna stopped when she saw her father waiting in the archway to the kitchen. He smiled at her the way he always had ever since she was a little girl, lips curling around his fangs and eyes twinkling—a hint of warmth beneath his stern exterior. He was tall and sinewy in stature rather than willowy like many of his brothers, and the oldest ever since his elder brother had met his end during the Renaissance. Her father still had a scar from that same night when one of the hunters' poisoned dagger split his skin from his lip to his chin, but none had managed to take him down then or since. Unfortunately, his brother had not been so swift.

"Father," she greeted him, smiling as politely and warmly as she could despite the deception at hand. There was a certain distance that he held being the future clan head—should anything befall her grandfather—and that he was more than five centuries her elder. They were close in some ways, and yet worlds apart in others, one of which being that all clan members addressed him with firm respect. In some ways she was jealous of her cousins' more laid back relationships with their parents, but in other ways not: she would rather Eric for a brother than Frederick.

"Lilly," her father said fondly as he walked over to them and turned to Dara to offer his hand. "And you must be Dara. It is so good to meet you. It is much cause for celebration that you are here."

"A pleasure," Dara nodded with a polite smile as she took his hand. "Your daughter is lovely inside and out, I couldn't have asked for more." Wait. That had not been what they went over. She cast a subtle, questioning glance over at Dara, but failed to find anything in her pleased, contented expression that would ease her own confusion. If Dara upped the ante, Lillianna's parents would be more than upset when they inevitably "broke up" before summer. The original plan was to allow their joint presence and closeness do the talking rather than forcing something that sounded fake—although what Dara had said didn't sound fake at all. There was something about those words that made Lillianna feel rather strange. As it swelled in her chest, she recognized it for what it was: pride. Looking back at her father, he gave her a knowing look. *Damn.* How she had felt must have shown on her face. How terribly embarrassing to be paying Dara to pretend to love her and still flattered by her performance.

Her father inclined his head to the both of them. "We have always wanted more children, and another daughter is just perfect. Come, nothing was spared for the occasion," he replied, guiding them to the dining room. There they were greeted by her Uncle Titus and Aunt Victoria who were just finishing laying down silverware along with one of their sons, Sergei. Each of them greeted the both of them cordially, expressing their gratitude and well wishes for Dara's presence, and Dara performed admirably if a bit bashfully, though Lillianna felt that made the performance even more believable to seal the deal.

"Tav's little girl has her own woman now. You've really grown up," Titus congratulated her. "Would that my sons could follow your example."

"Would that my own son could follow her example," her father chuckled under his breath in a rare joke.

Lillianna tried to hold herself back from puffing up again, but it was difficult. After nearly five decades of waiting and being the youngest of Clan Markov, they were finally noticing that she had grown up, even if just for a purported engagement. His other son was missing, and if she was lucky perhaps he would not show up at all. But that was too good to be true, and Lillianna knew it. When Eric popped into the room carrying a bottle of wine from the cellar, Lillianna quickly intercepted him to confirm.

"He's not here?" she whispered as she pulled him aside, feeling unwarrantably optimistic. It was not like Frederick to miss family events, as unpleasant as he made them.

"Don't get your hopes up too much. Fred said he had a phone call," Eric whispered back, looking disappointed himself. "Wish his car had broken down on the way over instead."

Lillianna had to stop herself from groaning in response, but there was no time for commiseration as the devil himself, Frederick Markov, walked back in the door and flung his scarf and coat onto the rack with what he probably thought was a sophisticated flare, but in reality was just trying too hard. Immediately Lillianna stalked back to Dara's side to stand watch. She placed a hand across her back as if to brace the both of them for the coming unpleasantness.

As Frederick walked to the dining room, he saw them and slowed, then stopped. For the briefest of moments, Lillianna thought that he might make a biting remark or snide comment, but there were eyes beside her own on him and he knew it. Instead he smiled wordlessly, smarmy and sly as his fangs peeked from behind his lips, but if he had widened the expression any further it would have begun to turn into a snarl.

"Good to see you, *Lilly*," he said, then sauntered past both her and Dara without any further comment.

Lillianna forced her face to remain neutral, but her grip on Dara's waist tightened anyway. There had been animosity in their relationship before, but something was different now—something she could not quite place.

"Good to see you too, *Frederick*," she heard Dara say quietly beside her, clearly noting that she had been ignored. And though Dara certainly assumed he could not hear it, his vampiric hearing definitely did. Lillianna smiled as he paused for a moment and huffed, then went to stand beside his mother.

"Time to eat," her own mother announced merrily as she appeared with a platter of food from the kitchen.

"What about grandfather?" Lillianna asked, keeping Frederick in her peripheral vision as she spoke. "He's not coming?"

"He wanted to be alone tonight. Said the moon reminded him of Amélie," she informed her with a sad, sympathetic smile.

"Oh." There was a solemn moment that fell over the room at that, but it quickly cleared up as the rest of the food was laid out as distraction.

There were slices of tender, marinated beef that lay in a bed of shallots and pearl onions soaked in wine sauce. An overflowing basket of rolls buttered with salted sweet cream was laid out beside the main dish, as well as small bowls of creamy tomato bisque garnished with fresh basil. Dara looked positively delighted as she piled her plate high with slices of beef and rolls, and Lillianna found it difficult to be upset about Frederick or concerned about her grandfather when Dara was clearly so very happy with the spread.

Thankfully Frederick was quiet as they ate, leaving the bulk of conversation to his far more agreeable parents. Sometimes it was hard to believe Titus and Victoria were related to him, seeing as neither had the sort of itchy desire to irritate or taunt that their son possessed. Somehow their son always managed to be on his best behavior whenever they were paying attention to him, which was something he used to skillfully to make it appear as though *she* had started the argument instead.

As per usual, Eric's usual boyish self had vanished in his father's presence, replaced by someone so respectful that Lillianna would have thought he had a twin had she not known better. As for herself, everything was going excellently as she fielded questions about Dara and how the two had met and worked together at the office. Dara added a little smile and helpful comment every now and then, and everything was going fine.

"So then it was Eric's master plan after all?" Titus asked jokingly. "I heard it through the grapevine, though it wasn't very quiet."

"Well, he seems to think so," Lillianna replied with a chuckle.

"He bribed me with gift cards to make sure I transferred in," Dara commented. "He had me worried about what I was signing up for."

"I was trying to make sure the initial impression didn't scare you away," Eric corrected, the edges of his mouth already tugging into a smug grin. "She was rather scary when you first walked in there, wasn't she?"

Lillianna had opened her mouth to correct his wild ideations when suddenly Dara spoke first.

"Yeah, she really was. I thought my days of having a life outside work were over," she said, her voice wistful yet amiable. The tone of truthfulness in the statement shocked Lillianna at how much she had already forgotten.

Lillianna shut her mouth so quickly that she felt the taste of her own blood, and then the memories came flooding back. That all seemed so terribly long ago when she had growled at Dara, recognizing her instantly as the young woman who had not been watching where she was going in the clinic and spilled precious blood all over her clothing. But she had been mistaken back then—the precious blood she had smelled had not been in the shattered vials, but inside Dara's own veins.

"But you'd say it was worth it, don't you think, Lilly?" Eric said, smugly addressing her.

"Yes," she admitted begrudgingly but kept her voice light. She could not be too poor a sport about her own behavior toward Dara, and she was the one who had suggested keeping things as authentic as possible. When she turned to glance at Dara she was not sure what she was expecting to find considering she was her scary boss that had then bribed her to act as fiancée to cover up her own, stupid mistake, but she was pleasantly surprised to find Dara smiling fondly at her as if the memory was somehow humorous rather than traumatic. Suddenly feeling very grateful, Lillianna reached to curl her arm around Dara's shoulders and pull her closer with a tug, resting her head on Dara's soft, chestnut hair for just a moment. Even in front of others, maybe even because of the others, everything seemed to simply slide into place easily. "Yes," she repeated more surely. "Very worth it."

"She certainly seems lovely, and I'll bet she's delicious," Frederick said, eyes glinting and his mouth curling into a subtle smirk.

Lillianna tensed, gripping Dara's shoulder tighter than she had intended as the very air around them seemed to stiffen. Had Frederick really just subtly suggested that Dara—for all intents and purposes her *mate*—had blood worthy of a taste as casually as he might recommend a vintage of wine? *No one* discussed the taste of blood bonded mates after they were chosen—it demeaned their new status. No one did, except, apparently, Frederick.

Instinctive, possessive anger pulsed through Lillianna's veins, threatening to spill over across the tablecloth in an angry surge to charge at her cousin. Dara whimpered as her grip became too tight. Someone's fork clattered to their plate. Everyone at the table had gone quiet as the last remnants of conversation died out and were replaced with uptight silence. Some looked on with an anxious awkwardness, but many more glared at Frederick for the off-color remark.

"Frederick," Uncle Titus said, his voice low and warning. Frederick appeared to instantly remember himself at his father's reprimand.

"All the best, of course," he said, smiling broadly in an attempt to smooth things over, but the poor excuse for a smile still bordered on a sneer. His eyes then darted down the table to Eric. "And how are you doing on the hunt for a mate, oh-so-accomplished matchmaker?"

"She hasn't wandered into my life yet, but if she does I'm not telling you about her even after the ring's on," Eric said, waving him off. "Anyway, when was the last time you even took an interest in someone? I don't recall it being entirely..."

With the matter seemingly settled, dinner continued on, but the tension did not entirely dissipate, and Lillianna caught Frederick looking in Dara's direction again more than once before he felt her eyes on him and turned to look at her directly. He stared back at her in a manner that Lillianna was unused to, even during the height of their petty rivalry decades ago before their grandfather had told them to tone it down, and what she found there unnerved her. No taunting mirth or petty irritation glimmered in his eyes, just revenge, but for the life of her Lillianna could not imagine what in the world for.

* * *

"I'm glad that's over with," Lillianna said when they reached the bedroom. After digestifs and small talk, she was grateful to finally have a break.

"It wasn't that bad. They seem nice," Dara commented. "Well, most of them."

"They are nice," Lillianna agreed. "But it's just a lot to, well, you know." She shrugged, unable to voice the last part of their secret agreement aloud, nor the bit about how after Frederick's display she had felt antsy about having any other vampire in Dara's remote vicinity at all. Thankfully, shortly after dinner Titus's family had all left to Leon's place again along with Eric to spend time with her other relatives for a while longer. Lillianna had been invited too, but she had politely declined due to fatigue both feigned and real. "You did good," she said, her words both about their ruse and yet also fitting perfectly into the ruse itself. "They liked you."

"Did they?" Dara beamed as she retrieved her toothbrush from her luggage. "I mean, I was hoping they would. I was a little worried."

"I don't think there was anything to worry about. Everyone you work with at the office likes you already, so it makes sense that it'd be the same here. Even I like you, and I never cared for anyone Eric brought on to the team before." Somehow the realization made her feel proud, but that confused her. Dara was definitely better than the other assistants, but it wasn't like Lillianna had accomplished anything herself by that. It was all Dara's doing.

"No one?" Dara asked, a certain curiosity in her voice. "Katie's pretty nice, isn't she?"

"I don't even remember which one Katie is. All of his assistants are so interchangeable. I can't even remember which one is which," Lillianna said. Laying down on the bed, she stretched out and closed her eyes to gain a brief respite from the day. She could hear the whir of the electric toothbrush as Dara finished brushing her teeth, then the soft footsteps down the hall as she went and returned from the bathroom before she spoke again.

"Aren't you going to get ready for bed?" Dara asked. Lillianna felt the bed shift under her weight as she sat down on it.

"It's a little early for me. Sleep disorder, you know," Lillianna explained, opening her eyes as she turned to look at her. Dara was wearing a set of fleecy, gray pajamas printed with polar bears adorned with crimson ribbons. There was just something so dorky and adorable about the design. "Those are so like you," she chuckled, shaking her head.

"Well, sheesh, I didn't think anyone was going to see them! If you wanted me to wear sexy pajamas you should have told me!" Dara replied with mock indignation.

"No, no, they're cute, I promise. But sexy, well—" The image of her reaching out a hand to pull Dara into her arms flashed through her mind, bidding her to not-so-gently tug at the hem of her top and throw the ribboned polar bears on the floor.

"Well?" Dara asked, giving her a jesting look. Lillianna realized she had been staring.

"—well, they're kinda sexy I guess, in a forbidden sort of way?" she mumbled, confused by the sudden thought. No sooner had she spoken the words than she wanted to smother herself with her pillow. Her brain must have stopped working to have said something so stupidly inappropriate.

Dara blinked at her as a rush of blood went to her face. "Um…is that so?" Silence quickly followed, but Dara did not take her eyes off her—just long, agonizingly slow blinks. When Lillianna had said to keep things as authentic as possible, she had not intended like *this*. Moreover, it was not a great way to start a night of sleeping in the same bed. Lillianna had already envenomed Dara without permission and she didn't need her thinking that she was going to be doing *other* things without permission too. She had self-control, damn it! Time to change the topic fast. Lillianna grasped for the first thing from dinner that came to mind.

"You really thought I was scary when we first met?"

"Like hellfire," Dara admitted. "But then you turned out to be so nice."

"Nice?" Lillianna said, perking up. She wanted to be convinced of that. Being intimidating was something she had always wanted to be before, but that was to her cousins, not Dara. When it came to Dara she wanted to be…something *more.*

"I do less overtime for you than my last boss, actually. I mean, I guess I shouldn't be saying this or you'll make me do more?" Dara joked.

"I don't intend to do that."

"Well, thank you." Dara reached to turn off the bedside lamp.

"Wait," Lillianna said suddenly.

"Yes?" Dara looked over expectantly.

"Sorry about Frederick, he's—" Lillianna began, pausing in frustration at how difficult it was to explain the past danger and animosity without vampirism. "—never been this bad. We always gave one another a hard time about everything, but now he's just being downright nasty. He's usually over everything by the next day, but in case he isn't…please tell me."

It was true that what had happened at dinner was not normal even for Frederick. He never made such a scene when his parents were watching, much less in front of her own father, the future patriarch. Even she had been able to resist retaliating when faced with such an audience, as much as she had felt the urge to.

"I will. Thanks for looking out for me," Dara said softly. "Good night."

The lamp clicked off, and darkness swept through the room. Despite the curtains being drawn, Lillianna's vampiric senses could still see Dara's outline in the darkness as she laid her head down on the pillow and closed her eyes. Her steady breathing slowed as the minutes drew on until the cadence matched the gentle rhythm of sleep.

Lillianna was grateful that Dara seemed far more relaxed here in her presence than she had been at her apartment, and by no means did she want her to be uncomfortable, but at the same time she sort of wished it was a bigger deal for Dara—at least in the same way it was for herself. Dara had not made any fuss about the plans for sleeping in the same bed, and of course Lillianna had not either, but now that she was confronted with the reality of Dara's sleeping form something felt so monumental about it all.

While at the atelier she had taken lovers every now and then, but those had been shallow connections and in the end amounted to little more than a convenient and less hassling source of fresh blood. Since joining the company there had been no time for lovers, nor much desire for fresh blood since it no longer held the appeal it once had when weighed against the disgust of dependency. However, even back in those days before at the atelier, Lillianna was fairly certain it had not felt like this.

The first day of their trip was over with and a success. She should be happy about that, but as she watched Dara sleep on the other side of the bed, she could not help but feel a touch of melancholy coil its way into her heart at the realization that their time together like this was limited. She could tell that it was not just her family that would be sad when they broke up, but herself as well. She rubbed her forehead as if to physically push the erroneous thoughts from her mind, but they would not budge. It had only been one day of pretending and now her brain was scrambled worse than before. Falling into the role of devoted fiancée was fooling more than just her own parents, but herself as well as the instincts of her counterfeit blood bond worked double time to trick her into believing that this was real. Even now she could hear Dara's gentle, sleeping heartbeat and smell the scent of her skin, something that made Lillianna want to protect and devour her in equal measures. She wanted to stay here near Dara, but even with how much blood she had drunk this morning before getting into the car for their trip it did not feel like enough. With some reluctance, she peeled herself away from the sumptuously tempting time bomb asleep on the bed and headed downstairs to retrieve something sanguine to sate herself with.

152

Chapter 15

Blinking awake to morning light seeping in from the thickly curtain window, for a moment Dara forgot where she was. The floral wallpaper, thick blankets, and unfamiliar ceiling were all completely foreign until she spotted the little lion curios on the wall shelves, bags of luggage nudged against the wall, and Lillianna herself across the bed from her, wrapped haphazardly in stolen blankets despite having her own thick, flannel pajamas.

Her dark hair was lightly tousled by sleep, and her clothing had been ruffled as she tossed and turned in the night. Her top was pulled up partway to reveal a hint of a rather toned stomach that Dara could not help but guiltily admire. She shivered, belatedly realizing she had awoken early because she was cold. Lillianna was using even half the blankets she had taken, but Dara did not want to wake her by tussling for them.

Deciding to simply start her day instead, Dara hopped out of bed, taking care to not disturb Lillianna, then washed and dressed for the morning before she made her way downstairs. She had been so exhausted after the road trip last night that, Lillianna beside her or not, it had been impossible not to just fall asleep. Now she was feeling refreshed, and quite hungry as she made her way to the kitchen. Soon the scent of roasted coffee filled the air, but still not a single soul stirred in the house. After pouring herself a steaming mug, Dara opened the fridge to look for milk and noticed some peculiar plastic bags filled with dark liquid leaning against the juice. They looked like drink pouches for kids at sports games, except the Markovs did not appear to have any young children around. Perhaps someone was feeling nostalgic for some artificial fruit punch flavoring, except the color of the liquid was so dark and concentrated that it did not look tasty anymore. In fact, it was such a dark and earthy shade that it looked a little...*raw*. Dara grabbed the milk and shut the fridge.

When she was finished preparing her coffee, she threw on her coat from the rack and took her steaming mug outside to enjoy on the back porch step. Warmth radiated from the ceramic vessel to her fingertips, staving off the brisk winter air. Outside the house the world was not nearly so bereft of company; a couple of brilliant crimson cardinals twittered on nearby trees, and an errant blue jay settled down on a branch to watch her. Even with many of the trees missing their leaves, the silhouettes of wintry austerity held a certain elegance to them, and Dara could only imagine what it looked like in the height of summer when the trees were crowned with foliage.

When the coffee had cooled enough, Dara took a sip. The refined taste was creamy and pleasantly sweet. She savored it as she gazed out across the meadow that served as the Markov's backyard. A small plot had been cleared for a garden but it currently lay empty in the cold weather. A store of fire wood lay near the edge of the house, filled to the brim. Trees ringed the edge of the meadow, with a gap in them that led to a trail into the woods.

As Dara was contemplating where the path might lead, the back door creaked open and Dara turned to see Lillianna walk to greet her. Her tousled hair had been easily combed back into its standard sleek state, and her pajamas had been exchanged for a dark navy double-breasted peacoat that sveltely fit her frame. She offered Dara a friendly, if a bit sleepy, smile.

"You're up early," she commented as she settled down beside Dara on the step.

"Did I wake you? I'm sorry. I know you need to sleep later," Dara said.

"It's alright. I'll take a nap later if I need to. Have you eaten yet, or just coffee?"

"Just coffee," Dara replied, taking another sip. "Have something in mind?"

"Pancakes?" Lillianna offered.

"Sounds great," Dara accepted eagerly, standing up to follow her back inside.

"Do you like chocolate chip?" Lillianna asked as she fished through the lower shelf of the pantry and found the pancake mix.

"Very much," Dara answered as she set her mug down on the counter. "What do you need for it? Eggs?"

Lillianna checked the label on the box. "It says to just add water."

"Then let's add milk instead. They'll be better that way," Dara suggested as she reached for the fridge door.

"Wait, that's alright! I'll get it," Lillianna exclaimed as she practically threw herself at the fridge to get to it first. "You can just, uh, chop the strawberries. Here's a knife and a cutting board."

"Uh, okay," Dara said, still unsure of what had just happened. "Sure."

"Don't worry about it. My parents are just, uh, very particular about their fridge?" Lillianna explained, attempting to fill the awkward air between them, but it was so stilted and obvious that something was off. Were the Markovs hiding contraband in their fridge? Drugs in the orange juice? Dara glanced back to her mug on the counter. She didn't feel weird...*yet*.

Ugh, she was letting her imagination run wild and away with her again. Although, even her imagination could not have cooked up pretending to be Lillianna's fiancée for some reason she did not know.

She should just enjoy the simple domesticity of making pancakes together, but instead she chewed on that thought as she chopped the strawberries. However, soon the niggling thoughts drifted away once more as the scent of cooking batter reached her nose and her stomach growled happily at the coming breakfast.

Once finished, they settled down into the breakfast nook along with their pancakes covered in a drizzle of berry syrup, chopped strawberries, and a hefty dollop of whipped cream on top. It was picture perfect, and tasted even better.

"The house is so beautiful. Has your family lived here a long time?" Dara asked after wolfing down half her pancakes.

"Almost two hundred years now I think. Though it's much more modern now because they rebuilt a lot of it after there was a fire," Lillianna informed her. Though she had been the one to suggest pancakes in the first place, Lillianna did not seem as enthusiastic about them as Dara was. She kept glancing back toward the fridge instead.

"Wow, so it's been in your family for generations then."

Lillianna gave her an odd look. "Generations? Oh, yeah, I suppose."

"It's kinda cool how secluded it is, but commuting must be terrible," Dara mused. Her pancakes were nearly gone now.

"The company has another building in the other direction that's much closer. That town's where my parents get groceries too."

"Oh? I'm surprised you don't live closer then."

"Well, it has a grocery store and an office building, but not much else I must admit," Lillianna chuckled, shaking her head. The fridge had been forgotten and her attention was fully focused on Dara now. Dara smiled; she liked that. "I prefer my cities to actually have things in them to do."

"I didn't know you had time to enjoy what the city had to offer," Dara joked.

"We go to all those restaurants," Lillianna recalled. "And there's the zoo, remember? Although you're right, it's been ages since I went there." Her expression turned pensive as she looked over out the window, the last pancake uneaten and forgotten as her fork fell to the plate. "Maybe I've taken things for granted a bit."

"Well, it's not like I am the pinnacle of a busy social schedule either," Dara admitted.

"Then maybe we should go together to the zoo when we get back. As a new years resolution to get out more or something. Would you want to?" Lillianna asked.

"I would love to," Dara replied a little too quickly. She may be a fake fiancée, but the invitation was a welcome reminder that the rest of their friendship was real. She wasn't sure if allowing her massive crush to continue to grow was a great idea, but now that she knew that Lillianna actually liked women it was not as though this train was going to stop. "Do you also like aquariums or maybe—"

Her question was interrupted when at that moment the front door swung open loudly and a chorus of young men's voices filled the den as they traipsed inside.

"Eric!" someone hollered. "Where are you at?"

"Coming!" he called, his voice soon accompanied by hurried steps on the staircase. "You brought the table? Chips? Lucky socks?"

"I brought your defeat," someone said with a laugh.

"Never!" Eric declared. "I can't lose. My love life's failings ensure my success in cards." Hoots of laughter followed the joke.

"What were you saying?" Lillianna asked Dara as the volume of voices died down once more.

"Don't worry about it, we're good. Do you want to see what they're up to?" Dara said.

"I *know* what they're up to," Lillianna said with a sigh. "Gambling where Grandfather won't catch them. He only hates it if he sees it, so their little club hangs out over here. It's the only thing they'll wake up early for."

"Hey, Lilly!" Eric called, poking his head around a corner to spot them in the breakfast nook. "You want to join us?"

"Maybe some other time," she declined politely. "I want Dara to myself today."

Her hand reached across the counter to cover the back of Dara's own, her thumb brushing against Dara's wrist casually in a manner that gave her a delicious bundle of butterflies in her stomach. A smidgen of guilt bubbled its way to the surface of her heart. Who was she kidding? She didn't want to be Lillianna's friend; she wanted this to be real. Maybe she should stop this train....next month, when she was not being paid to be Lillianna's fiancée. Dara threaded her hand through Lillianna's long and slender fingers, pulling tight and squeezing, and Lillianna squeezed back.

The moment was interrupted by Eric who was still there despite Dara immediately forgetting about him. "Now you're just showing off." He rolled his eyes playfully and continued, "When are you going to return the favor and set me up?"

"When such a woman exists," Lillianna scoffed, before whispering to Dara. "Let's go before they get rowdy. Are you up for a walk?"

"Through the forest? Sounds lovely," Dara accepted.

She hummed happily as she went to the coat rack to uncover her jacket from among the many coats now stashed there. As she plucked hers from the rack, there was much conversation in the den as Lillianna's cousins set up their chips and cards at a large table. Dara looked over with mild interest. She recognized Sergei with his slender frame and unassuming attitude, but could not recall the name of the stockier cousin next to him despite knowing Lillianna had shown her a photo of him before the trip. On the other side of Sergei was Frederick, the only cousin that did not look like he was having any fun as he sipped at a glass of something dark and...*viscous?*

He turned and their eyes met, his lips curling into a sour slant when he spotted her and eyebrows crushing together before he gave a silent scoff and turned back to his drink in disdain. He muttered something under his breath, and Dara could just barely make out the words his lips formed. *"Human livestock."*

Dara wrinkled her nose in disgust and huffed to herself. Buttoning up her coat, she walked to the door where Lillianna was waiting and smiled brightly at her, determined to enjoy herself. She got one preciously short vacation to pretend to date her boss, and Lillianna's stupid, misogynistic ass of a cousin wasn't going to ruin it.

* * *

The piercing winter sun was too bright for Lillianna's eyes as they walked out onto the trail and inhaled the brisk winter air, but having some time alone was worth it. She held Dara's hand protectively as they left the house behind them, and made no move to let go even once they were out of sight.

Dara walked along beside her, clearly enraptured with the wintry beauty of the forest as her eyes roved over the landscape. At times, Dara reminded her of a cute little puppy that was too adorable for its own good, but if she wandered off somewhere she might find a new person to play with, a new boss to work for, or a real lover to date. Lillianna did not like the sound of any of those options, but least of all that last one. Surreptitiously, she cast a glance downward at her companion. Unlike a puppy, Dara was very much attractive. Her duffel coat hid her figure more thoroughly than any sweater, but Lillianna could still see the swell of her breasts and the hint of the curve of her hips beneath it.

159

"I can remember Sergei, and I think one is named Alexander? Who was your other cousin again?" Dara chattered as they walked along into the forest. Fallen leaves swirled along the ground when roused by the wind, but their coats kept them toasty warm despite the chill.

"Julius," Lillianna informed her, "but don't worry about it. None of my cousins are going to be upset if you forget them except probably Frederick, but that's all the more reason to."

"I would if I could," Dara replied with a defeated sigh. "I see now why you reacted like you did that time at the office."

"You do?" Lillianna asked, alarm creeping into her voice. Had he tried to drink Dara's blood again?

"It feels like he has it out for me," Dara continued.

Lillianna let out a soft breath of relief. There were plenty of other things to dislike Frederick over besides attempted blood drinking, she reminded herself. "He's very two-faced, but he has always shown the jerk version of his face to me." Lillianna held Dara's hand a little tighter. She did not like the idea that there was something about Dara in particular that had set Frederick off. The man went for tall, leggy red-heads, so it was not like she was his type. "But make sure you're never caught with him alone, just in case."

"You make it sound like he's dangerous."

"Well, I mean it'd be good to not find out, right?" Lillianna did not like to consider it herself even, but it had to be said. Vampires were magnitudes stronger than humans and even dhampirs, and Frederick had never held a high opinion of their more mortal counterparts.

"That's true," Dara agreed, though it was clear she was still worried.

"I won't let him do anything to you," Lillianna promised. "And even if it seems like Eric and I don't always get along, I'm certain he wouldn't let anything happen either."

"He's a good older brother, huh?" Dara said, sounding reassured. "He was trying to look out for you when he made me your assistant."

"Yes. He and the others can get all protective because I'm the youngest," Lillianna sighed. "And the only girl born in generations."

"Wow, no other girls at all?" Dara commented. "They must have been really happy when you were born."

"They were," Lillianna agreed, then sagged as she remembered, her breath white in the frosty air. "And had quite a lot of hopes and expectations too."

"Well, you seem to be living up to them splendidly."

"Am I?" Lillianna asked, unable to help the bitter edge that crept into her voice.

Dara looked at her oddly. "I mean, yeah? You've got a great job, do good work, and are a really talented painter too."

"Most of my family has done better."

"You mean the Louvre and the Vatican? You don't need to be famous to have done well for yourself," Dara pointed out. "Isn't the work its own reward, or something like that?"

"Those platitudes sound great until you get there," Lillianna sighed, remembering how dissatisfied she had been when the cold reality of the situation had dawned on her. She understood that her family cared about her and did not want to risk the hunters being on their trail, but it still stung. "I'm trapped being second best, no, dead last, forever."

"I don't understand." Dara stopped and cocked her head to the side, concerned.

"I wasn't—I'm *still* not—allowed to even try to exhibit. I could train and practice as long as I wanted, but it was only ever going to amount to a hobby with a leash." Lillianna did not normally speak of this with anyone, and despite it being Dara she could not help but be defensive. Her family had often told her that she would understand when she was older, that it was wise and for the safety of all, but she already understood that. She understood and she hated it.

"Not allowed?" Dara asked, confusion evident. "Why?"

"It's not safe—" she began to say before biting her tongue. The hunters had watched for centuries for the telltale signs of an artist that had simply reappeared with a new pseudonym a century or so after their supposed death. Every counterfeiter had been investigated *just in case* they were actually the true artist "back from the dead." The Markovs had been intertwined with the art market for centuries and had been unwilling to give it up despite the dangers, but when her father's eldest brother, the last of the old guard, had fallen, the remaining Markovs had walked away to mourn their dead and honor their memory. Now there was just her, born centuries too late to a family whose heroes she was forbidden to follow in the footsteps of, and the only thing left was to seek recognition and respect through alternative avenues—the office, like everyone else.

"Not safe?" Dara was becoming alarmed now. "Is your family part of the mafia or something?" she asked in a hushed tone despite the emptiness of the forest.

"Goodness, no," Lillianna exclaimed.

"Witness protection program?" Dara guessed again.

"No, not that. It's more like a family feud," she attempted, though that only partially described it. She was by no means related to them, but the hunters had an eternal war against her mere existence simply from being born into the wrong sort of family.

"Am I in…danger?" Dara whispered again, glancing around at the empty forest.

"No! That's the point of me not exhibiting paintings in the first place. Everyone is safe. See? That fear is why I had to give it up. I understand that, and I'm not going to endanger anyone, but it still makes me upset."

"Oh."

It all appeared to click for Dara then. She looked down at the ground, the whistling of the wind through the trees the only sound in the quiet forest as both of them searched for something more to say. As the silence grew longer, a feeling gnawed at Lillianna's heart until she couldn't take it any longer.

"I'm sorry," she said, feeling foolish. This had been a perfectly good walk before she opened her mouth. "I didn't mean to bring the mood down." Feeling like she did not deserve it, she let go of Dara's hand and let her arms drop to her side.

"No, I understand," Dara said, looking apologetic herself. "You're right, the platitudes don't amount to much when you're living them. Stuff like 'it's better to have loved and lost than never loved at all'—crap like that, you know?"

"Your ex?" Lillianna asked, interest suddenly piqued. A possessive urge began to growl inside her, and she did not have the strength nor desire to silence it.

"Oh, well, no, I just mean, like, in general," Dara said nervously before adding, "We should keep walking to stay warm."

Lillianna nodded and stepped forward, but Dara's admission remained on her mind. The trail soon brought them to the top of a hill with an old, low fence across it that had been constructed decades ago. They leaned out over it, enjoying the view of the campground clearings and forest below. Aluminum roofs of camper vans poked out of the trees in places, glimmering in the winter sun, and Lillianna could see specks of movement down below as the human campers went about their day.

"Lilly, look!" Dara exclaimed, pointing to a college of crimson cardinals among the branches of a tree a short ways off. Their puffed up breasts shown vibrant in the winter sun.

"Lilly?" Lillianna asked, her mind snagging on the sudden change. Dara never called her that nickname.

"Oh, sorry. Everyone else calls you that, so I just…" Dara trailed off, looking a little lost. "Should I not?"

"No, it's fine. I don't mind. I was just surprised, that's all," Lillianna replied quickly. And, surprisingly, she really didn't mind. The change was unexpected, but not unpleasant despite the fact that for years the diminutive nickname had been a reminder that her family still saw her as a little girl, youngest of Clan Markov, rather than the adult woman she really was. But somehow from Dara the syllables struck differently. Her voice kept all of the endearing elements of the name and none of the patronizing undertones. "I like it," she finally decided, earning herself a pleased smile from Dara.

"Well, good, I like it too," Dara said.

Among the scenery of the office, Lillianna had been unable to see Dara as anything but her assistant who smelled deliciously of blood. She had thought she was only overly fond and protective of her because of her usefulness and because she needed Dara in order to get ahead at the company, but that was not true. Her smile, the way she blurted out what was on her mind when nervous, and the earnest way she worked had all wedged their way into her heart. Like how the colors in a painting changed perception depending on the hue of the colors beside them, seeing Dara here against the winter sky rather than office walls made everything feel much clearer than it had been last month, last week, and even last night. She could not tell if the blood bond made her feel this way, or if the venom simply slipped from her fangs because she had felt this way all along, but at this point it was ceasing to matter.

Considering how to proceed was a different question, and she did not like how the future slunk around on the horizon like a wild jackal. Humans generally were not fans of vampires beyond the bounds of a movie set. Which, considering Lillianna's track record so far of accidentally envenoming her, perhaps that ill reputation for her kind was not unearned. There were exceptions of course; her mother had been dying when her father's venom had quite literally saved her life all those years ago. He was her hero then and now, but Lillianna was just a leech.

That last thought did not have time to fully settle in her mind before she shoved it away. Maybe this was just reality, she told herself. Vampires just had to drink blood, and she just had to have Dara. She still wasn't sure about any of it, but it felt nice to just focus on that one goal.

"It's beautiful, isn't it?" Dara asked as she gazed dreamily out at the clear blue horizon.

"Yes," Lillianna replied, her own gaze still focused on Dara herself against the winter sky, her chestnut hair lit with golden highlights from the sunlight. "Very beautiful."

Chapter 16

Through the window of the study, Dara had watched the sky turn from wintry ice blue to an orange glow streaked with pink to now as the colors finally began to darken and fade from the sky. It was very beautiful, but also distracting. Between Lillianna being on one side of her and the window on the other, Dara's ability to focus on the game they were playing had suffered.

After dinner, they had sequestered themselves in the downstairs study to drink mulled cider as they desperately tried to best Lillianna's mother at a dusty, ancient board game she had pulled from an equally ancient closet. After Lillianna had warned her that her mother was "really quite good at this game," they had ended up playing two versus one to try to even the odds. Even despite the advantage, Lillianna had already been knocked out in an earlier round, and Dara was fading fast as Natalia Markov's pieces continued to advance across the board.

"Your turn," Lillianna's mother said as she set down her piece. She was clearly winning, but her tone remained calm and tranquil rather than gloating.

Dara lifted one of her pieces and moved it a few squares over, waffling for a moment on her decision before setting it down. Reaching for her mug to take another sip, she found it disappointingly empty.

"I'll get you more," Lillianna offered, noticing her obvious dissatis-faction.

166

"Thanks, Lilly," Dara said, enjoying the way the name rolled off her tongue. It felt surprisingly intimate.

Lillianna smiled back at her as she collected both their mugs and headed to the kitchen, her footfalls fading into the background as Dara focused on her next move. *Ahem,* correction: her last move. This was not looking good.

"It was a good game. You learn quickly," Lillianna's mother praised her.

"I don't know about that. You thrashed us," Dara replied, shaking her head.

"Oh, but I have a lot more practice. You'll get there, I am certain, and sooner than you think—certainly not a century like it took for me."

"That's too modest," Dara replied, chuckling at the hyperbole as she helped clean up the game pieces.

"No, really! Although I must admit Tav let me win far more often than he probably should have in those years, though you wouldn't think it just by looking at him." Lillianna's mother finished putting everything back in its box and placed it in the center of the desk for later. "Speaking of, I should probably go find him." As she spoke, she reached a hand to her neck and stroked it absentmindedly before bidding Dara farewell.

After she left, Dara went to go find Lillianna. She had been rather quiet ever since they got back from the walk, but had hovered near her all throughout the evening anyway. Now, without her so close, Dara missed her. She didn't want to waste any bit of this trip and its perfect excuse to be near her without a report in hand. Going back to "normal" after this was going to be a monumental hassle. As Dara walked past the den noticed that Lillianna's cousins had stopped their gambling and were presently putting on their coats in preparation to brave the winter weather. She was almost to the kitchen on her quest to find Lillianna when she spotted her through the archway standing beside the cooling pot of mulled cider on the stove, two filled mugs in her hands. Dara could also hear Eric's voice speaking to her, his words becoming clear as she grew closer.

"...have to get to the campground before it snows too much and get a bite to eat. Leon said they're holding a bonfire down there and we want to catch them outside the campers."

"There should still be enough to drink to hold us over past the solstice, and it probably wasn't Alex who drank them all," Lillianna defended, sounding repentant as she fidgeted contritely.

"Better to play it safe. Besides, you're not the one going thirsty if we run out. You've got Dara. Oh, speak of the devil," he said, spotting Dara in the doorway. His coat was already fully buttoned and he was just finishing putting on his gloves.

"Hey guys," Dara greeted them both, stepping into the kitchen.

"Dara," Lillianna sputtered, looking quite surprised. "Why are you here?"

"Because your mother won again. Geez, the woman's a pro," she replied, shaking her head.

"Eric! We're leaving!" someone called from the front.

"Oh, gotta run. Have fun you two." Eric winked at Lillianna before following his cousins out the door and into the cold.

"What was that about?" Dara asked.

"How much did you hear?" Lillianna queried nervously, holding out her mug for her to take.

"They're heading to the campground to...I don't know? Drink the campers' beer and eat their snacks? Did you guys run out of groceries?"

"No, we have food, but uh—well, we own the campground," Lillianna admitted, her eyes shifting back to the door that her brother had just left out of.

"Huh." It should not come as a big surprise that the Markovs owned the campground, and yet she could tell from the way Lillianna spoke that this was not about modesty, but secrecy. That last thought stung, but Dara tried her best to ignore the discomfort. It was none of her business, so she changed tack. "He mentioned something about the solstice? Do I need to know anything about that?" she prodded.

"Oh, we celebrate the winter solstice with a big dinner and candles and stuff. It's not that big a deal," Lillianna explained, but that seemed like a pretty big deal to Dara. She was here over the holidays, and this was the Markov's holiday of choice. She didn't want to embarrass herself by not knowing anything about it when the time came.

"Isn't celebrating the solstice usually something mostly Wiccans do? Witches?" Dara pointed out, growing urgently curious.

"Well, I wouldn't say it's Wiccan, and definitely not witchcraft, though I suppose one might call it pagan. It's really just a family tradition."

"What do you guys do?" Dara asked, still curious. Her understanding of all things pagan was primarily gleaned from cheesy horror flicks, and this was a new experience for her.

"Well, there's a big dinner," Lillianna explained. "After that we go outside and recite some things." Her voice was stiff, almost cautious, as if all it took was one wrong word and everything might be revealed. But what? Was this really so embarrassing?

"Like a prayer?" Dara asked, confused. That sounded rather more serious than she had been led to believe.

"No, not really." At first it seemed that Lillianna was going to brush this aside too. Her eyes darted toward the door her brother had left out of, then back to Dara. She shifted her weight from one foot back to the other, and Dara had all but given up when she suddenly blurted out more. "Well, it's sort of like a prayer I guess. It's a hope for the coming year to be better than the last, and for the family's good health. But the words have been passed down for centuries with very little changes so you would probably think it's weird."

Dara had never seen Lillianna so bothered by something, even under the pressure of a deadline. At first, she wasn't sure what to do, or if there was even anything she could do. She reached out, her fingers brushing against the back of Lillianna's hand before becoming brave enough to take it. "Hey, you don't have to be scared about this. I mean, I know it's new for me and all, but it doesn't mean I won't like it."

"Yeah?" Lillianna looked down at her, visibly relaxing as she squeezed Dara's hand back. "I'm really not used to this. I don't think I've even mentioned it to anyone before."

"No one?" Dara asked. "Not even your exes?"

"I never thought to," Lillianna said, looking down before raising her eyes to look directly into Dara's. She gave her a sad, almost apologetic, smile that did not match her words. "They weren't important. They weren't, well...you."

You. Staring into those ice blue eyes, Dara nearly forgot to breathe. Something fluttered in her chest. That feeling of being special, unique, different from the others. Little by little, Lillianna was opening up to her. She blinked, forcing herself to breathe. *Snap out of it, Dara.*

Like hell she was different—of course she was. She was the only one Lillianna had paid to pretend. She could not believe this. In one moment Lillianna was being heartfelt and honest, then in the next she was effortlessly saying words she did not mean. Forget just being a talented painter, she was a supremely talented actor too. Unless... unless it wasn't an act.

Dara looked back up at Lillianna, noting the way her dark hair had been pulled back over one ear and the first few buttons of her shirt were undone. She could see the artful curve of her collarbone, the way it connected to the sinew of her neck, and the graceful way her eyelashes fluttered as she blinked at her in silent expectation. In retrospect, Dara could nearly cringe at the childish optimism of her prior thought. With looks like this, Lillianna could surely do better than her whether that was someone with a better figure, better face, or better bank account.

"Are you sure everything's okay? It's not that weird?" Lillianna pressed for reassurance.

"Everything's fine. I'm sure the solstice will be lovely," Dara assured her. She knew that they were not supposed to talk about their monetary bargain while here, but while Lillianna wanted to be reassured that she was normal, Dara wanted assurances and explicit reminders that this really was all just pretend. She forced her eyes away from Lillianna, and the troubling emotions that arose there, on over her shoulder to the windows above the kitchen sink. The dusky violet sky glimmered against the glass as a swirl of movement drifted through the air. "It's snowing," she noted.

"Already?" Lillianna turned around to see for herself.

"Will Eric and the others be alright?"

"It looks pretty light, but I'll go check." Lillianna went to put on her coat and took her mug of warm cider with her outside to look at the weather, and Dara, having nothing better to do, decided to do the same.

Outside, flakes of soft, white snow fell against an amethyst sky. Most flakes melted as they hit the porch and ground, but in a few areas they were already beginning to build. The dark pines of the forest were crowned by a yellow moon, nearly full. The pines were sure to be swept into a thick frosting of snow by morning, but for now the forest was silent with not even a whistle of wind to punctuate the quiet blanketing of snow.

Dara and Lillianna stood side by side on the porch, close but not touching. They were only a few mere inches apart, but it still felt so very, very far. Dara sipped at her cider, the heat of the liquid warming her bones and staving off the chill of the weather, but it could not hold off the feeling that was beginning to well up inside her chest. It was a longing she was familiar with, one she had felt many times throughout her life, and one she had thought she had finally come to terms with. But unlike her ex, her father, or even now her mother who drifted away from her in a process that was wholly normal, Lillianna was right here in front of her, actively giving her attention that she did not want to end. Against the twinkling tapestry of the stars, the city, her job, and everything else just seemed so small and manageable. But without the noises of the city to distract her, everything she ever wanted seemed so much further out of reach too. The feeling threatened to swallow her whole when combined with the overwhelmingness of her desires.

No, things did not have to be like this. Things were going to look up for her. She would get her own place someday, and hopefully someone to live there with her too. She did not want to let go—her heart was stubborn like that—but she was going to have to. When she got back to the city, she was going to set a new years resolution to go on more dates, even if it currently felt like going to the gym four times a week in January would be a more achievable resolution. Glancing to the woman beside her, she found Lillianna lost in thought as she gazed toward the heavens. Dara wanted to know what she was thinking about now, tomorrow, and always. To share in her fears and her hopes and dreams. She had already had a little taste, and now she wanted more than she was rationed.

"So what do you think?" Dara asked, her words feeling unnaturally loud in the stillness of the night.

"Hm?" Lillianna snapped out of her reverie.

"About Eric and the others. They'll be alright?" Dara repeated her question from earlier.

"Yes. They'll be fine." Lillianna said.

"That's good." Yawning sleepily, Dara finished the last of her cider and set the empty mug down on the flat, wooden railing of the porch.

"Tired?" Lillianna asked, placing her own mug down beside it.

"Yeah, but it's so pretty out here. Maybe we should get your parents.

I'd bet they'd like to see it," Dara suggested. "I'll go look for them." Lillianna held out a hand to stop her. "No, we don't need them. I mean, I like my parents, but—" Lillianna breathed out a heavy sigh of quickly frosting air. "—I like it better when it's just you...and me."

"Oh." In the darkness of the night Dara thought she could see Lillianna's cheeks color from more than the cold. Lillianna smiled, flashing her sharpened teeth that glinted in the light of the moon, but then her bravado faltered.

"Or is it not enough when it's just me?"

"You're more than enough," Dara said immediately, unable to stop herself from telling the truth.

"Yeah?" Lillianna murmured, reaching a hand up to brush a lock of Dara's hair from her face. A shiver rippled through Dara's spine, but not because of any winter chill. "I'm trying to not be scary."

Dara could not help but giggle at that. "It's because you're so tall. It's hard to imagine you ever not being at least a little intimidating."

"What if I made myself a little shorter?" Lillianna asked, crouching down slightly and inching forward to come closer to Dara's eye level.

"It's not a bad thing to be tall." From this close, Dara could see a sprinkling of frost on her dark eyelashes. "Sometimes I wish I was a little taller."

"I think you're perfect the way you are," Lillianna murmured quietly. She was only a few inches apart from her now, and there was a dreamlike quality to the whole scene as Dara stared back, spellbound. Her lips parted, but no words came out. Then there was no distance between them at all.

Lillianna brushed her lips chastely against her own, hesitant at first but then emboldened as her lips covered her mouth. The kiss was velvet warmth, slow and sweet, and Dara's touch starved senses drank it in hungrily. The kiss quickly grew more demanding as Lillianna's tongue traced her lower lip, and Dara moved to deepen the kiss herself.

The longing in her chest had been replaced by a wild swirl in her stomach. All thoughts she had slipped away. Her senses reeled, short-circuiting in the moment as the kisses drugged her with delicious sensation.

"Yoohoo, Lilly! Dara!" Eric's voice called from a dozen yards away. The spell broke. Dara sat breathless and confused on the porch step as Lillianna pulled away from her.

"Eric, What the hell are you doing here?" Lillianna yelled back as her brother walked out of the woods and into the meadow.

"I live here," he offered sulkily as he continued to walk closer, but Lillianna's unamused look made him try again. "Leon called and told us the bonfire was canceled anyway so we got lucky and grabbed some deer. I see you were about to grab something yourself though, don't mind me."

Lillianna flinched at those words and cast an agitated glance at Dara, who was still too dazed to process what any of it meant. She wanted to talk to her about this—all of this—but she did not even know what to say, and certainly not in front of Eric. He was nearly to the step now, and Dara noticed a rust-colored stain below his lip smeared all the way to his chin. It looked a lot like—

"Nevermind, I don't care what happened to the bonfire. I'm *busy*," she snapped before turning back to Dara and grabbing her arm. "Let's go."

Dara bumbled along behind Lillianna as she was led back into the house, now unsure of if she had just dreamed the whole thing up with the help of the cider. One moment Lillianna had been so gentle, and then at Eric's arrival everything had rapidly deteriorated into flustered agitation. No, not just agitated—*panicked,* but Dara could not fathom why. She opened her mouth to ask, but before she could even think of the words to say her chance slipped by.

"Ugh, I forgot the mugs," Lillianna remembered suddenly, barely five steps from the door. She let go of Dara's arm. "Be right back."

Before the door even closed again, Dara could hear Eric hassling Lillianna again about something while Lillianna, still clearly agitated, hissed words back at him. Dara was straining her ears, trying to figure out what they were talking about, when Lillianna's mother swept into the den from the staircase.

"Something wrong?" Lillianna's mother asked, looking toward the door Lillianna had just left through.

"Nothing," Dara insisted reflexively. Receiving a concerned look in return, Dara suspected that she probably looked as lost as she felt. Thankfully, beyond giving her a concerned eyebrow raise, Lillianna's mother did not push it. Instead she looked again back to the door and sighed, placing her hands on her hips as she considered what to do, if anything, about her adult children bickering on the porch. She seemed mostly unruffled about the whole thing, though still rather annoyed, and it was then that Dara noticed the mark on her neck. It looked to be a wound that was in the process of healing—one that had not been there earlier during the board game.

"You hurt yourself," she stated bluntly.

"Huh?" Lillianna's mother looked at her, confused for a moment before realizing what Dara was talking about. "Oh no, no. You know how it is," she explained, blushing in a way that made her look an awful lot like her daughter. "Their teeth are so sharp, but even if they're vigorous everything heals up by morning."

"Huh?" Dara cocked her head. She didn't really get what she was talking about—*wait.* Oh no, *oh god,* that wasn't a wound, that was a hickey! While Dara had been living out her fantasies on the porch, Lillianna's parents had been enjoying their own sort of fantasy. Dara just wanted to crawl into a hole, or a grave, or at least under a large pile of blankets. She was overwhelmed with an urge to simply go to bed early and come morning pretend this conversation never happened.

It did not matter that Lillianna's mother looked young enough to be her sister, these were still her parents!

The door swung open again to save Dara from her own social faux pas. "Sorry about that," Lillianna said as she returned with the mugs. Eric was close behind her, rolling his eyes where she could not see him.

Lillianna's mother cleared her throat as the prior conversation with Dara was swept under the rug. "Everything good, you two?" she asked her children.

"Everything's fine, Lillianna replied quickly. A hint of the agitation was still there, but it was quickly stabilizing. Eric rolled his eyes again in the background, this time harder, but he nodded to his mother in the end that it was, indeed, nothing, or at least *he* thought it was nothing. To Dara, what had transpired a mere minute or two before was everything and more. Lillianna addressed her mother again, "Just tired. I think we're just going to head to bed early, right Dara?" She turned to Dara expectantly.

"Sure," she agreed immediately, eager to be alone again and away from both their stressors.

Dara quickly traveled up the staircase with Lillianna close behind her. They had just entered the bedroom when Lillianna stopped, pausing behind her in the doorway as she shut the door softly behind her. Dara turned back to look at her, and, for a brief second, thought she saw a hunger lingering in Lillianna's ice blue eyes, cold as a winter storm and twice as dangerous. It was breathtakingly beautiful and seductive, and Dara's breath hitched at the sight.

She immediately found that the words to all the questions she wanted to ask were too shy to leave her mouth. If she asked them, she might get answers, and suddenly she did not want to hear an assurance that everything was pretend, or that Lillianna had simply gotten too far into her role. Dara wanted to just keep pretending and stave off her inevitable disappointment just a little longer—or forever. She stepped forward, coming closer into Lillianna's space, but then Lillianna stepped back.

"I just remembered something I have to do," Lillianna said suddenly, reaching for the doorknob with haste. "Outside."

"It's snowing," Dara pointed out, her words coming more easily when they were not about the elephant in the room.

"I know," Lillianna replied, a hint of the nervousness from earlier returning. "But I'll be fine. I know these woods. Sleep well, okay?"

"Lilly, wait—" Dara began, but Lillianna did not even wait for her to reply before she scuttled out of the room and down the stairs at an expeditious pace.

Somehow, even without words, Dara had gotten her answer, and now she wanted it even less than she had before. She brushed her teeth in a mute daze, changed into her pajamas, and laid down on the bed with a book she had packed that was a poor excuse for a distraction. The trip had barely begun and her world had already been turned upside down so many times that it was spinning. When this first started, she had thought that it was probably a bad idea. Now she *knew* it was a bad idea, but that was simply because no amount of money was ever going to allow her to get over this. Even if she would be finally able to afford a down payment, all she was going to do was sit in her new place and mope that she was not Lillianna Markov's actual fiancée.

* * *

Droplets of ruby blood dripped across the snow beneath the quivering body of the deer as Lillianna drank her fill. The blood was wild, gamey, and distinctly inhuman, but the pulse beneath her lips was real and strong. When she had drunk enough, she released the beast and stood. The animal staggered to its feet and stumbled, wandering dazed back into the forest. In a few minutes it would regain full consciousness, though it would remain woozy for the rest of the night.

She watched as its hooves printed tracks leading into the forest until it meandered, lost, behind a thick copse of barren trees and a rapidly building snowbank. Flakes still swirled in the air around her, quickly working to cover up the fresh tracks and bloody evidence at her feet. The deer had struggled wildly before Lillianna's saliva had soothed it, and her hypnosis could only do so much on an animal. Wasteful spurts had stained the scuffed snow beneath her but were quickly fading from view as the snowfall continued on. She wished everything, all her worries, cares, and concerns, could just disappear under the snow along with it. Heaving a sigh, she turned to head back to the house.

Standing once again on the porch and breathing in the frigid air, she ran her tongue across her teeth, feeling the sharpness as saliva flooded into her mouth. Breathing deeply, she willed herself to calm. She had fed and she did not need more, but that did not help with control when she wanted to feast on Dara in a wholly different fashion. She could not sleep beside Dara, not like this. She found her far too appetizing in more ways than one.

Chapter 17

Dara woke in the morning and immediately realized that, though the bed was quite warm, it was also quite empty. She stretched out along the bed, still feeling tired but knowing it was time to get up. She had slept terribly, sometimes overheating, other times restlessly waking as her mind lingering on both the kiss and the shaky, insecure feelings that had come after as she lay awake in bed. She should get up and take a shower, but down the hall she could already hear the water running in the bathroom so she instead allowed herself to loaf in the snug cocoon of quilted sympathy.

She drifted back to a half-sleep, barely noticing when the sound of the shower ceased and down the hall a door creaked open. It was only when she heard the scrap of wooden drawers being opened that she cracked an eye open to find Lillianna, clad in only a towel, rifling through a dresser drawer for clothing. Her bare shoulders were pale and smooth, but held a muscular definition that seamlessly blended into the slender curve of her neck. Long, lean legs led to toned thighs of which Dara could see far more of than she had ever seen in a business skirt at the office, but beyond that everything was mostly hidden by a fluffy, white towel. "Mostly" because Dara could still see the outline of, well, everything. She gulped, trying not to stare, but found herself unable to look away. As a compromise, she forced herself to look at Lillianna's face, which was a poor idea because it turned out to be far more embarrassing than just ogling her body. Lillianna was staring back at her with a mix of confusion and keen interest, though her gaze did not quite meet Dara's eyes.

"Hey Lilly," Dara sputtered out, very much awake now. Lillianna blinked slowly, then her gaze refocused on Dara's face. "Good morning."

"Good morning," she repeated back. "Sleep well?"

"No."

"No?" Lillianna tilted her head in concern at Dara's blunt answer, forgetting all about the shirt she held in one hand that she still needed to put on.

"I had a lot on my mind," Dara explained. *Like how you would rather wander around in the snow than be anywhere near me last night.*

"Me too," Lillianna admitted, looking away as she retrieved a pair of pants from the dresser. "We can talk about it if you want."

"We probably should," Dara agreed, though the knots in her stomach protested wholeheartedly. "I wanted to know why you—"

Just then Dara's phone on the bedside table began to ring wildly, causing them both to nearly jump as the expectant tension crumbled. The phone's screen lit up with her mom's name and Dara remembered now that she had told her mother that she was going away on a business trip; she was probably extremely worried about her poor daughter being overworked.

"Do you need to take that?" Lillianna asked, peering over at her phone.

"Yeah, I probably should," Dara said, both reluctant and relieved as she picked up her phone.

"We'll talk later once you get dressed," Lillianna said, grabbing her things and leaving.

Once I get dressed? Dara reflected, confused at the choice of words. *Doesn't she mean once she gets dressed—oh god no.* Dara looked down to find that sometime in the night, probably when she had overheated, she had decided to unbutton her top. The bed had been empty, and, being barely coherent, it had seemed like a good idea at the time. It wasn't like much had been exposed—just the center of her chest and stomach—but Dara still felt like she had been practically seen naked. She was nowhere near as athletic as Lillianna was, and did not want to advertise her scrawny physique.

"Hey, Mom," she said wearily as she answered the phone. "Yes, I'm fine. Yes, really. No, it's nothing too hard. The nativity? I put it in the garage. It's in the big box to the right with the blue tape..."

* * *

"Hey Lilly, do you want to join us?" Eric asked, pointing to the card table where he had already started to set out cards in order from ace to king. "We're starting up a game of faro."

Lillianna sighed dejectedly as she looked disdainfully over at the cards. "You know I prefer games where there's at least a little bit of skill involved."

"There is skill!" Eric insisted impishly.

"Besides how well you can cheat," Lillianna said, rolling her eyes but smiling a little despite herself.

Though she had often found Eric's distracting nature annoying at the office, she could appreciate it now when she desperately needed a distraction. Even if she knew she needed to talk to Dara, there was no real excuse or explanation to give her about how she had behaved yesterday on the porch. A blood bond was the preferred type of mate for a vampire, and now Lillianna fully understood why. There was something irresistible about Dara, even beyond her other natural qualities. However, such a match was not a guarantee that things would work out—a potential match had a personality and desires of their own of course—and that was something she was becoming more acutely aware of since last night.

But the way Dara had looked up at her like that, the way her lips had parted just so, and then leaned forward to meet her ever so slightly had made her think Dara wanted her. And she did, at least in some form—that much was proven when she had kissed Lillianna back earnestly. What it did not prove was that Dara wanted her beyond some surface level physical connection. The kiss may not have even been that big of a deal to her. Dara was cute and probably had plenty of exes before she ever walked into Lillianna's office, but thinking that did not make her feel any better about the situation. Just now, she had wanted to walk back over to Dara, finish off the rest of those buttons, and push her back down on the bed in a heady, overeager rush of affection and attraction, but had willed herself to keep in check. This wasn't any way to treat a potential mate. Dara was supposed to agree to these things, not just have Lillianna envenom and take her whenever desire possessed her. Lillianna needed to do better. *Be* better.

"Give me some chips," Lillianna relented at last as her thoughts grew both overwhelmingly troubling and tantalizing as her daydreams began to wander back to Dara's bare midriff and chest. If Dara had just moved a little more, then she would have been able to see more than just the side of her breasts…and she needed to stop thinking about that.

"We got ourselves a game, boys," Alexander crowed heartily as he slapped the table. "Lilly's finally going to play."

"Are you sure you have the time?" Frederick said scathingly from across the table. "I thought your mate needed caring for. Have you filled her water trough yet?"

Lillianna bared her teeth at his brazen contempt as her protective side flared up. "Dara is well cared for, glad you noticed."

"As any prized heifer should be," Frederick sneered.

Eric looked over in horror at what was transpiring verbally as Lillianna's grip on the table tightened. Her knuckles whitened as she strained against the table, but just as she was about to snap back another one of her cousins spoke up first.

"Don't act like you're not jealous, Fred," Alexander jabbed. "Lonely, are you?"

"I don't want a human mate, nitwit," Frederick spat back scathingly.

"Well looky here at the only one whose parents were both vampires. You know they weren't even planning on that happening, right? And it causes problems with feeding," Alexander pointed out. "The only real benefit was fighting off hunters was easier back in the day. But you don't see hunters around now, do you? Most of the holy orders are extinct, and half the clans don't even take precautions anymore."

"I'd prefer a dhampir myself," Sergei chipped in.

"You'd like anyone at all is what I heard last," Julius mocked.

"Hey!"

"Maybe if Freddie got a vampire girlfriend he'd join her clan instead of ours and we'd miss him."

"Oh, the horror."

"Shut up, all of you," Frederick snarled, his face an angry, embarrassed scarlet.

"Hey, we're just joking. Like you were, remember?" Alexander stated innocently. An awkward silence fell over the table as he looked between Lillianna, her knuckles still white, and the sour, sanguine expression that was masked over Frederick's face. "You *were* joking, weren't you?"

"*Yes,*" Frederick grumbled reluctantly, clearly seeing no other choice. Lillianna had to resist the urge to smile smugly lest he lash out again.

"Oh, are you busy? Is now a bad time?" Dara's voice came from the stairway. Her phone was still in one hand as she held back cautiously and glanced between the faces at the table.

"No," Lillianna said, rising and turning away from the table, grateful to have a smooth exit after Frederick had ruined her chance at distraction. The knot in her stomach was quickly reforming, but she kept her tone upbeat and voice level despite the nerves she felt about the upcoming conversation with Dara. "I was just about to come check on you."

"Prized heifer," she heard Frederick mutter bitterly behind her. Lillianna resisted the urge to kick him and instead kept walking forward. The last thing Dara needed was to see a brawl between two vampires.

Damn you Frederick, Lillianna thought. And damn his stupid desire to win at everything too, especially when he had already lost. Patently ignoring him, she made her way to Dara and took one of her hands in her own as she offered her a tentative smile. Did Dara want what she wanted? Did the mother of night smile upon her this day? This was it, this was—

Without warning, the front door swung open, and in came her grandfather flanked by both her father and her Uncle Leon. Her grandfather was from an era where one preferred to never dress down for any occasion, and was wearing a royal blue three piece suit. His sons wore more austere clothing and were clad in simple dark turtlenecks and peacoats. Next to her father's comparatively bulky, muscular frame, her grandfather was slender and elegant, but Lillianna knew he could more than hold his own in a fight against hunters, and had done so many times in the past.

"Children," he greeted, smiling warmly in what soon turned to a displeased frown as he spotted the cards laid out across the central table and her cousins encircling it. "Misbehaving, I see. Building another card castle, was it?"

Someone coughed. It sounded like a death rattle. Then a low, chorusing mumble. "Sorry, grandfather."

"You all need to be more like Lilly," grandfather admonished. "A mate before her fifth decade even."

"She was gambling too—" Frederick started to say.

"*Silence*," their grandfather ordered. "Now put that away. If we are to play games it is the civilized kind. Ones that do not lead to loathsome quarrels." Finished with his grandsons, he turned to Lillianna. "Lilly, it is so good to see you again and meet your mate. I heard that you had been keeping her something of a secret."

"This is Dara," Lillianna introduced before apologetically explaining, "It all happened a bit fast, so I couldn't help but leave it a secret."

"It's good to meet you," Dara nodded cordially. "It was indeed rather sudden, but thank you for having me."

"Suddenness is not a problem. Everyone knows at a different time. Amélie and I did not know each other long before we…" His voice trailed off and a faraway look entered his eyes. "Ah, how she would have loved to meet you both."

"I'm sorry for your loss," Dara offered, still looking confused. Lillianna resisted wincing. She had never thought about how she was going to explain the way her grandfather *looked*—not the suit, but how he appeared to be late thirties at the very oldest.

"Thank you. We keep a piece of her here with us still, you see that painting over there?" He pointed to a picture of a heroic angel fighting against a many headed serpent. "She painted that one. Used me as the model for the angel even, ah, but without my beard. I didn't wear one back then."

"Oh, you're right. I can see the resemblance," Dara said, craning her neck to get a better look. Without his beard, Lillianna's grandfather looked even younger in the painting.

Lillianna's father tapped her grandfather on the shoulder and whispered something in his ear. "They haven't even eaten yet?" he said with a disappointed sigh before turning back to Lillianna and shaking his head. "The things gambling will do to a man. You all must be famished. Let us eat."

* * *

The sky had long grown dark again by the time Dara managed to slip away from the gathering and up the stairs to be alone and rest. She was somewhat regretful for making the excellent dinner look bad with her excuse of a "stomach ache," but she also did not want to say that she was just far too introverted spend another moment with this many people at once, let alone someone she knew was a big deal such as Lillianna's grandfather. If she had thought meeting her parents was stressful, this was something else entirely. The man was the chairman of the entire Markov company! Having the chairman be chuffed to meet her would normally be a good thing, except the man could barely contain his enthusiasm that she would be joining them at the solstice gathering for the first time, and she still hardly knew what it was. Aside from the mention last night, Lillianna had remained rather tight-lipped about the solstice gathering—no, *ritual* as her grandfather had called it, if the man was even her grandfather at all.

Physical exhaustion combined with unfamiliarity rolled over Dara in a wave of weariness. She had begun to feel a sense of dark foreboding about the upcoming solstice, but she could not quite place why except for the reverent tone used to discuss it, the secrecy, and that it was, well, *pagan.* Dara chided herself for not being more open-minded. Magic and the occult wasn't real, even if some people really thought it was. Celebrating the solstice was as harmless as getting presents from

Santa...right?

Her thoughts circled about warily as she shut the bedroom door behind her, sealing herself off from the Markovs. After meeting Lillianna's "grandfather," she just could not shake a growing feeling of unease that there was something very odd going on. Sure, Lillianna's mother looked great for having several adult children, but no amount of good genetics could make someone look that young when they were grandfather to someone Lillianna's age. That man couldn't be her grandfather, but if he wasn't then where *was* Lillianna's real grandfather? Perhaps he had already passed on, but so far there was no one that Dara could count as elderly attending the gathering at all. Vaguely she recalled movies where bathing in the blood of innocents allowed one to keep a youthful visage forever. Speaking of which, if this were a movie Dara would have been brought purposefully to be the sacrifice this year and—*ugh*. She had watched far too many bad horror flicks in college and now it was coming back to haunt her. The theory was so absurd that Dara chuckled to herself, the laughter dispersing the foreboding feelings that were clustering in her gut. Lillianna's grandfather had played solitaire with the cards he confiscated from his grandsons, not pulled out a deck of tarots with an ouija board. She could hear the chatter of their voices below as he drank wine and spoke with his family, and nothing about them seemed sinister at all. All that this was, was that she was exhausted and very, very stressed about that one thing she did not want to think about—Lillianna's kiss.

Dara pulled the curtains to look out the window across the wintry landscape of night. Fresh snow blanketed the landscape, laying the land to sleep before the solstice on the morrow. Just then, she noticed a figure, tall, slender, and distinctly feminine in shape beneath its large coat marching with purpose through the snow. The figure was reaching the tree line now, the outline of the body blending in the darkness with the dark trunks of the trees as it slipped into the forest and altogether disappeared. Lillianna had doubly assured her that her family knew these woods like the backs of their hands, but Dara still felt uneasy at the sight. A snowy wood at night was nowhere to be going alone. And what if it was Lillianna wandering into the woods? *No, it might be one of her aunts. They walked here, after all.* She could go downstairs to check, but that meant seeing everyone again, and she was still too tired for that. And Lillianna... No, she did not want to think about that at all. The more space there was for hope in her heart, the more room there was for fear to grow. It was beautiful and tempting like a box of chocolates wrapped in barbed wire.

Whoever was in the forest would be fine just like Lillianna had said; Dara would just have to trust her. Though the night was still young, Dara laid down on the bed and closed her eyes. Just a little reprieve, and she could find the strength to go back downstairs and socialize a bit more. She breathed deeply and tried not to think about anything.

Dara woke to a knock at the door. It creaked open on its hinges before she had even a moment to orient herself. Blinking blurrily in the lamplight, she looked around to find Lillianna kneeling beside the bed.

"Hey. Are you feeling okay?" Lillianna asked softly, her hand reaching out to lay across Dara's forehead with an equally soft touch. "You don't have a fever."

"Yeah, I'll be fine," Dara replied, but her stomach could not help but quiver at the casualness of the touch. "I think I was just too tired after dinner."

"I was worried it was the soup," Lillianna said, moving her hand down to the edge of the pillow.

"No, definitely not. Wait, your mother doesn't think that, does she?"

"She might, but I'll tell her she has nothing to worry about when she gets back."

"Gets back?" Dara asked, thinking of earlier. "Where did she go?"

"She and my father went...out," Lillianna said, her words a slow, careful cadence. "To get ready for tomorrow."

"Tomorrow." Dara's eyes focused on her. "You mean the solstice. Could you tell me more about that? I don't really, well, like surprises—not like this anyway. And I need to make a good impression, you know?"

"I understand." Now Lillianna's hand retracted from the bed altogether. "The solstice is a time for new beginnings. To try again, to start anew."

"Makes sense that it's so close to the end of the year. Stuff has to end to start over," Dara nodded.

"So that brings us to what I wanted to talk about," Lillianna said quietly, hanging her head. "I want to start over with you."

"But starting over means that something has to end, like you just pointed out," Dara pointed out, the uneasiness from early coiling up inside her gut once more. She did not like where this was going at all. Everything Lillianna was saying sounded like a farewell, and deep down inside her heart that was not what Dara wanted to hear.

"Yes," Lillianna continued to look down, avoiding her gaze. "I have not been...well, very good to you. I'm really not that great of a boss."

"What's that got to do with anything?" Dara sat up on the bed. She had heard something like this before when her ex broke up with her a year ago, although Lillianna's version was far more sincere. She had clearly reconsidered her decision to kiss her last night, and now Dara's pipe dream was over without having even done anything. "Nobody's perfect. You're a fine boss."

"No, I'm not." Lillianna looked up finally and met Dara's gaze. Her ice blue eyes were apologetic, searching, and yearning. "I've been terrible to you. I just keep taking things, and you're just too nice to tell me no."

"No, it's fine—I'm fine. I don't want to stop you—I—I—I'm in love

189

with you." Dara could not think of anything else to say, and for a moment she did not fully process that she had actually said it.

"You...are?" Lillianna asked, a curious, eager, unbelieving edge to her voice. The soft, apologetic yearning in her eyes had been replaced by the hard-edged glint of something else—something hungry and terribly famished.

"...yes?" Dara hesitated, terribly confused by the swift change in outlook and searching for positive signs.

"That means it's okay?" Lillianna leaned in closer, her hand raising to stroke the side of Dara's cheek ardently. "To take more?"

Something in Dara's brain short circuited at the close proximity. She could feel Lillianna's warmth through her hand, and hear the hint of raw vulnerability in her voice. She would give her anything she wanted, so long as she just didn't leave. "Everything," Dara whispered back, only half-believing it would work.

The touch became possessive as Lillianna's hand slipped from Dara's cheek and snaked down her arm, running long, nimble fingers along her forearm and pausing just above her wrist. She leaned forward, their lips pressing together and the kiss quickly deepening as Lillianna boldly sought to devour her. Dara was so distracted by the kiss and intermingling of their tongues that it almost did not register that earnest hands were tugging at her sweater and the shirt beneath it. She had said "everything" but this was so fast. It felt like a dream. Maybe it was.

"Um," she said breathlessly when they broke apart, not even sure what she was going to say.

Lillianna had already moved to press a heated trail of kisses along her jaw. Her lips landed on Dara's neck, nipping kisses against the skin until she settled into a rhythm of sucking along her pulse with such intensity that it was sure to leave a mark. Dara released a soft groan of pleasure at the pressure, her hands grappling about Lillianna's shoulders and holding her close. She could smell the sweet vanilla of her perfume mixed intoxicatingly with the natural scent of her skin. Lillianna raised her head to nibble at Dara's ear. "I meant to wait," she whispered, her voice a low, demanding growl, "but I don't want to wait."

She pulled away for a moment, swallowing hard and biting her lip with pointed canines before looking at her again with those enigmatic blue eyes that held hidden the swirling emotions within them: hunger, caring, heat, and quickly eroding caution. Something sparked to life within Dara, as bold and reckless as her earlier declaration. She leaned forward, hands grasping at the material of Lillianna's shirt, and pulled her into a clumsy, yet still heated, kiss.

The next moment Dara was flat on her back, pinned against the mattress as Lillianna straddled her and kissed her with a voracious hunger as if she had been starved of touch all her life. Her hands cupped at her breasts and stroked at her stomach before moving down along her body and latching onto the hem of her sweater once more. In moments, Dara's sweater had been discarded and short work was being made of the shirt beneath.

"Wait," Dara yelped, immediately reaching for the lamp's switch. The light vanished, leaving her to be stripped bare in the all consuming darkness. A low, disappointed rumble greeted her in the pitch black gloom, but the lamp stayed off as Lillianna kissed her hotly again before her mouth traveled downward to her neck.

Dara felt an indescribable thrill as her lips swept over her neck, her teeth barely grazing the skin and leaving a trail of fiery sensations in their wake. She slid her hands over to cup each breast before latching on to tease a taut nipple between her teeth. Every stroke and grazing nip across Dara's skin felt like a wildfire across a dry kindling forest as she was explored. Lillianna leaned up to kiss her on the lips once more, and Dara returned it with incautious fervor, reveling in the security

191

of touch and sensation.

"I want to see you," Lillianna uttered, her voice low and deep in the dark, but she did not reach for the lamp. The curtain rings scraped harshly as they were thrown open, and moonlight flooded into the room and over Dara's body. Exposed and unexpectedly vulnerable, Dara's first thought was to shrink away, but when she looked up at Lillianna she could not help but remain in place. Lillianna's ardent gaze brushed over her with the heat of a flame. Her ice blue eyes were full of heated desire, never looking away even as she slowly pulled her own garments over her head and tossed them aside to reveal a smooth, toned stomach etched in moonlight. Dara had never had anyone ever before look at her with such intensity and fire. The desire was palpable as Lillianna leaned back over her with a prowling grace and stroked a hand across her cheek. Her gaze dropped from her face to her neck to shoulders before finally sliding to her breasts with a satisfied smile. "You're beautiful."

The beautiful one is you, Dara thought as she was forced by a complicated roil of emotions in her stomach like a storm of butterflies to look away.

"Dara," Lillianna said, her voice rough. Dara's insides tingled at the way her voice caressed her name. Lillianna's hand guided her head back toward her. Dara looked up, and then her heart lurched madly as their lips met once more.

Their tongues danced inside her mouth as Lillianna's hands continued to roam. Dara's own hands fumbled across her back, wanting more and trying to draw ever closer, but was thwarted as Lillianna shifted and slid down again to nibble again on her breasts. She hailed Dara with a downpour of craving, caressing touches, then suddenly shifted again and Dara's sensitive, swollen nipples were left wanting as Lillianna moved with urgency to the area that pleaded for her touch the most. Her lips seared a path from Dara's breasts down past her navel to momentarily halt at the waistband on her pants.

Dara shivered at the heady sensation of Lillianna's fingers threading across her stomach, and then nodded urgently in the darkness between breaths. Her pants were quickly done away with, but her underwear was removed more carefully, reverent even, as Lillianna slowly revealed her and dipped her own head to explore. She roamed over Dara's thighs with her lips, teeth, and tongue before finally settling down between them. Lillianna explored, tasted, touched, licked, but nothing was enough to sate Dara's growing need. She raised her hips impatiently, and was rewarded with a tantalizing lick and shiver as Lillianna ran her tongue deliciously across her center. Laving her tongue over her in another testing taste, the pace began to rapidly increase. Dara squirmed at the sudden ferocity of attention, but Lillianna held tight to her as jolts of pleasure crackled through her body and sent tingles up her spine. In alternating rhythm the touches became more tender, each nibble and caress pushing her further along the slope of her climax without allowing her to tumble over the edge.

"More," Dara moaned as she thrust her hips up and her head back into the pillow.

A finger entered her slick entrance easily, and then another, curling against her inner walls as Lillianna continued to suck at her with a fiery intensity. Dara shuddered in ecstasy, gasping at the pure excess of emotion and physical pleasure crashing over her as the fingers twisted inside of her ever more tightly. Her hands scrabbled at the blankets and bedsheets, finding no purchase great enough to anchor her as she was coiled into pure ecstasy.

The pulsing, liquid heat in her core released, coursing through her veins in a dizzying rush of euphoria and bursting sensations. Lillianna continued to suck and thrust as Dara rode out the wave of her climax until she was left feeling cloudy and contentedly exhausted. Lillianna pulled herself up off the bed once more to lay next to her and stroke her face. Dara closed her eyes, leaning into her touch and nuzzling the palm of her hand. She felt Lillianna's hot breath on her neck, and then a slow, sucking kiss near her collarbone.

"You like that, don't you? My neck," Dara giggled, exhausted. Despite the lightheartedness of her words, she felt Lillianna tense next to her.

"Well, no—I mean yes, but," Lillianna began. "I just—" She sucked in a breath, considering her words. "—want another taste."

"Huh?" Dara's eyes fluttered open.

Lillianna was no longer laying down next to her. Instead she was leaning over her with an even more intensely hungry gaze than before, if that were even possible. They kissed, Lillianna's tongue exploring just as fervidly as the first time, and Dara melted all over again.

Chapter 18

When Lillianna awoke in the morning, the winter sunlight slipping in through the undraped window hurt her eyes, but as long as she held Dara in her arms nothing could ruin her mood. Curled into the curve of her body, Dara was fast asleep. Lillianna closed her eyes once more, savoring the pleasant sensation of another's skin against her own, and wished that this could just last forever, but Dara awoke all too soon. She yawned, opening her eyes, and looked surprised for a moment when she saw Lillianna beside her, but then quickly donned a shy smile.

"Good morning," Dara said, snuggling into her a little bit more.

"Did you sleep well?" Lillianna asked, nuzzling her cheek back.

"Yes—" Dara began to say, but her stomach interrupted her with a loud gurgle. "—er, sorry."

"I'll make you breakfast again," Lillianna suggested, but that only embarrassed Dara further.

"That's okay, you already do so much for me," she replied quickly.

"I do?" Lillianna asked, confused. She was pretty sure Dara's incredible ability to quickly produce financial documents was the entire reason she was on track for promotion. "Isn't it the other way around?"

"I mean, I wanted to do something for you last night and, well—" Dara fumbled as her blush continued to grow. "—I didn't mean to fall asleep."

"That? Don't worry about that," Lillianna dismissed. "There will be plenty of time to make up for that tonight." She leaned over to kiss Dara, slow and sweet, and she felt the sharp tips of Dara's canines on her tongue. They were growing dull...more human. A surge of possessiveness rippled through her chest, then the urge to envenom Dara again swept through her. She pushed it back, willing herself to be patient—at least concerning that piece of things. She shifted under the blankets to straddle Dara once more. "Or maybe even right now." But before she could make any more lurid suggestions they were interrupted by a loud knock at the door.

"Lilly! You need to get up. Mother wants you to go to the store. She needs some things," Eric's voice called through the door.

"Can't you?" Lillianna called back, irritated at being interrupted.

"I'm hauling firewood already! Anyway, get up!"

"Okay, okay," she grumbled, turning back to Dara as she rolled off of her. "Sorry. If it wasn't the solstice, I'd spend all day with you. I still would even, except my grandfather will be very upset if I skip."

"That's okay, we still have later tonight," Dara said understandingly. "But...Is that man really your grandfather?" she asked as she got up off the bed. "He looks so...young."

"That's normal, he's—" Lillianna paused, realizing she had planned no way to explain this. *'He's just a vampire,'* was not in any way something she could say at the moment. "—he's a Markov. We all age well. Good genes."

"Did he have kids really young too?" Dara suggested, clearly trying to rationalize it away in her own mind, which was helpful. "And I guess your parents did also."

"Yeah, I guess so," Lillianna said, facing away from Dara as she threw on her shirt. What else had her grandfather said yesterday that was suspect? Hadn't he referenced her almost being fifty? Had

Dara noticed that? She glanced back to Dara who was still innocently still sitting on the bed with the covers across her chest.

No, she should not be further covering this up; she should be preparing to tell Dara the truth anyway. Except, preparing...*how* exactly? The question settled like a stone to the bottom of her stomach, only softened by the feather-light feeling that buoyed up in her chest when she remembered making love to Dara. Even if she had been able to ask someone for advice, there was no one in her family that could tell her anything relevant; human culture was vastly different now than it had been when the last Markov mate had been welcomed into the fold.

The prospect of keeping the flame alive for the centuries to come was a daunting prospect, but at this moment Lillianna could not truly consider the alternative. Letting go of Dara right now sounded like an equally devastating failure. As much as the intensity of the feeling she felt for Dara frightened her, she did not want to run away, though she could not eliminate the possibility that Dara might. Lillianna was a vampire, and just *a* vampire at that, not even a particularly impressive one as her ancestors had been. Somehow she had to convince Dara that she was worth it, even after she knew what Lillianna really was.

"Hey, Lilly?" Dara's voice brought Lillianna back to the present. She was toying with a loose thread in the duvet and worrying her bottom lip with her pointed-but-quickly-dulling teeth. "We're dating, right? I mean, since last night—?"

"Shh," Lillianna hushed her, and she could tell from the look on Dara's face that she had suddenly remembered that they were supposed to be engaged already, not just begun dating. After a surreptitious glance toward the door, Lillianna took a step forward for privacy and whispered, "Yes, we are."

"Good," Dara smiled, but then her forehead creased as she remembered something. "Could you tell me more about the solstice when you get back?" she requested. "I didn't hear all that much before we—" she gestured her hands wildly. "—you know. I want to look good in front of your family, even more now than before."

"Of course. That's mostly my fault that we didn't get to it," Lillianna agreed. "I'll be sure to make it up to you." She gave Dara one last kiss on the forehead and then went to prepare to make the long trip to the store and back.

* * *

Dara's boots crunched in the snow as she made her way through the outskirts of the forest, careful to not stray too far from the house. The snow was no longer powder, having become far icier as it melted and refroze under the sun's mild heat. Blue jays hopped along the branches of the trees to keep her company. Some stopped to give her a solid chirp as she passed, inspecting her with dark, beady eyes, but quickly moving on when they did not find whatever it was they were searching for.

Back at the house, Lillianna's mother was busy in the kitchen, Alexander and Julius were peeling potatoes, and even Sergei had been put to work rolling out dough. Dara had watched Eric stomp out into the forest to get firewood, and at that point she had decided that it was a rather fine day for a walk herself. As the guest of honor, she was not required to participate in any of the preparations, but it still felt odd to be hanging around the house when most everyone else was busy. Plus, she was pretty sure her happiness showed on her face, and she didn't need everyone in the house noticing that something had changed.

She and Lillianna were dating now, and she could hardly believe it. It didn't seem real, but now even the ring that sat on her left hand felt realer than it ever had—except it wasn't, *at least not yet,* she reminded herself. But goodness, Lillianna paying her to pretend to be her fiancée had to be the most roundabout way of asking a woman out that Dara had ever seen. She still did not know why Lillianna had asked her to do that, and now the secrecy stung when she recalled it. Maybe liking her *was* the secret, except that seemed far too simple. Lillianna may have a few quirks, but she was not *that* quirky. Now that they were dating, Dara wanted to know everything and to be the first person Lillianna told. She wanted to be there for her if something was bothering her, but maybe it was just too early for that. At least for now, Dara was Lillianna's girlfriend and she should just be happy. Besides, she was probably just blowing things out of proportion like she had been last night.

Dara recalled that she had been expecting an awkward, possibly heart-wrenching conversation, but then she had been roughly pinned to the bed and nipped all over instead, which was frankly a better outcome than she could have ever hoped for. She smiled at that recollection and everything that had come after, but her daydreams did not get far before she came across hoof prints that intersected her path in the snow.

Curious, she followed the tracks through the forest as her idle mind rehearsed her pleasant daydreams once more, but then all semblance of serenity disappeared when the deep tracks toppled over into an intense gash in the snow. The deer had slid wildly across the ground, punctuating the scene with wet, crimson smears and droplets of blood that recorded the deer's struggle as it rose and staggered into the forest beyond. The sight of blood across the once-pure snow unnerved Dara and sent a tremor through her breast. Judging by the color, it was scarcely shed even a few hours ago. Had something attacked the deer? Wolves, maybe? Dara did not see any lupine tracks in the snow, just another set of boots. Another person had been this way, and they had turned around after encountering the deer's tracks. Dara could not blame them for doing so. Finding bloodied snow like this was creepy, and whatever had injured the deer could still be nearby whether it was an animal, a sharp rock, or slippery ice.

Backing away from the unsettling scene, Dara decided to cut her journey short as well. She turned around and began to quickly march back to the house. A few steps into her hasty retreat she realized that, aside from the crunch of her own step, everything was deathly quiet. The blue jays had disappeared, and even the wind seemed to hold its breath as the winter landscape lay silent. Arriving soon at the house, she quickly shut the door and leaned against it, simultaneously feeling relieved and extremely silly at having been spooked so badly.

Inside the house, everything was just as she had left it. The wafting scent of cooking meat and baking pie alighted on her nostrils. The potatoes had been peeled and moved on to the next step as Alexander and Julius congregated in the den. Sergei was speaking to Frederick about something, but his brother was not listening. Instead Frederick was staring at Dara, having taken a disconcerting interest in her as she removed her scarf from her neck. His intense gaze did not meet her eyes, instead staring somewhere just below her chin. *Ugh.* What a creep, ogling her like that. She had been thinking of reading a book downstairs in one of the comfy chairs in the den, but hiding out in the bedroom on her laptop was going to be a lot more relaxing.

* * *

Lillianna groaned, willing the traffic to go even a little bit faster. In front of her was an endless expanse of cars on what would normally be a stretch of barren and empty pavement. It was not even rush hour yet, but despite that there was no end in sight. The car moved forward at a snail's pace, slowly moving past a sign posted on the side of the road. "Free Holiday Concert!" was printed across it in big, bold lettering just above "Next Exit."

Damn it.

The stalling gave her extra time to think about what to tell Dara, but while searching the store shelves for her mother's gourmet olives she had already had quite a lot of time to think about that and come up dreadfully short. She wanted to ease her into this, but even in her head nothing sounded good. She was just going to have to try to play off the solstice as her weird family's kooky tradition and ease Dara into things later, once they were back in the city and there was plenty of time to gently reveal the truth without being in the middle of a vampire lair. That also gave her more time to work on convincing Dara that it was worth giving up part of her humanity to be with her.

The car continued to inch forward as the sun slunk lower to the horizon, but eventually—*finally*—she reached the road to the campground. Zipping through trees and stray campers to finally arrive back at the house, she jogged up the icy steps as quickly as she could without slipping. She was impatient to see Dara again and growing resentful for how lacking today had been in that regard. Everything felt nicer around Dara now, like a halo of warmth, and she wanted to bask in her glow.

"I have the olives," Lillianna said after she made her way to the kitchen and handed the shopping bag over to her mother.

"Thank you. Wood fired and grilled, right?" Her mother scanned the jar, before making a satisfied sound.

"Do you need me for anything else?" Lillianna asked, though she really hoped there was nothing more.

"Set the table, would you?" her mother requested. "And then after that go get Dara. She's been upstairs for most of the day."

Now *that* was a task that Lillianna was happy to help with.

* * *

Dara was just finishing up some online shopping—expensive chocolates as a celebratory a gift to herself—when Lillianna abruptly bounded through the bedroom door.

"Dara," Lillianna exclaimed, kissing her forehead and pulling her into a tight hug as the laptop fell by the wayside. "I missed you."

"I missed you too, Lilly," Dara said, welcoming her back. She nestled her head into the crook of Lillianna's neck, hugging her back.

"Anything happen while I was gone?" Lillianna asked. "They didn't try to put you to work, did they?"

"No, nothing really, except—" Dara hesitated, not wanting to bring down the mood but also remembering that she had said she would tell Lillianna if there was trouble. "—except, well, your cousin."

"Frederick?" Lillianna asked. Her tone was still close to neutral, but Dara could feel her body tense against her. "What did he do?"

"He was leering at me," Dara admitted. "He's pretty creepy."

"Again?" Lillianna growled. "He should know better a thousand times over than to—" She stopped herself before she said anymore and forced herself to relax her grip on Dara's sweater. "I'll tell my father tomorrow when the solstice is over. After that we can just head back early."

"Already?" Dara asked, unable to hide her disappointment that their little vacation would be over so soon. Sure, Frederick was a pain, but back home all she had was her absent roommate to keep her company, while here she got to stay in the very same room as Lillianna. "Is he really that big of a problem?"

"It really bothers me. You won't have to go back into work right away or anything," Lillianna offered, clearly missing the point. "Though honestly, I'm glad you don't like him either."

"Why does your family put up with him?" Dara asked.

"Half the time I don't think they know what they're putting up with, and the other half of the time they're far too forgiving," Lillianna lamented, pulling away. "Frederick is on his best behavior around them usually. It's only when they're not looking that he thinks he can do this, but I'm going to make sure he stops. This is too much, even for him." There was an air of finality to Lillianna's words, perhaps even almost a dreadful determination to those words, and Dara wondered if she should have even mentioned it.

"Thanks, Lilly." The mood was thoroughly dead already, but Dara decided to steer the conversation to what she hoped were clearer waters. "So, the solstice? We're having dinner, and then I think I heard someone mention we're going out?"

"Yes, we go out into the forest. There's an altar deeper into the woods."

"An altar? Like, uh, sacrifices?" Dara questioned half-jokingly but still seriously concerned. The image of the bloody deer tracks immediately flashed through her mind. "Nothing's going to get hurt right? No animals?"

"No, no animals. It's not scary. The altar looks a little like Stonehenge but much smaller," Lillianna explained, but her tone had become nervous despite her own assurances. "My family chants some things, we sit there for a bit, and then we go home. No big deal."

"No rituals to call fire down from the sky?" Dara commented playfully, probing for more information. "Or speak with the dead?"

"None that I know of. We're not witches."

"And here I thought that it would be so much more spooky with how much you held out on me."

"No," Lillianna shook her head, clearly relieved at Dara's easy response. "It's just a little, well, weird. The words in the chant and stuff are strange, so just ignore them."

"What kinds of things do they say? Some sort of earth mother goddess reference?" Dara asked, still curious.

"Not an earth goddess, just Mother Night," Lillianna clarified. "The main chant, the only part you have to say, is *the blood is life, your love eternal, your blessing divine.*' After that my grandfather says some things about eternal night and—"

"Eternal *night?*" Dara asked, unable to help herself. She distinctly recalled that usually the solstice in older traditions was a celebration of the rebirth of the sun, not a wish that it would never return.

"Yes?" Lillianna looked to her cautiously, clearly thinking she had just misstepped. Dara could not blame her for being worried about what she might think, that chant actually *was* spooky, and she had not even touched on the whole *the blood is life*' line yet.

"Well, that's not so bad," Dara offered in an attempt to support her. She still wondered if that was all there was to it, but she did not want to set Lillianna ill at ease. Reacting now would be akin to laughing right after promising not to. "It's not like it's going to take all night, right? They'll be time for us later."

"Yeah, there will be." There was a glint in Lillianna's eye as her head tilted to the side and she leaned down.

Dara leaned forward too until they were just a hair apart, and then Lillianna closed the gap with a kiss. A dreamy intimacy clouded over Dara's mind as the kiss sang through her veins as Lillianna's lips worked to persuade her that there was nothing in all the world that mattered. It was with great difficulty and much willpower that Dara cut it short.

"We'll miss dinner," Dara reminded her, still hovering close.

"Oh," Lillianna breathed. "I suppose we shouldn't, especially not when my mother has worked so hard on it. Plus, I think they'll notice that the guest of honor is absent if you don't make it."

"Right, they probably would," Dara agreed, lingering there for another moment before reluctantly breaking away and heading to the door.

It was strange how things could contradictorily feel so intimate and yet so oddly incomplete, as if the puzzle pieces fit together perfectly but one was left conspicuously blank. It seemed like the source of all of Lillianna's worries was the solstice and accompanying ritual after all, but her explanation sounded reasonable and Dara could understand where her concern came from. As for the rest of it, she would have to wait until tonight to try to get another clue as to Lillianna's purpose in their fake engagement. What's the worst the secret could be, anyway? It's not like Lillianna could be hiding that she was already married. No, the worst that could happen was that Dara got ahead of herself and screwed everything up on her own. Lingering concerns about the plotlines of late-night horror movies returned to the forefront of Dara's mind, but she shooed them away. This was reality, not fiction.

Chapter 19

Numerous wax candles set along the table cast a warm, gentle glow, causing the dinnerware to glimmer under the light. The platters of meat, rolls, and buttery potatoes had been emptied and only a few sprigs of sautéed asparagus and slices of decadent cheesecake remained, but neither Dara nor anyone else had any more room left for them. She was contemplating whether or not she would be able to sneak a slice away for later when a chime rang through the dining room as a metal knife tapped on glass.

"Well, it's about time we get started then, shall we?" Lillianna's grandfather announced, looking pointedly between both Lillianna and herself. "To welcome our newest member properly."

There was a murmur of assent as he stood and the others around the table dutifully followed suit. One by one the candles along the table were snuffed out and strands of smoke coiled to the ceiling. Coats and scarves were pulled from the racks as the Markovs assembled by the door, and Dara stayed close to Lillianna's side as they departed.

As they walked out into the forest and a chorus of boots crunched across the snow, she kept looking to Lillianna as if to await a signal of some sort, but there was nothing she found there. In the fading rays of sunset, Lillianna's expression was resigned as she marched along, her brow creased ever so slightly by the disturbance of thought. Her worries bled over into Dara's heart and mixed with the already potent feelings of apprehension and jittery excitement.

The procession continued into the forest following the trail and soon passed the bloody, smeared hoof prints in the snow, but none gave any heed or notice to the now dark, rusty stains. Dara herself could only afford them a passing glance in order to keep up with the long strides of the much taller Markovs. It was not long after that before they departed from the trail entirely. All the trees looked the same as the minutes ran together, until they finally came to a small clearing in the trees just big enough for the many Markovs to comfortably ring the edges but small enough that one might walk the forest for years and never find it.

In the center of the clearing a horizontal stone slab, ringed on the sides by its vertical brothers, lay sleeping between the trees under a heavy coat of snow. Lillianna's grandfather swept his hand across the snow, revealing a series of intricate, deep grooves in the stone underneath. Dara did not recognize the majority of symbols carved into the stone, only the waning moon carved in the middle of them.

"May you watch over us always," he intoned. "Mother Night, the first and the last, our protector, our guide without light."

He held up both hands and exposed the palm of one while extending the index finger of the other. His fingernails, though Dara could have sworn were normal before, were now sharp like claws. The keen nail of his index finger sliced through the flesh of his palm, and ruddy droplets of blood dripped down upon the altar.

Dara had to hold herself back from gasping at the painful gesture, but all around her no one else seemed affected, not even Lillianna who had averted her gaze staunchly to the ground. The man was still speaking, but it was hard to focus on anything he was saying as Dara watched morbidly as the blood seeped into the stone around the waning moon. As it settled the liquid changed from a robust cherry red, to deep burgundy, then finally black as it hid the waning moon from view. The symbol had been transformed into a new moon, obscured and invisible against the sky of stone.

"The blood is life. Your love eternal, your blessing divine," Lillianna's grandfather chanted, his recitation complete.

All around her the words were repeated in unison, but her own mouth was frozen in shock. Perhaps that was for the best, because if she had been able to speak she would have immediately proclaimed that this was freaky as hell and dear god *please stop*. No wonder Lillianna had been stressed; her family was acting out a Halloween horror skit while everyone else in the county was eating gingerbread and singing carols. Dara hoped to high heaven that somehow whatever was congealing on the altar was fake, but she knew it was not.

After finishing his chant, Lillianna's grandfather's hands dropped to his sides as he wished them all luck and good tidings in the year to come, and just like that the ritual was over as if nothing out of the ordinary had even happened. There were a few more murmurs of thanks and reciprocal well wishing and then the group was on its way back through the forest to the house.

Dara wandered along with them, feeling unsteady with what had just happened. She was so dazed that it took her by surprise when a hand reached out and squeezed her own reassuringly. She looked up and though Lillianna said nothing, the consolatory look she gave her communicated plenty. Dara summoned the warmth to smile back and counted the minor blessing that at least Lillianna was not the one leading the ceremony. The amount of dissonance had been overwhelming enough already. Lillianna's grandfather had been extremely convincing as he recited the lines—a true believer. And that blood... Dara shook it off. It did not matter. The solstice ritual was over, and she was simply walking away from it all instead of being sacrificed like in her wild imaginings. Some people just got way too into these things, but in retrospect it was kind of cool to watch—at least from afar.

* * *

As soon as they got inside, Lillianna hurried to herd Dara up to their room to get away from everything that might be objectionable about her existence. At the solstice ritual she had sensed Dara's heartbeat quicken as she stood beside her, but there was nothing she could do besides endure in quiet shame that everything about being a vampire was damnably uncomfortable for everyone else. Dara's still-human senses could tell that something was wrong intuitively, but in the end it had gone off without a hitch. Now it was all over and Lillianna was in the clear.

She shut the bedroom door behind them, sequestering them off from the rest of the world. Dara sat down on the bed and Lillianna took a seat beside her. Even if it weren't for the obvious weirdness of the solstice ritual, Lillianna would still have been immensely grateful to be home and alone together. Things just felt right once more.

"So who is Mother Night?" Dara asked abruptly. "There was something about her blessing your family? I didn't catch all the words."

The question surprised Lillianna. She had been hoping to sweep this under the rug as quickly as possible, but Dara's curiosity provided an unforeseen opportunity. If Dara still wanted to talk about it, maybe Lillianna could make vampires seem less freaky.

"I'm not sure that I could answer that properly. I read the stories when I was a kid, but it's been so long that it's all fuzzy now," she said, testing the waters. "I have a book about the traditions back at my apartment though. I could let you read it if you want to know more." Maybe if she showed Dara the Markov codex with all of the instructions and explanations in a more clinical form that would be a good way to ease her into it.

"I'm surprised you don't have all this memorized," Dara commented as she thumbed the palm of her hand, recalling the gruesome gesture of the earlier ceremony. "That thing your grandfather did was crazy. It really freaked me out at first, but then I sort of felt like an anthropologist venturing to observe a secret witchcraft ritual."

"I told you, we're not witches. They're way more into fire and smoke at their ceremonies," Lillianna corrected, but she could not help but feel relieved. The shock was wearing off and Dara was taking it better now.

"You know some?" Dara asked, her curiosity growing. "Can we go observe that too?"

"I don't think the witches would take kindly to me attending anything of theirs," Lillianna admitted. The covens were not currently at war with the clans—or having much to do with them at all really—but she still did not feel like risking it. "I think you would be guilty by association."

"That's a shame," Dara lamented, laying down on the bed. "It would have been cool to see some variety. Well, as long as I'm not being burned at the stake or something."

"Isn't my own weird family enough?" Lillianna joked. "You want to go meet more weirdos?"

"Jealous?" Dara teased, poking her side from where she lay. "You're my favorite weirdo, you know."

"I'm happy to hear that." Lillianna leaned over Dara on the bed and planted one arm on either side of her. Dara had gotten through today, the most important part of the whole trip, and Lillianna wanted to make it up to her. "Do I get special privileges for that?"

"Of course," Dara said encouragingly, giving her a coy look.

Lillianna could not resist. She kissed her, drinking in the sweetness of the sensation as she repositioned herself to straddle Dara across the bed. Trailing kisses along her jaw, she moved to her neck as she got lost in a rhythm that was already becoming familiar. She palmed Dara's breasts through her shirt, eliciting a soft moan as she explored despite the hindrance. She sucked at her neck and Dara moaned again encouragingly, but then Dara tensed beneath her. The bundles of muscle in her neck bunched up in pain, relaxing for a split second only to tense again as Dara emitted a loud yelp. Lillianna pulled away from her as if burnt, and then—and then? *Oh no. Dear night, no!*

Lillianna did not understand what had happened. Dara's hand grasped at the punctured flesh of her neck as hot, liquid blood seeped out and stained the bedding. She was bleeding, and—Lillianna ran her tongue along her lips—she was delicious. Dear night, what had she done? All Lillianna could do was stare, still able to taste blood in her mouth as Dara observed her own blood-soaked hand in horror. Blood continued to gush down her neck and soaked the fibers of her sweater a deep crimson. Lillianna's eyes darted between Dara's panic-stricken face to the flowing blood and back again as instinct warred with reason. It had all happened so fast without thinking, and her body begged for another taste, but she couldn't—not while Dara was staring at her like the entire world was being engulfed in flames. It felt like a thousand baby snakes had hatched in her gut as Dara quaveringly met her eye. Droplets of thick blood began to congeal along her neck, but their temptations fell short as the bottom of Lillianna's stomach dropped out.

"You—you—it's not just pretend," Dara whimpered. The terror in her eyes plead with Lillianna to deny it, to will this entire moment out of existence. "You're going to sacrifice me on that altar!"

"What? No!" Lillianna blurted out, a semblance of vampiric dignity kicking to life at the accusation. "We're not cultists, we're vampires!" It would have been funny, had it not made the situation even worse as

Dara blanched at the declaration.

"You—then you were going to turn me into a vampire?!" Dara's shock deepened as the words sliced like a knife between them. Lillianna fumbled, wanting to erase the horrified look from Dara's face and assuage her own pain, but no ready solutions presented themselves.

"I—" she began, but her mouth snapped shut before she could say anything more. Avoiding the topic had been one thing, but she could not lie to Dara now. Though not exactly a vampire, it was true that she wanted Dara to be a dhampir, and also true that she had started the process both by accident and without asking.

You're changing back now though.

But I don't want you to.

It was an accident.

But I liked it.

I still want it.

I want you.

Lillianna's jaw felt like it was held by steel cables as she stood rigid in the tumultuous silence. Dara's bite wound continued to coagulate in the cool air as the vampiric saliva worked to encourage the broken skin to heal, but it did little to soothe Dara's erratic, hammering heart.

"You're not joking about this," she said at last, her voice shattering the stifled calm. Her eyes grew wider, if that were even possible.

"I would never hurt you," Lillianna said quietly, her eyes shifting to the floor as each word fell like lead.

"You just did!"

"It's healing. My saliva—" Lillianna swallowed, her mouth parched. "—it helps. Pain, swelling…" Her words trailed off, unwilling to say 'pleasure,' because that was not what this was.

A wave of morbid realization swept over Dara as she uttered a statement that was more an accusation than question. "You did this before. I had this—" She waved her hands aimlessly, still in shock.

"—dream?"

"I didn't mean to."

"But you did it. Oh god, I'm going to have to drink people's blood too?"

"No, you won't. I promise. Can't we just talk about this?" Lillianna asked, her voice pleading. "You won't be drinking blood. "

"I—I don't know." Dara stared down into her lap at her bloodied hand. She took a deep, steadying breath, and shook her head. "I don't know. I just want to clean this off," she groaned, overwhelmed by everything.

"There's hydrogen peroxide in the bathroom," Lillianna offered weakly while wincing at the large, crimson stain across her sweater. It was unlikely to help at this point, but would do more than she could.

Dara rose, her steps wavering and shaky, but she flinched away when Lillianna raised a hand to steady her. Quickly retracting her hand, Lillianna stood alone as Dara left the room and stumbled down the hall.

The rejection stung like a razor blade against her skin and heart, and Lillianna had never before felt so out of place. Even in the beginning when she had been indifferent and somewhat hostile toward Dara, she had never been so unwanted. She sucked in a steadying breath, trying to marshal her thoughts and come up with something intelligent and consoling to say.

A cacophonous slam came from the hallway as a door rattled on its hinges, followed by a fleshy thud as a body crumpled against the carpet. An inhuman snarl filled the air of the upper floor, and a split second later Lillianna leapt into the hall with a snarl of her own. Dara cowered on the ground near the bathroom, the barely coagulated blood flowing from her neck once more from the force of being thrown, gushing swiftly as her body pulsed with fresh adrenaline. Over her stood Frederick, fangs bared and eyes wild with raw, unbridled hunger.

"Get the hell away from her!" Lillianna shouted, her hands clenching and then extending as her nails rapidly sharpened to points.

Frederick's head whipped around to glare at her with unbridled fury.

"She's mine! You stole my match from me, you *bitch!*"

The utterance struck Lillianna like a brick. Her mind reeled. Eric had said something about rigging the selection against other matches, hadn't he? But he had never mentioned who, and Lillianna herself had been unable to comprehend any alternatives to herself. Dara was *her* blood match, her one and only. Yet a blood match never guaranteed that things would work out, it merely greatly increased the odds. She was not special; Dara had matched with others as well. Though Frederick...no. Night damn him, *NO!* Rage bubbled to the surface, sweeping away whatever feelings she might have had concerning his plight.

"She's not yours, Fred," she said, her voice cool, jagged, and deadly with rising magma beneath. "Get the hell away from her."

"She should have been *mine!*" Frederick snarled again.

His possessive rage ripped through the air and shattered the last vestiges of reason left within her as he lunged toward Dara. Faster than he could blink, sharpened nails raked the side of his face and scalp, slicing through skin and perfectly combed hair. Droplets of vampiric blood sprayed against the wall like a thousand rough-hewn rubies. A fresh scream escaped his lips that quickly turned into a roar as he changed course to charge at her instead.

Savage blows were exchanged one after the other as flesh ripped and began to reform. Vampiric blood sprayed upon the walls turned from ruby to obsidian as it cooled, darker than night and blacker than Frederick's failing heart. He may be an older and more experienced vampire than her, but it meant little when he had grown sloppy and neglected his training.

"*Mine,*" he choked, gasping as he fell to his knees, scrabbling to support himself with his hands.

Lillianna thrashed him again, and he collapsed, crumpling to the floor, quiet except for his slow, pained breaths. She stood over him, her nails still sharp and his rapidly darkening blood on her fingertips. She had protected her claim. *Hers. All hers.*

A whimper of fear in the background of her thoughts brought her back from rage to reality, and triumph turned to abject, plummeting disaster. Dara was still cowering in the corner by the bathroom door, huddled up and clearly trying to make herself as small as possible. Instinctively, Lillianna took a step forward to comfort her, but in response Dara tried to become even smaller as she shrank away. Once more Lillianna's heart sank through the bottom of her stomach and down to her feet as she took stock of everything around her: the blackening blood on the carpet and her nails, and the red blood dripping down Dara's neck whose flavor she could still taste on her tongue.

Downstairs there arose a commotion followed by the sound of footsteps as her family began to rapidly ascend stairs, but Lillianna could not bear to face them. She could feel their eyes burning into her back as she fumbled through her pockets in search of her keys.

"Here." She thrust her car keys at Dara. The back of her throat ached with defeat, vile and acidic, but she repressed the nauseated urge. "Take the servant stairs. Last door at the end of the hall. Just go."

Dara did not need to be told twice as she snatched the keys from Lillianna's hand and scurried off down the hall. In another moment she was out of sight, and the sound of her hurried footsteps on the back staircase quickly faded to nothing. Behind her, Lillianna's grandfather cleared his throat, and the silence became unbearable as she turned to face his judgment.

Lillianna steeled herself as she raised her eyes. Titus and Victoria's expressions were filled with shock and horror, her father's gaze was stony as his hands clenched into fists, clearly desperate to speak out of turn and mete out his own judgment, and her mother was devastated on the verge of tears. There was a palpable, morbid excitement among her remaining cousins in the aftermath of what had been a veritable bloodsport. Even Uncle Leon, who she had barely seen this season, was staring with a look of macabre fascination. Eric alone looked simply stunned and very, very worried. In the center of it all was her grandfather, his face a mask of inquisitive, troubled grief.

"I would have much rather my grandchildren were gambling than dueling," he admonished sternly. "But come, tell us, what was this about?"

"He threatened Dara," Lillianna sputtered out, her heart beating a hole through her ribcage as the hammer began to fall. "He tried to drink from her."

"It does not look like that worked out well for him," her grandfather stated bluntly as he walked forward to consider his grandson's prone form. "Unfortunate."

"I know we're not supposed to fight," she stammered shakily, hanging her head and clenching sweaty, bloodied hands. "I am sorry. I accept my punishment."

"No." Her grandfather shook his head. Behind him Lillianna could see her father's thick brows churning into a deep furrow at the simple word, but he held his tongue.

"No?" she asked, still wary.

"As much as I disliked—and still dislike—the old ways, I would not have our ancestors see me disrespect them from their graves. A duel is a duel, and Frederick has disappointed in more ways than one," her grandfather explained as he knelt down to check Frederick's vitals.

"What do you mean?" Lillianna asked, her eyes darting to Frederick's prone form and back again.

"I mean you won." Her grandfather looked up from Frederick and gave her a half-smile tinged with melancholy. "Congratulations, you're moving up in the clan."

Chapter 20

Dara kissed Lillianna with a fierce desperation as she was pushed back onto the bed. Time seemed to move in alternating periods of fast and slow as she savored her lips. There was a rush of pleasure, a pinprick of pain, and then she blinked. Something had gone very wrong, and yet it felt so very, very...right. A fierce, liquid heat spilled out across her neck. Immediately she reached to touch it before pulling back. Her hand was covered in her own blood, the liquid seeping into each crease of her palm and fingers. She panted, dazed as she tried to sit up. Blood dripped across Lillianna's lips and chin. *Her* blood. Even as Dara stared at her wide-eyed and in shock, Lillianna's tongue snaked out to lick the smear of blood from her lips. Her expression was confused, but her eyes were still full of damning desire. An icy fear twisted itself around Dara's heart and pumped glacial terror through her veins. She yelped in surprise, and the desire fled from Lillianna's face to be replaced by pained penance. The world spun and then faded to nothing. Dara awoke.

Cold winter sunlight greeted her eyes, and the plaster ceiling of her home had never felt so unwelcoming. She plucked at the covers, tugging at a loose thread that had begun to unravel, and breathed deeply as her racing heartbeat began to subside. However, the confusing mix of feelings settling in her gut stubbornly lingered: arousal, fear, and morbid fascination. She still did not know what to make of what had happened; sometimes she thought that she had dreamed it up completely with how the wound on her neck had completely disappeared. But there had been undeniable sincerity in Lillianna's eyes when she told her that the Markovs were vampires, and though Dara had realized with muted horror that she was telling the truth, that did not make things any better or even more comprehensible. Vampires didn't—*shouldn't*—exist, but it was that very line of thinking that had lulled Dara into ignoring all of the signs: the youthful, attractive appearances of all the Markovs, the dark colored bags of liquid in the fridge, their "sleep phase" disorder, and even the questionable things Eric had been doing late at night with his assistants at the office. Her decision to overlook all of the signs had culminated in complete disaster as she had been forced to drive along unfamiliar, icy roads late into the night fueled by coffee and paranoia.

After she finished the long, terrifying drive back from the Markov's mansion and the initial panic had faded, Dara had felt a sense of longing so strong wash over her that she wondered if she had made a mistake. Belatedly, she had recalled how horrified Lillianna had looked when she had realized what she had done. Lillianna had clearly not meant to bite her, at least that time, but what about the time before? *The time before...* Dara closed her eyes, trying to recall it, but all that she remembered was the vague rush of endorphins that had morphed into a sexy dream. That same sizzle of pleasure had been there the second time too, but it had only served to bewilder her as to why being bitten bloody felt *good.*

Dara looked at the time on her phone and winced; it was nearly noon. Maybe she was turning into a vampire after all, or maybe she was just stressed and sleeping her life away. Not that it really mattered when she got up since her roommate had managed to get some time off for the holidays and promptly vanished. Her own mother remained away with Jack, blissfully enjoying the holidays and making plans for New Year's Eve. Dara was certainly not going to call her mother up to vent about how disaster had struck her budding love life, but even if she could, what would she say? That she had slept with her boss and then discovered that the woman was a vampire? Ask her mother if she thought she should quit her job? She couldn't quit her job. Looking for a new one in this market would be a disastrous decision, and furthermore, she did not even want to quit. She just wanted things to go back to normal.

Back to when Lillianna had made her feel so special as her assistant and then lover, priceless even. Lillianna had wanted her more than anyone ever had, and Dara just wanted to cry about how it had only been for her blood. Eric had six goddamn assistants he must be drinking blood from, and it clearly did not matter which in particular provided it on any given day. The same would be true from Lillianna. The fact that Dara had feelings for her just made her an easy mark to take advantage of in a way far more questionable than unlimited overtime. Hell, maybe Lillianna was not even into her at all and bedding her had all been a part of the elaborate ruse to turn Dara into a literal snack. But if she put her foot down and quit Lillianna would just get another assistant or six, and Lillianna's lips, her glittering ice blue eyes, and that hunger directed at someone other than herself was something that Dara could not bear to even think about. She desperately wanted to cling to the memory of being special, even if reality pointed to her being just as interchangeable as the rest of the office.

"Maybe I should get a pet," she said aloud to no one in particular as she sat up in bed. Unlike her mother or roommate, a dog had the added benefit of not judging you for being broken up about a woman who was a ten except for the part where she drank your blood.

At that moment her phone buzzed with a notification, and Dara snatched it up embarrassingly fast. Her heart fell when she saw that it was not a message from Lillianna, or even a message from a real person at all. It was an automated notification from her bank to let her know that five thousand dollars had been deposited into her account. She sighed, deflating as she allowed herself to fall back against the pillow. A few minutes later she found the energy to punch out a simple text of "Thanks," but her thumb merely hovered over "send," never quite managing to press it. The money just did not feel like it mattered anymore.

* * *

"Thanks Alex," Lillianna said as she took the folder from him. "This will help a lot."

"You're welcome, Lillianna," Alexander said with a stiff nod. Normally right about now was when he made a casual remark about looking forward to the next holiday or even the weather, but he only turned on his heel and departed her office briskly. She wished she could put him at ease in her presence, but she couldn't. Perhaps just being "Lilly" to her family had not been so bad after all. Now she wasn't "Lilly" to anyone, even to Dara.

Lillianna skimmed through the folder before setting it aside and allowing her gaze to drift out her office window. Beyond the glass, the world was dreary. The holidays had come and gone, and now a gray January hung over the landscape like a permanent raincloud to match Lillianna's mood. The day was just starting, and it already felt overwhelmingly bleak.

"Hey, Lilly," Eric said, shuffling into her office with one eye still on their cousin as he scuttled down the hall. She sighed, having spoken to soon. There was always Eric to be kid sister "Lilly" to. "Something wrong with Alex? He seems a little jumpy."

"And Sergei and Julius too." Lillianna let out a resigned sigh. "I don't think they're ever going to get over it."

"I'm sure they will eventually. They were just shocked, and then grandfather..." Eric shook his head. "He always told us there would be no fighting, no duels. Back then it felt about as serious as his gambling ban. I just thought he meant nothing counted if we fought."

"Me too. I didn't realize that what he meant was he did not want to have to uphold the tradition, and that that was what he was afraid of." Lillianna recalled the disturbing memory and her grandfather's sad smile. His little grandchildren had grown up finally, after decades, and even despite him not wanting them to.

"You make it sound like Fred's dead, though I'm sure he certainly feels that way," Eric said, shaking his head again. "But if he was, he'd deserve it anyway. You really surprised me, you know. I didn't know you had so much fight in you."

"It's partially thanks to you, you know," Lillianna admitted, a soft, melancholic smile playing at her lips. "You told me all those stories about the hunters coming to kill me if I was a bad kid. There was also a time that I thought if I could just fight better I could exhibit paintings and it wouldn't matter if the hunters came for me."

"Glad to know all my teasing paid off," he said with a smile, but then his expression pivoted to become more serious—something that was rare for Eric. "Say, is Dara alright? She's been out sick for quite a while now."

"I think it was pretty bad," Lillianna said quietly, growing tense at the change of subject. "I'm not sure when she'll be back."

In truth, she doubted that Dara was sick at all—at least with any normal illness. Dara's horror at discovering the truth was etched deeply in her mind, and that was without even counting the subsequent shock that followed when Lillianna had beaten Frederick bloody. She had wanted to text Dara, but was at a loss for what to even say so instead she had spent the precious few days of vacation she'd had left worried sick about if Dara had made it home safe on the icy roads. At first it was somewhat of a relief when Dara had left a curt email, addressing her as "Lillianna," explaining that she "was out sick." After that Lillianna had quietly picked her car up from the curb outside Dara's home, but that was as close as she had physically gotten to her. Dara's sick leave had run out yesterday, and now Lillianna was readying herself for the other shoe to drop.

A resignation letter could come at any moment, and the worst part was that she knew she deserved it. Envenoming, the trip, her recognition of feelings—it had all been in the wrong order. It would have been nice to blame this all on her vampiric instincts, but that would be far too convenient—not to mention unquestionably false. What if it had been Frederick who swooped in and injected his venom into Dara? Even the very thought of it made her hackles raise. Accident or not, there would have been hell to pay. Dara was her valued assistant and no one should be doing that to her, but most of all Lillianna hated that it had been her. She had failed to recognize how she felt about Dara before it took a toll on her actions, and that had been her downfall. Her biting of Dara on the solstice had simply been the karmic reprisal she deserved. If she had recognized how she felt about Dara sooner, the proper thing to do would have been to give Dara space while Lillianna considered the next steps for a proper courtship. The very least she could do was give her space now.

"Lilly? Earth to Lilly?" Eric called to her, interrupting her self-flagellating thoughts.

"Sorry," Lillianna said, snapping back to the present.

"Worried about her?" he asked sympathetically. "You know, it wouldn't kill you to take some time off to go visit her."

"The project is already getting behind without her here, I don't want to make things worse for her when she gets back," Lillianna sidestepped.

"Oh, well that is true," he considered. "But I mean, are you and her—?" He hesitated, the question on the tip of his tongue. It was uncharacteristic for her brother to broach such a serious topic. He ordinarily shied away from such serious matters.

"I'm going to get sick too if I don't eat something," she remarked, leading the conversation back to shallower waters. "I didn't manage to get breakfast this morning."

"Oh, that reminds me. The catering got delivered early today. The bistro had a new sandwich on the menu and I'd love to hear your opinion on whether I should make it a regular offering. It's a steak sandwich with peppercorn sauce and this glaze…"

"Sure," Lillianna replied, though she did not actually feel hungry at all. She just felt numb.

* * *

"It was pretty good, right?" Eric asked as they headed back from the lounge. "The peppercorn really made it."

"Yeah, you should add it to the rotation," Lillianna agreed. "It's nice to change it up from my regular Italian sometimes." The peppercorn sauce was better that she had expected, and it had even managed to kick her flagging appetite back to life. While it had not completely healed her, it would be enough to get her through the day and remain on track with the Graves project.

Eric continued to gab about the brilliant combination of peppercorn and spicy fruit glaze and how it really brought out the flavors as they walked back along the corridor, but Lillianna's mind had long since drifted away back to the matters of work. First she needed to go through the file she had gotten from Alex, and then she would go over the figures from the email she got last night. After that she would—

"Hey, Lilly," Eric whispered, nudging her side to get her attention. He must have realized that she was not interested in the fine tuning of fruit glazes.

"Sorry, Eric, I just have a lot on my mind. I'm sure any choice of glaze will be fine."

"No, not that, although I do think you should consider my ideas more," Eric whispered again, "just *look*." He pointed dramatically toward the cubicles and Lillianna turned to look so quickly that she nearly hit him.

There was Dara, loafers and all, sitting at her desk and chatting amicably with one of Eric's assistants as her computer booted up. Unable to help herself, Lillianna made a beeline over to her desk immediately.

"Hello," Dara said as she noticed her. "I hope I haven't caused too much trouble by being sick. And sorry for being late today, I had some car trouble." Her chestnut hair looked duller than last time Lillianna had seen her and dark circles had begun to form under her eyes, but despite looking rather worse for wear the sight of her made Lillianna's heart sputter back to life.

"It's fine," Lillianna said quickly. "It's terrible that you've been sick."

"Yeah, it was pretty rough," Dara nodded. She was polite but firmly neutral, and her tone held hardly any of the warmth that Lillianna had grown used to in their time together. "But it sounds like you've been okay here?"

"Yeah, I've been okay," Lillianna found herself saying. That was a lie, but her next words were not. "I'm glad you're back."

Dara hesitated, looking back up at her again, her gaze inscrutable. "...yeah. So what did you need me to work on?" She clicked through her email, not finding anything in the barren folders.

Lillianna badly wanted to ask what was on her mind, but was just as much afraid of what that might be. She had seen Dara's left hand. The ring was gone. "I'll bring you the papers," was all she could say.

Lillianna went back to her office and grabbed the folder that Alex had brought her earlier before quickly returning. She felt impatient to keep her eye on her, like if she was gone too long Dara may take the opportunity to bolt while unattended. She handed her the papers and watched her scan through them.

"Ow!" Dara pulled her hand away and squeezed her thumb. A droplet of ruby blood emerged from the tiny paper cut, and Lillianna felt pulled toward it like a moth to flame. She forced her gaze away and back to the papers, but Dara had already noticed and was staring at her now. Out of the corner of her eye, Lillianna could see that she was curious, concerned, but most of all worried. Lillianna swallowed back saliva, forcing everything away.

"So, this data…" she began, going on to explain the information in minute detail to force herself to remain focused. She would definitely keep her hunger under control this time, even if it may be too late.

* * *

"Coming to lunch?" Katie asked as she stood up from her desk.

"Go ahead. I'll be there right after I finish this up," Dara replied, hitting the send button for the printer. She headed over to collect the fresh copies before peeking inside her boss's office. Lillianna was currently brooding and tapping her chin as she considered some especially frustrating data. Dara sighed. Now was as good a time as any.

It had been a couple days since her return, but things were still just as stilted and awkward as the first. It had taken all of her resolve to get back in here, and she was still not sure what she had been expecting, except probably something more frightening. Perhaps for the Markovs to send trained assassins after her to silence her for learning their secret, or for her to develop a sudden craving for raw meat and blood pudding. After all, vampires in movies were alternating parts sexy and villainous. Lillianna really had the sexy part down, but there had been no sudden reveal of Machiavellian tendencies or schemes. Instead Lillianna had become distant, and her expression when Dara stepped into her office was as detached and unapproachable as she had been when they first met months ago, if not more.

"Here you go," Dara said, dropping the papers down on the side of Lillianna's desk.

"Thanks. Good work," Lillianna replied, giving her a polite, neutral smile. Then a soft, longing expression that Dara had seen often these last few days crossed her face and broke through the facade. "Enjoy your lunch."

"Thank you," Dara replied out of habit, but she did not really mean it. The unspoken rule between them to not talk about anything and everything that had happened, while a relief at first, was now becoming unbearable. Dara just wanted to yell at her to—to—to what? What did she even want from her? An apology? That wasn't going to rewind time. She wanted to go to lunch with *her,* not Katie and the others. "Lilly—Lillianna, I think we should talk—" Dara began, but then a fresh flash of hurt crossed Lillianna's face. Dara could not bear it. "—about the projected figures for next quarter, after lunch."

"...sure."

Dara hightailed it out Lillianna's office in the most graceful save she could muster before retreating to the employee lounge to hide. Curse her cowardice for not wanting to just pull the thorn out. Things like

227

this hurt before they got better, but she just didn't want it to hurt and especially not for Lillianna, which was doubly stupid. Dara was *not* the bad guy here. Lillianna was the one who bit her and kept massive secrets. Sure, she had also protected Dara from Frederick, but that situation would not have happened in the first place without all these vampire things going on.

As she ate, Dara wished she could be as carefree, ignorant, and happy as Katie and the others. It seemed like they did not have a care in the world, and the more time she spent around them, the more she suspected that they really didn't. Dara knew what she had seen late that one night at the office, but no matter how many hints she dropped, Katie appeared none the wiser as to Eric's true nature, and her canines were distinctly blunt. As unpleasant as it had been to learn the truth, it set Dara apart and meant that she was different from the others—special even—and that thought, while frightening, also comforted her just a little.

* * *

Finished for the day, Dara wearily logged off her computer and bid Katie farewell for the evening. Would Eric be drinking from her coworker's neck tonight? Would she remember any of it in the morning? Dara did not know anything anymore, and she was starting to care even less. She slumped against the elevator wall on her way down to parking, making a mental list of everything she needed to do when she got home. Write a thank-you note to Jack for the scarf he had gotten her for Christmas, cook dinner, and then maybe collapse on the couch. She needed to figure out what to do about Lillianna too, but that was a headache all on its own. Her mind kept hitting a snag and whirred uselessly when she tried to come up with a plan on how to proceed.

The elevator dinged and she shuffled out into the parking, walking along until she got to her car in her marked space—one of the perks of being an assistant on the sixth floor. Opening the driver's side door she set her bag down and got in. She turned the key in the ignition, and then—nothing. Dara frowned, turning the key again, and again, but it would not start.

* * *

Lillianna's pencil lead snapped, and she growled in frustration as she tossed her notebook aside. That was the sixth time in the last few minutes, and, while she probably shouldn't be sketching anyway, work was becoming increasingly difficult to focus on. None of it even felt like it mattered anymore, so she instead pulled the company directory up on the computer, typed in a keyword, and clicked through the profiles until she got to the one she wanted.

Dara's employee photo, clad in familiar glasses, cheerfully smiled back at her from the screen, and Lillianna lamented that she should have taken photos with her back when she had the chance. Now the time for casually enjoying one another's company had passed, and even Dara's cute glasses were gone. She had thought that she had been happy back then simply because she had been getting ahead on the Graves project, but in retrospect that had not been the case at all. She just liked being with Dara.

There came a knock at her office door, and Lillianna looked up hopefully, but her hopes were dashed when she saw her brother patiently waiting outside the door instead. It was then that she remembered that Dara had already gone home for the day. Lillianna frowned as she realized something else. It was odd that Eric actually waited after he knocked; he never did that.

"Come in."

"Hey Lilly," he said, greeting her as usual as he slipped inside her office. He had the papers she had asked for, but he did not immediately set them down on her desk. Instead he glanced around her office, his eyes meandering until he caught sight of her open notebook on the side of her desk.

"Oh no, what happened to the poor thing?" Eric asked, pointing at the discarded notebook. On its pages a sketched lion had been impaled by a half-dozen hunters' spears and lay bleeding in the snow.

"Karma," Lillianna stated bluntly, reaching over to flip the sketchbook shut.

"Oh." Eric looked around the room again awkwardly and noticed her screen. Lillianna quickly minimized the employee directory, but he had already seen it. "Aren't you going to talk to her?"

"We do talk," Lillianna stated defensively, wishing he would keep out. This already hurt enough without her pain being public.

"About more than spreadsheets?" Eric questioned. There was a long, stubborn silence between them, but just when Lillianna thought he had gotten the message he spoke again. "You know, I had a nice secretary back in the fifties. Sweet, lovely, and a hard worker too. Everything I ever wanted."

"She sounds perfect," Lillianna commented flippantly.

"She was. Can you imagine why she's not here with me now?" Eric asked, giving Lillianna a hard look.

"Because you decided one's not enough?"

"No. It's because she's dead." There was a poignant silence as Eric looked at her, and Lillianna looked back in bewilderment. She had never heard of this before. Eric continued, "She had a car accident while I was still trying to make up my mind. She would have lived through it if she'd been a dhampir, but I just hadn't asked yet or done anything. I know it's different because you already made her a dhampir, but what I mean is you should just do something, Lilly. I don't want to see you lose her."

The pause between them was heavy now, like a dozen thick blankets made of wool. Lillianna had always assumed that Eric remained single because he preferred immature gambling binges and his six assistants to being partnered, not because he had missed a golden opportunity.

"She hates me now," Lillianna spat out. This wasn't her golden opportunity, and if it was she had tarnished it.

"For protecting her from Frederick?"

"No," Lillianna sighed, and nothing really mattered anymore. "She's not a dhampir—not a full one anyway. I didn't tell her before. She didn't know about vampires," she said, the words finally spilling out. She didn't care anymore about what her family thought, or said, or did. The only person in the world that mattered was Dara, and Dara was gone.

"Oh." Eric clearly wasn't expecting that. "You have your work cut out for you then, but still, you're a high ranking member of Clan Markov now, who wouldn't want you?" Eric joked, but his tone quickly turned somber again when he saw that she was not amused.

"None of that matters now," she said morosely. "Even if I thought it did."

"You should just talk to her," he encouraged. "It might go better than you expect."

"It might go worse, too," Lillianna protested. "Could you do it if you were me?"

"No, definitely not," Eric said. "I would rather fight hunters for my life." Then, in a gesture that altogether surprised her, he stepped forward and pulled her into a warm, solid hug. "But you could defeat hunters, and you can do this. You have already gotten much further than I did."

The strength of his embrace reassured her, and Lillianna smiled softly at his words. "Thanks."

"How about you just take the rest of the day off? Rest up for the big battle ahead," Eric suggested as he pulled away. "I think you could use it."

"Yeah," Lillianna agreed. "I think I'll do that."

After he left, she pulled up the employee directory and took one last look at Dara's smiling face before shutting down her computer. Then she collected her bag and headed to the elevator down to parking.

Chapter 21

The lighting of the enclosed parking was dim as Lillianna strode across the cold, concrete floor, but there was a renewed vitality in her step. Eric's unexpected pep talk had bolstered her courage, and, though the cold weather nipped at the collar of her coat, she felt warmer than she had all week. She would go home and rest like she had promised, but immediately after that she was going to sit down and figure out how to fix this mess. She was so caught up in her own thoughts and planning that she almost did not notice the person standing on the other side of her car. Chestnut hair bobbed behind the sedan. Dara! Her heart skipped a beat at the serendipitous timing, though the space for her assistant should have been empty a long time ago.

"Dara?" Lillianna called over to her. "Is something wrong?"

"Car trouble," Dara explained as she turned around to face her.

"Do you need jumper cables?" Lillianna offered. This was a much quicker potential opportunity to mend things with Dara than she had expected, and she was not going to just let it slide by.

"I got it to start this morning, but unfortunately it's worse than that," Dara told her. "I already called to have it towed to the shop, but it's going to take a while to get picked up. There's traffic from an accident down that way."

"I can give you a ride. I mean, if you want," Lillianna amended.

"Well—" Dara hesitated for a moment, and at first Lillianna thought

233

she was reaching for a gracious way to refuse her, but then she relented with a nod, "—alright." She smiled politely, revealing dull canines. "If it's not too much trouble. Thank you."

Dara was notably cautious as she slid into the passenger seat and settled down. In her peripheral vision, Lillianna could see her cast a guarded glance over in her direction, but she pretended not to notice the attention. *Normal, just keep everything normal,* she reminded herself with a deep, calming breath as she turned the key in the ignition.

A misty, drizzling rain hit the windshield as they exited the enclosed parking, and Lillianna flipped the windshield wipers on. They drove with only the cadence of the rain to fill the silence as they made their way through packed intersections and back to sleepy surface roads. Soon they were drawing close to Dara's neighborhood, but Lillianna did not want this brief time they had together to end. Spotting a glowing sign off to the side of the intersection they were stopped at, she took a chance.

"Do you want to get something to eat?" She asked, feigning casualness as she motioned to the Chinese restaurant's sign. "Takeout maybe?"

"Sure," Dara replied neutrally.

Lillianna pulled into the parking lot and hopped out with her umbrella. Dara had declined to come inside in favor of waiting in the car, but maybe that was for the best. She still needed to think of something to say before this ride ended because, unfortunately, Eric was right. If she left things as they were, she was just going to wait forever until Dara slipped away regardless. However, as much as he had bolstered her courage, her mind remained empty, and she still felt ashamed that all she had to offer was a limping apology.

When Lillianna made it back to the car with food in hand, she found Dara looking away out the passenger side window. Raindrops splashed against the glass as cars sloshed by on the road and Dara remained melancholic. Lillianna swallowed back her unease as she opened the door and settled back down into her seat. She could not delay any longer. She should have called or texted Dara ages ago, even if she had been terrified of what she might say in return.

"Here," Lillianna said quietly as she laid the takeout boxes down on the armrest between the seats like a peace offering. "I…I'm really sorry."

Dara turned away from the window to blink at her owlishly. "What do you mean? Were they out of teriyaki?"

"No, they had it," Lillianna corrected as shame and fear welled up inside her, threatening to push her back into cowardly hiding. She was not going to run anymore. "I mean—I mean what happened back at my parents' house. I shouldn't have bitten you. I won't do it again." The words came out in a rush, but she had finally said it.

Dara's mouth opened, then shut again, then opened once more to finally speak. "That's—that's not the point."

"But I am truly sorry," Lillianna repeated, confused by Dara's response and racking her brain for what else she could have possibly done wrong. There was too much.

"It didn't have to be my blood," Dara accused. "It could have been anyone's."

"Your blood is special," Lillianna tried to explain. "That's why I had so much trouble. Frederick did too, but he's—"

"Dead and buried?" Dara finished for her. It was clear from her expression that her memories of the man were not fond.

"No." Lillianna shook her head. "It takes a lot more than that to kill a vampire. He's been sent away."

This answer seemed to frighten Dara more. "What if he comes back?" she asked, her voice beginning to waver.

"He can't. He's been made the charge of another clan, a distant ally of ours. He will serve them as a second chance to prove himself, but if he ever tries to cause trouble again they will kill him." Lillianna released a heavy sigh. Titus, Victoria, and Sergei were never going to look at her the same again, even if they understood why it had happened. Dara was—had been—her mate, and Frederick had attempted something horribly taboo despite that.

"Does your family—do they know?" Dara questioned. "That I didn't know?"

"No. There was too much of a mess after you left. It was the least of anyone's worries."

"Even yours?" Dara looked hurt.

"I was worried about you. I wanted to call you, but I—" Lillianna hesitated, wanting to say more but with nothing to offer. "—I just didn't think it would help."

"I don't think I can do this. I don't know how Katie or anyone else does it, alternating giving blood with the others." Dara's eyes were now glistening with moisture as she looked away.

"They don't know. Eric makes them forget that it happens."

"And you? Why didn't you just make me forget? Are you still going to?" Dara pressed, her eyes darting back to her with pained reproach.

"No, I wouldn't even if I could," Lillianna refuted. "I don't want you to forget."

Outside on the street, headlights flickered and horns blared in a discordant rumble. Everything Lillianna had worked for at her job these last few decades did not matter at all. No amount of skill or however many promotions she could obtain or accolades she might receive would ever fill that void: they were all mirages that moved further and further away the closer she got to them. But Dara was right here, almost within reach, and she would do anything to have her stay. "I love you."

"Me?" Dara asked, her voice small. "Why me?" she asked again, worrying her bottom lip with her teeth. "I don't have any special talent aside from making spreadsheets for you, and I get paid to do that."

Lillianna's brows furrowed together in consternation. She had prepared herself for rejection, not to be told she should not like her in the first place. "I don't understand. When did talent become a prerequisite for affection?"

"I mean, I'm worried about how you might feel next year, or the year after that. Don't vampires live a long time?" Dara asked, the moisture still stubbornly clinging to her eyes.

"Forever, provided nothing catastrophic happens," Lillianna admitted somewhat reluctantly. It was something she herself had not wanted to think about in the midst of her desperation. The romance had taken corporeal form so abruptly that she had not even had a moment to truly enjoy it before it was suddenly over. Yet somehow she was supposed to make that brief flame last forever—to shield it from rain and snow and never let it go out. It would potentially be a lot of work, but she had a feeling it would be worth it. "I want it to be you," she decided, her resolve bolstered even as Dara's flagged. "And although it may feel a bit sudden to say forever, if it's possible I would like us to take the time to find out."

"I want to believe you, you know? That's what makes me think maybe I shouldn't," Dara said, her expression conflicted. She began to reach her hand up to Lillianna's face but then stopped midway. "Can I?"

"Yes?" Lillianna answered. She was not sure what Dara was asking, but she was not about to refuse her either. Dara's hand reached to her mouth, her thumb running along her lips and pushing back to reveal the pointy fangs beneath. She pressed at the sharp point, drawing a tiny droplet of blood that Lillianna could immediately taste. The savory scent of sauce and chicken wafting through the car paled in comparison to the flavor of rich, red blood and her gums itched for a more substantial bite, but Lillianna reigned it in. There was so much—

too much—on the line. Her heart was left hammering with tempting, sweet adrenaline and disappointment when Dara's hand, and with it the promise of blood, was abruptly pulled away. Dara cast her eyes downward as her wayward shyness caught up with her.

"Promise me that you won't do this—this blood thing with anyone else," she requested, her voice full of indefinable emotion.

"I don't. I won't."

Lillianna waited until Dara looked up again and held her gaze. There was a vulnerability in those deep brown eyes she urgently wanted to comfort. Lillianna leaned forward across the divide, and as she drew close the vulnerability in Dara's eyes shifted to something far more needy and wanting. Lillianna had intended to hold back, to be soft and gentle, but her willpower had been tested long enough. She kissed her so thoroughly that the discomfort she had felt in her gut for the better part of the week melted under the heat. The kiss began to escalate as Dara moved to make her own demands, struggling to overcome the armrest that separated them. The poorly placed takeout boxes were jostled by her efforts and tipped, tumbling down onto Lillianna.

Lillianna frowned as she pulled away, disgruntled at the spilled food for interrupting their moment and extinguishing the mood. Although the chicken had at least stayed inside the box, now her work blazer had teriyaki sauce down the front.

"Sorry," Dara apologized, panting and looking contritely at the mess. "It's like that time I spilled stuff all over you in the clinic."

"It does look like that, doesn't it?" Lillianna groaned, assessing the damage. "Thankfully this time it did not involve glass." Dara laughed at that, her smile real and genuine. Lillianna could not help but smile herself. "We'd better go eat and get this cleaned up then."

* * *

When the conversation winded down and the hour grew late, Dara moved to clean up the takeout boxes and throw them in the trash. With Lillianna here, her house that was normally empty felt like a real home—one where there was warmth and laughter and smiles realer than any amount of money could buy. She had had a home like that once, but it was one that she barely remembered from her childhood.

"Thank you again for the food," Dara said gratefully, though more than food she had simply appreciated the returned company.

"No problem," Lillianna replied, standing up from her seat. "I suppose this is good night then."

She moved to leave, but after opening the door she halted. The wind blew an icy chill through the open doorway, the night as cool and unwelcome as the drafty currents of loneliness settling once again into Dara's heart. She followed Lillianna to the door, lingering there in a protracted and reluctant farewell. Tonight had been more than she had hoped for and, even if she could not rewind time, Lillianna had turned out to still be herself, vampirism and all.

"What I said before—please give it some thought, alright?" Lillianna asked.

Dara nodded, but she had already given it a lot of thought. The delay in communication that had followed their mishap at the Markov's mansion and then the subsequent anticipation of when or if they may speak to one another again had already taken its toll on her. Despite her remaining trepidations, at this moment she did not want to be without her comforting presence in her life. Lillianna turned away from her to leave, but did not make it even a single step before Dara gave in to her longing and wrapped her arms around her waist.

"Dara?" Lillianna questioned. "What's wrong?"

"Can't you stay? Aren't you still hungry?" Dara asked, trying to cram as much insinuation into her voice as possible.

"We just ate," Lillianna pointed out as she swiveled around in Dara's arms to face her.

"You're a vampire," Dara pushed more bluntly.

"You were terrified before. I don't want to hurt you," Lillianna refused.

"Does it actually hurt?" Dara pressed, trying to unravel the tangled reasoning in her heart. "It felt good that one time, at least as far as I can remember."

"The initial bite does, though only for a moment." Lillianna sucked in a breath, and Dara could tell that she was struggling with the suggested offer. She liked that she had that effect on her, even if it was just for blood. "What's gotten into you?"

"I just want to be, well, useful I guess, and—" Dara swallowed back her pride as she looked away. "—irreplaceable." Dara had never said that final word aloud before—never admitted it for the world to hear. Now that it was all out in the open she felt naked and exposed.

"You *are* irreplaceable," Lillianna assured her, holding onto Dara more tightly. "That's why you don't need to force yourself."

"Thank you," Dara whispered. "I just keep thinking there must be a catch. I keep thinking—" She caught herself. It had been a mistake in years past to reveal that weakness. "Sorry, I'm being a bother."

"No, you're not. It's okay. If you're that worried, you must like me a lot, you know?" Lillianna smiled, her fangs glimmering in the front porch light. They had been attractive before Dara had known what they were for, then frightening once she realized, but now they were just teeth again, a quirk and not a threat.

"I do." Uncertainty held Dara for a moment, worries teetering on the precipice, before she swept the insecurity aside and let it scatter haphazardly in the wind. "Even if it scares me sometimes, I want you too."

"There will be time to grow used to that. We can take our time with everything, not just blood," Lillianna encouraged.

"What if I'm feeling impatient?" Dara asked. Before Lillianna could answer, Dara reached her arms up to link around her neck and pull her close. "Can't you stay?" she asked again.

"I really shouldn't bite you," Lillianna repeated, but Dara could see her will begin to crumble the longer she remained within her embrace. "At least not tonight."

"It's not for blood. It's just, well, I never got a chance to do you too," Dara whispered in her ear as she leaned in close. "And I'd like to."

Lillianna gave her a long, slow blink before breaking out into a sharp smile once more. "I'd like you to, too."

* * *

Later that night, long after the world had wound down, Dara awoke. Stars twinkled outside the bedroom window, their light clouded by frost that clung to the glass. Beside her, Lillianna was stretched out on the bed sleeping peacefully, the lion's share of blankets wrapped around her.

After gently tugging back a portion of the blankets, Dara laid beside her quietly, watching the rise and fall of her chest with each breath. Still sleeping, Lillianna licked her lips and mumbled a string of unintelligible words, clearly dreaming about something delicious—perhaps even Dara herself. Dara smiled at that idea; perhaps she should ask her in the morning if she remembered.

In the morning... What a wonderful thought; Lillianna would still be there when morning broke and beams of light streamed through the window. And she would be there the morning after that, and after that too—Dara could count on her. Maybe she would even be Lillianna's real fiancée someday, though that was still a ways off. Dara wiggled over on the bed to get closer, then brushed a kiss across Lillianna's forehead.

"Mnnn...Dara?" Lillianna murmured, still half-asleep, and likely still dreaming. "Come here."

She reached out to encircle Dara in her arms, pulling her against her chest. Dara could feel Lillianna's heartbeat against her body, strong, steady, and safe.

"Lilly?" Dara whispered, sleep tugging at her eyelids.

"Mn?"

"I'll tell you tomorrow," Dara decided, drifting off again to sleep. Because Lillianna would be there tomorrow, and that was all that really mattered.

Epilogue

It was a beautiful May day with clear blue skies when Dara emerged from her car carrying a small box. A balmy breeze rolled over her as she skipped up the steps to Lillianna's studio and pulled the key from her pocket. It was Saturday, which meant Lillianna would be busy painting. As Dara made her way back to the main workspace she passed a number of Lillianna's prior works in the hall—oils of lions sunbathing on rocks, tigers prowling through thick jungle foliage, and panthers wading through rivers. It had surprised her when Lillianna had started painting again, even working less to make time for it, but it also made her very happy too. Dara liked to think that maybe she had something to do with the sudden change and that she was being a good influence. Coming to the end of the hall, Dara popped her head into the main workspace. The scent of turpentine and pigments filled the air, and soft, natural light filtered in from a high window, illuminating the empty workspace.

"Lilly?" she called but there was no answer. Wet paints were still on the palette half-mixed and the brushes laid out were not yet cleaned; Lillianna must have just stepped out for a moment. Dara came inside the room to wait, settling down on one of the benches pushed up against the wall, and could not help but catch sight of the painting Lillianna was currently working on. Her jaw dropped.

A woman, almost completely disrobed, was relaxing on a chaise longue with a sultry expression across her face. Rich burgundy cloth was draped across the most revealing bits, but nothing at all was covering the woman's breasts. Most shockingly of all, Dara recognized the woman. It was herself.

Her shocked staring was interrupted when the door to the studio opened again.

"Dara?" Lillianna asked, noticing her immediately.

"What—what's that?" Dara sputtered, wide-eyed in shock as she pointed at the painting. She was quite certain she had never posed in such a sultry manner before in her life. Lillianna painted majestic lions and other large cats, not naked women, and especially not *her*.

"Oh, that," Lillianna looked over at the painting. "It was going to be a surprise gift, but I guess you caught me."

"It's for *me?*" Dara asked, bewildered.

"Well, sort of?" Lillianna answered. "I'm going to put it in the bedroom."

"But I'm right there next to you in bed already?" Dara sputtered again, horribly embarrassed. "And why am I naked?"

"Well, it was supposed to be a portrait, and then—" Lillianna gestured awkwardly. "—anyway, lots of women were naked in the paintings by old masters. The female form is very beautiful."

"But those women aren't around to see those paintings today!" Dara pointed out. "And—" she bit her lip, giving a glance back to the sultry painting. "—do I really look like that?"

"Well, I had to paint some of it from memory," Lillianna admitted, though the true meaning of the question seemed to breeze right past her. "But I do think I got it pretty accurate. See, I remembered your mole right here," she added, pointing to Dara's inner thigh.

"I mean, am I really that attractive?" Dara asked again, staring at the painting. Outside of the sultry expression, she also looked way, way too pretty.

Lillianna looked at her oddly. "Of course. In what universe would I not find my wife attractive?"

"Well that's true," Dara agreed. Lillianna did tell her quite often that she liked her, but she had never translated those words of endearment into *this*. "I just think that this sort of thing would look better with, uh, *you* in it."

"Me?" Lillianna blushed. "No, I don't think I've ever made a face like this."

"What?" Mortification filled Dara as she realized the implication. "You mean I *do?*"

Lillianna quirked one of her perfect eyebrows at her. "What do you mean? Of course you do—all the time."

"I—that's—" Dara was at a loss for words as her face grew unbearably hot. That was a lot to take in. "Anyway, um, here!" She thrust the small box she had brought into Lillianna's hands.

"What's this?" Lillianna asked, but Dara remained silent as she opened the box. A cake was revealed, made of cream and decorated with slices of strawberry and dozens upon dozens of candles. Lillianna frowned. "Dara, what happened? The poor thing has been stabbed to death."

"I had to fit fifty candles," Dara explained. Lillianna gave her a look, clearly not getting it. "It's your birthday, remember?"

"Oh." Realization swept over Lillianna's face.

"The cake and frosting isn't very sweet, but that's just the way you like it," Dara continued, producing a knife, some matches, two forks, and paper plates from her bag. "I wanted to make sure we celebrated it this year, even if it was just something small."

"Sorry about last year," Lillianna apologized. "Birthdays aren't really that important for vampires. We record them of course, but after a certain age we all start to forget a little more of the mundane things like that."

"Your mother mentioned something like that to me recently, about her work as the archivist," Dara nodded. "I think it's a shame that as soon as your cousins mature a little they will immediately forget again." The comment earned a chuckle from Lillianna.

"Well, I suspect they started forgetting earlier than usual. And it's not like I'll forget everything. I would never forget you." Lillianna eyed the skewered cake again. "Or this cake."

"I wanted to have the actual candles at least once before there were too many to even try to fit," Dara explained sheepishly. "There's no way I could fit a thousand candles on there."

"When I'm a thousand, if you want regular candles instead of numerals I'm sure we can find a way," Lillianna smiled as she settled down onto the bench beside her with the cake.

Lighting all fifty candles was quite the ordeal, but somehow Dara managed. "Make a wish," she instructed, and then Lillianna blew them all out. Smoke swirled from the extinguished candles up into the air, coiling up toward the ceiling.

"What did you wish for?" Dara asked curiously as Lillianna set the cake down on the side of the bench.

"I thought the current tradition was that my wish won't come true if I tell you?" Lillianna teased.

"Oh, don't be superstitious. It's not like the supernatural exists or anything," Dara said playfully.

"I'm sure it doesn't," Lillianna chuckled. "But if you must know, I wished that my thousandth birthday would be a good one." She pulled Dara into her arms and held her close in a warm hug. "But as long as you're there, I'm sure it will be."

Extended Epilogue

Sign up for my newsletter at bonus.michellestwolf.com to get a
bonus extended epilogue scene as well as updates on my writing!

Vampire Aphrodisiac
An Extended Epilogue for "The Accidental Bite"

Of all things, Dara did not expect vampire blood to be a literal
aphrodisiac.

To make matters worse (or better?), no one bothered to mention that
little fact to Lillianna either.

Acknowledgments

For Cassandra, who encouraged me and made the cover even though she was already way too busy.

For Rhys, who was determined to make me believe in myself and would not allow me to falter.

For Shane, who proofread on a tight schedule and was always there to lend an ear.

And for Sarah, who does not know much about writing romances, but has supported me every step of the way anyway. I would not be here without all of you.

About the Author

As a child, Michelle St. Wolf read every vampire and werewolf book she could get her hands on. When she got older, she discovered paranormal romance and fell in love. In her own writing, she enjoys exploring a touch of the forbidden, a little bit of destiny, and just the right amount of cozy combined with darkly beautiful women.

When not writing, Michelle spends her time snuggling with her tiny dogs, drinking milk tea, and growing blackberries and basil in her garden.

You can connect with me on:
🌐 https://michellestwolf.com

Subscribe to my newsletter:
✉ https://bonus.michellestwolf.com

Made in the USA
Columbia, SC
20 February 2024

6b9b4701-b17f-4357-8d55-4d9b61b0a0abR02